Professor Spindlebrock's

Little Blue Book of Traveling Spells

Joseph D. Lyman

ISBN: 978-1-7363739-0-3

Library of Congress Control Number: 2020925564

Typefaces: Libre Baskerville, by Rodrigo Fuenzalida, SIL Open Font License v1.1; Antique Book Cover, SIL Open Font License v1.1; Lime Glory, by FF user Lime; FFC License; Akura Popo, by Twincolabs Foundation, FFC License.

Images: Cover photography by Nathan Anderson, Free Commercial Use License; Chess piece models by Blendswap.com user Kilt2007, Free Commercial Use License; "Mystic Celtic Knot Flourish" a derived work from public domain vectors; All other images, modifications, and elements are original copyright works.

Pinpoint Management, LLC. Fulton, Missouri

To my Grandfather, Paavo Airola, for leaving a legacy of writing and publishing. To my Dad, Dan Lyman, for leaving a legacy of entrepreneurship and music; I love and miss you. To my wife, Stephanie, may we always cherish the magic we have together. And, to all the dear family and friends who lent their support, thank you.

CONTENTS

Chapter 1

The Wrong Book in the Right Hands

I f you would have approached me on my fourteenth birthday, and asked what the single most meaningful event of my life was, I would have had a ready and somber answer. Indeed, for more than a decade of birthdays after that one, I couldn't imagine that anything else might be able to shape my life so emphatically. But even the most formative experiences cannot remain peerless, as anyone who has passed through enough of life can tell you.

As I sit down to catalog the circumstances that brought me to the uncommon place which I presently occupy in this strange world, one in particular stands out to me. It was perhaps a simple thing, especially in comparison to the events of my childhood years, but it was formative nonetheless.

The story I'm about to share started—as so many stories do—when I hit rock-bottom. I had been stumbling slowly downward for a number of years without really knowing it, when, in the second year of my doctoral studies, my life took a turn. I had struggled through a Bachelor's degree in forensic science, then fought through a Master's degree in forensic anthropology that took more than a year longer than it should have. In those days I was fairly determined, and since my goals were quite particular, I passed up several job opportunities in the pursuit of more schooling. When I set out on my educational track the economy was good, and I had no thought for the mountain of student loan debt that was amassing. Everything seemed as though it would eventually work out, if I could just push myself through to my thesis.

The course of study itself was more than usually difficult, but life decided that simple academic challenges weren't interesting or painful enough. For reasons I still don't comprehend, my PhD adviser took to disliking me in a most acute way, which he tried at first to hide. Eventually his disdain for my very person could no longer be contained, and he openly rejected me. He took it upon himself to disparage my character, skills, and aptitude to all of his colleagues, the most influential set of people in my target industry. At the lowest point, when my options were feeling more and more limited and my liabilities weighed heavily, my mother and father passed away suddenly and unexpectedly. Circumstances demanded that I find a way to organize and cover the costs of funerals that crushed me even to attend.

At first I was numb to the whirlwind of circumstances that seemed to be consuming my life. The destruction felt as if it were bearing down on all fronts. After the funerals passed, the weight of my challenges came down on me with a staggering and overwhelming force. I lost myself and turned to drinking, something I had vowed to eschew since suffering at the fists of an abusive and alcoholic father. The only thing I hated more than that calamitous liquid was the growing emptiness and fear. If only I would have taken the opportunity to heal my relationship with my father before he had passed. If only my mother was there to help me cope with the pain of that missed opportunity.

The alcohol buried my grief for a while, replacing it with calloused indifference, reckless behavior, and several run-ins with the law. My life was in vertigo, a disoriented sliding both corporeal and mental. Dreams of employment in criminal justice—the family trade for three generations— seemed further and further out of reach as I slipped into an abyss. I abandoned my studies and quit my part-time job. Unable to pay my portion of the rent, I deserted my roommates and traded my comfortable and pleasant home for a dingy room in a derelict old building downtown. The only redeeming quality about the shabby dwelling was, I thought, the proximity of the liquor store. So it was in that dark period of my life; I was not myself.

After some months, my savings and small inheritance were as exhausted as I was, and I was compelled to seek employment. Coming home from an unfavorable job interview one afternoon, I bumped into an old friend from high school, who was exiting a thrift store near my building.

Our conversation was brief, but somehow instrumental in getting me out of my rut.

"Thomas? Thomas Martin, is that you? It's me, Benny, from high school!"

I hadn't recognized him at first, but the name and face clicked, and I mustered what remained of my recently unused social skills to start a conversation.

"Benny, right! Man, it's been a long time. How have you been?"

"Great, doing great! It's so good to see you, we used to have such awesome times! What have you been up to, I don't see you online at all! Most of my friends have an account on —, are you on there?"

I explained that I didn't do the social media thing much. Our conversation went the way they generally go with old friends, and we wound up talking about our life paths, including education and careers.

Benny, as it turned out, had dropped out of college to pursue an opportunity in the tech industry. His connections eventually led him into the world of rare collectibles, where he was making a reasonable living for himself. He spent much of his time scouring various haunts for treasures, and the rest of his time obsessing over them with others who shared his passion. The most interesting items he collected, the rest he sold online. He was thus able to make his hobby his livelihood, and I envied him. I accompanied him on several of his outings, and while he was busy seeking out his curiosities I began to seek out my own. Books fascinated me, and it so happened that our adventures frequently took us into shops where I could peruse volumes of all ages and genres. I made several purchases on a whim. Recognizing my interest, my old friend helped tutor me in the hobby of collecting.

Within a short time, I was able to transform my casual interest in book collecting into a passion, and from a passion into an adequate paying occupation. Now that I was working again I was able to secure a small but clean apartment as well as my own transportation, and start to pull myself out of the emotional mire that I had been slogging through. I found joy and pleasure in my new pursuit, and applied myself with all of the energy I had previously invested in my studies. The simple investigative work of hunting down rare and valuable books was enlivening and distracting, and for the most part sufficient to my simple monetary needs. All was going reasonably well, considering the depths of despair that had so recently overwhelmed me.

This brief glimpse into my circumstances and personal affairs is really only necessary and justifiable as an introduction to the events that ushered me into an entirely new existence. This book is about the amazing things I have discovered and experienced, and the remarkable people I have come to know and love. My goal is a selfish one in many ways. I wish to get all of these mysteries out of my mind and onto paper, to know that someone out there understands them at least as well as I do. I said that my life took a turn; I will now explain the curious and unexpected arc that turn flung me into.

Hunting rare collectibles for a living required travel. On one excursion I found myself in central New York state, where Benny was meeting up with a few of his fellow collectors. He had free room and board with one of his colleagues, and invited me to benefit from the savings. I tagged along with the expectation that I might locate a few worthwhile shops, and I was not disappointed. I happened one afternoon upon a small book store in a town called Dryden. I recall having greater hopes than usual upon turning from the main road onto the gravel driveway; an unexplained thrill of optimism caught me, and I drew in a sharp and clear breath as I surveyed the building. It was a rustic, re-purposed red barn, with only a small sign indicating to the passer-by that it housed a cache worthy of book lovers, rather than a stockpile of hay and farm implements.

A small metal bell tied to the door cheerfully announced my arrival as I entered, in competition with a stuck doorknob and a set of rusted hinges. Tightly packed aisles of aimlessly shelved books were visible beyond the cluttered entrance, which boasted an over-sized antique wooden store counter, and a worn out couch facing a dust-and-grime-glazed window. The interior of the store was a perfectly enchanting mess of literary miscellany, bespeaking the hope of wonderful discoveries lurking in every cobwebby corner.

I eagerly began pouring over book spines on the nearest shelf as I called out to see if anyone was in the store. A few minutes passed before the door noisily opened again, and an elderly woman stepped gingerly through. She introduced herself as the owner, asked a few questions about what I was looking for, then informed me that she would be on the couch reading until I was ready. Winding slowly through the dark and dusty rows, I rifled through the collection for hours, conversing with the owner from time to time and amassing a mountain of finds. It was clear that this shop hadn't been gone over by collectors for several years; the books I would bring home from that one visit would easily finance my hobby-job for another several months.

As the day drew to a close, the need for food and rest outgrew the compulsion of the hunt. Reassuring myself that I could always come back another time, I wended my way toward the entrance. Arms loaded, I twisted my body delicately through the cramped walkways until I was almost to the long aisle that led down the middle of the barn.

And then I saw it.

Peeking out from under a neglected pile in a forgotten corner was a small, dark navy-blue volume, bound in leather. Its size, color, and gold-stamped title revealed it to be a book of great worth; a first edition of Marmion, by Sir Walter Scott. I had seen pictures of books just like this one in exotic private and museum collections online. Connoisseurs the world over were searching for remaining first editions of this well-known title that now sat before my very eyes. It was worth ten times the combined value of every book I then hefted, making it an absolutely unbelievable find.

Setting everything down on the floor, I carefully removed the books that were sitting atop the Marmion and gently picked it up. Anxious and amazed at my fortune, I glanced at the cover only briefly, then placed it in with the rest of my finds and continued to the entrance to pay the shop owner. I was nervous that she would take notice of the Marmion and refuse to part with it. To my great surprise, I watched as she tallied the volumes all up at the same price, rambled off a modest total, took my payment, and set a small hand-written receipt on top of the pile. I walked out of that red barn in Dryden feeling an exuberance which I hadn't felt in ages.

Racing back to the house where we were staying, I was barely able to contain my excitement. Benny, knowing that I had been out searching for books, was ready to help carry my purchases in and go through them with me. I intended to let him discover the Marmion on his own, just to see the surprised look on his face. We took the books to the bedroom, where he proceeded to flip through each of the volumes, showing dutiful interest and excitement at each one. When he picked up the small, dark navy-blue book, however, he showed absolutely no interest at all, brusquely setting it aside without a word before moving on.

Naturally I protested. I picked up the book to show him precisely what it was, thinking he must have somehow missed it. When I saw the cover my heart sank; it wasn't the Marmion. I hastily tossed it aside and started madly rifling through the rest of the books, but it was no use. The copy of Marmion was nowhere to be found. The only volume that resembled it at all was the one that my friend and I had both rejected. I came back to it, turning it over in my hands in hopes of somehow finding that it really was my prize, and finally flopped down on the bed and let out a long, disappointed sigh. Holding the book above me I took in the title for the first time. It read, "Professor Spindlebrock's Little Blue Book of Traveling Spells."

Chapter 2

Learning to Mend My Suitcase

Stubborn as I am, I refused to believe that I had mistaken this silly little book for a first edition Marmion. I searched the pile again, this time removing all the dust jackets and carefully examining each volume. I combed every nook in the bed, the room, and even the car. My suspicions turned to the shop owner; pulling out the receipt, I counted up all of the books that I had purchased, to make sure the tally matched. The idea of going back to the shop and confronting the owner crossed my mind, but I had scrutinized our dealings with the greatest interest when they first happened, and couldn't bring myself to believe that I had missed some trick of the hand. Reluctantly, I had to admit to myself that I had made a mistake.

With excuses of feeling suddenly ill, I cut the trip short and headed back home, sorrowful. I thought that life would carry on in spite of this new disappointment, but those neural pathways of escapism started to recommend themselves once more, in a complex process that we distill into the purposefully ominous word "temptation." The thought of drinking wasn't the only one that tormented me anew; depression, anxiety, and grief resurfaced. I reasoned that if one small setback was enough to throw me off-kilter, perhaps my life still needed some serious work.

As I fretted over my situation one day, I again picked up the odd little book that wasn't Marmion. A rare mood seized me; I felt like some light and distracting reading, and I thought of the book I had ended up with. It crossed my mind that it was likely of the comedic variety, based on the title, and desiring to laugh for the first time in a long while, I dug it out of my collection and flipped through the front matter.

The publisher was listed as, "David & Sons, Toronto Canada," a house I had never heard of. The book was a few decades old, and had seen at least five printings. Judging by the condition of the binding, the volume had hardly been opened, but it was signed. It was made out, "To my good friend Carmichael, may you never find yourself lost and alone. Yours, C.C. Spindlebrock."

I scanned the table of contents and found a chapter that sounded amusing: "Mending and Repairing on the Go." Flipping to the listed page, I read the opening paragraphs of the chapter, which described many potential opportunities for fixing various things using magic while traveling: a hole in your trousers, a broken shoelace, a suitcase that won't latch, and a list of other common concerns.

I skimmed the chapter casually, amused at the ornate incantations and their accompanying explanations. The author seemed preoccupied with minute details relating to the performing of the incantations, and was particularly interested in repeated descriptions of "the subtle difference in tone and gestures required to perform repairing incantations effectively both with, and without a wand." As I read, I recalled that I did in fact own a suitcase with one broken latch; a minor annoyance that was too unimportant to worry about. Chuckling to myself, I went to my closet and located the suitcase nestled between two boxes on the floor. I took the book in one hand, and cleared my throat. With a flourish, as similar to the one described in the "wandless" directions as I could manage, I recited the incantation exactly as it was written.

No words can adequately describe the shock, surprise, and even terror, that gripped my whole heart when upon uttering the incantation I looked down at the suitcase and watched as the slightly bent and oblique latch restored itself to perfect straightness. My mouth fell open and I watched slack-jawed as the small hole where the latch caught—which had been worn, twisted, and indented from years of misuse —popped out flat and smooth, its edges sharpened to a perfect little rectangle. Then, to top it all off, the latch flipped itself closed neatly, and secured itself with a sharp click.

Thankfully, no one saw what followed. I dropped the book. Stammering incoherently, I stumbled backward, tripped over my coffee table and fell into my desk, knocking it over and upsetting its entire contents onto the floor. I lay there dazed for a few moments, struggling to come to grips with what I had seen, and then I took a spectacular mental leap over the great chasm of what I had observed with my unquestionable senses, and clamored onto a small mental outcropping called denial. There in my mess of papers and office bric-a-brac I burst out laughing, continuing until my eyes watered. Drawing in a few sharp breaths and collecting myself, I began to wonder at my own mental state; first the escapade with the Marmion, and now this delusion.

Resolutions began to take form in my head as I excavated myself from the clutter. I decided then and there that what I really needed was to face the problems that had led me to squander my time and sanity in purposeless hobbies. I had embarked on my journey into adulthood with lofty goals, goals that would have made my father proud. Why should a few challenges and setbacks stop me from pursuing my dreams? I would plow through the obstacles and disappointments, and confront the individuals that stood between me and my chosen career. My hobby could stay a hobby, but I was going to galvanize my soul so that I could do something worthwhile in this world.

I righted my desk and slowly undertook the restoration of its garnishments while I expostulated with myself out loud.

"This squandering of time," I argued, "has led me to a mental breakdown, which was made manifest in two hallucinations."

I interrupted my cleaning to hold up an ordinal index finger.

"First, that I had found a rare book which I so longed to find."

A small gesticulation produced a second ordinal finger, which I shook dramatically at the disheveled room.

"And, second, that magical spells and nonsense could somehow be real enough to have a tangible effect in a world governed by physical laws."

My eyes shot around the room in search of some vindication, some proof that I was at least on the path of healing, and not completely insane. The closet door was still ajar; there, I reasoned, I would find my justification.

I scrambled over to the closet to find solace in my old suitcase. It had been my tireless friend on many a journey, with its busted latch which had served no useful purpose for years. Countless attempts to close the thing had multiplied the annoyance so much that I no longer even tried to secure it on the broken side. It would still be broken, just as it had been, I assured myself.

Grabbing the suitcase roughly, I carted it to my bedroom without so much as a downward glance. I plopped onto my bed and took a deep breath, assuring myself that the imagined magic was nothing more than the effect of a worn out mind. Drawing a few more calming breaths, I situated the case so that I could examine it clearly.

My heart sank as my focus settled on the latch, which appeared to be in perfect repair. My hand moved over it slowly as I struggled to appeal to some sense other than my sight. My eyes darted from one latch to the other. The one that I was sure had been broken was now in better repair than its counterpart. I opened and closed the latch several times, observing that it worked perfectly, as if it were brand new. Flipping the case over I examined the empty innards, the outer shell, the pockets—everything—looking for some kind of explanation. It was doubtlessly my suitcase, previously with the annoying broken latch, in all other respects unchanged.

At this point I set the suitcase aside and left my apartment to get some fresh air. For an hour or so I sat at the park thinking. What if I was crazy? Certainly things could be worse. I'd get some help, some much needed counseling. I would finally come to grips with the problems that had been plaguing me. Nothing bad could come from asking for help. I had all but made up my mind to start searching for a psychiatrist when another thought popped into my head.

What if magic was real?

I laughed out loud for the second time that day, startling a jogger as she passed. What if it was real? What if you really could say a few magic words and do things without having to really do them? What if there was more to the world than just science and math and proof? It was a far-fetched idea, but at the brink of desperation, I figured it was worthy of consideration. The alternative was not as appealing, though it seemed much more reasonable.

With nothing to lose, I went back to my apartment. I spent some time tiding things up, and finally settled in my room with the suitcase and Professor Spindlebrock's Little Blue Book of Traveling Spells sitting side by side on the bed in front of me. I took a deep breath and reread the chapter on mending, this time in earnest. I memorized the incantation that I had previously used, then set the book aside. Examining my trusty old suitcase one last time, I focused sharply on the second latch. With a flourish, I recited the words and watched intently as the metal straightened itself up a tiny bit, the opening unbending and evening out on the edges. The latch-arm tightened its spring and closed itself neatly, just as the first had done; the spell had worked. I tested out both latches; they operated with smooth perfection, as if they were brand new.

Even if you're unacquainted with magic, I've not asked you to believe anything spectacular up to this point. But, I must make a particular request of my non-magical readers to take me at my word from here on. This mending of my suitcase, though absolutely and unbelievably astonishing to me at the time, has come to be but a comical memory compared to what I have witnessed since. An entire new realm of possibility was opened to me in an instant, though I was not prepared to receive, understand, or accept it. My hope is that you will have an easier time than I did, in accepting the new realms of possibility that must be introduced in order to share my story. Open your mind and explore; what you expect to encounter in your own life, and how you deal with it, might be irreversibly altered by the things I aim to reveal.

Chapter 3

Publishers and Baristas Know Nothing

After this first experience with magic, fear and ignorance took hold of me. Desperately desiring context and understanding—and some assurance that I was not insane—I resolved to obtain answers. The only way to get answers, I figured, was by conversing with another human being, one who understood what I was seeing and feeling; I needed to speak with someone familiar with magic. I decided that I would attempt to contact the author of the book, a Professor C.C. Spindlebrock.

The obvious best place to start was with the publisher, David & Sons of Toronto, named in the front matter of the book. Unfortunately, I quickly found that they were not a well-known publishing house; their business was not listed anywhere. I scoured every resource I could think of, and even enlisted the help of my knowledgeable book-collecting friends. I consulted the the city of Toronto business offices, searching for an entry in their database that was anything close to what I was looking for. Nothing supported the existence of a publisher by the name of David & Sons.

Out of ideas for finding the publisher, I began searching for professor Spindlebrock himself, but that effort was even more futile that the first. General directories and online listings, starting with Toronto but expanding as far and wide as I could manage, all yielded no results. The idea to look at faculty lists came to mind, since I was searching for a professor; I browsed through listings for every university I could dig up, but came up empty-handed.

It eventually occurred to me that my searches were likely in vain for one simple reason: neither David & Sons, nor professor Spindlebrock, wanted to be found. Clearly, this was not a book that had been released to a general audience, and clearly it was not released by a publishing house that wished to be known far and wide. I considered giving up my searches, but how could I? This was magic, something that until a short time ago had existed only in storybooks and movies. It was real, and there had to be more to it than traveling spells. No matter what it took, I was going to find either the publisher or the author, and I was going to know more.

On a whim I packed the book, my passport, and some clothes into my now perfectly repaired suitcase; if I couldn't locate David & Sons online, perhaps I could find them in person. An old roommate, who I still kept in touch with from my undergraduate years, was living in downtown Toronto and working at the US Consulate. He had repeatedly extended an invitation for me to visit any time, so I called him up and asked if I could stay with him a few days while I worked on a research project.

A training meeting had my friend stuck in D.C., but he offered to arrange for his doorman to give me a key, so that I could use his apartment while he was away. The details were worked out amicably in a brief phone call, and I boarded a flight to Toronto within a few hours of the idea entering my head.

The flight was short, and felt doubly quick as my mind raced with thoughts of magic. I caught a taxi to my friend's apartment and was about to unpack and get settled, but the moment I pulled the book out of my suitcase I had an overpowering urge to continue my search for David & Sons, coupled with an overwhelming feeling of confidence that I'd most certainly find them. I grabbed the book and left the building.

With a sort of reckless audacity I decided to simply walk around the city, book in hand. My wandering inexplicably took me directly to Queens Quay, near the harbor, to a strip of small businesses behind an auto dealership. Most of the establishments were common to a big city industrial district, but I eventually came across one which stood out to me as out of place: Dave's Signs & Copies. I looked down at the book I was carrying, and then back at the sign shop. Something just felt right. I tucked the book back under my arm and climbed purposefully up the wide concrete steps before me.

A clanky brass bell affixed to the top of the door announced my arrival as I entered. The cramped lobby held a few self-serve copy machines lined up against a wall that was otherwise bare and featureless. The next wall was even more exceptionally plain, apart from a handle-less door, and a tiny window-counter presumably for taking payments. There was a young lady visible on the other side of the opening, to whom I addressed myself, nervously:

"Hello, um, excuse me. I'm looking for a publisher?"

She was fiddling with a cell phone, and didn't stop to acknowledge my presence. Re-thinking my approach, I produced the book of traveling spells and set it on the window-counter, then cleared my throat decisively.

"Specifically," I said, pulling myself together and glancing around the tiny shop to make sure I was alone, "I'm looking for David & Sons. I need to speak with your editing staff about a somewhat urgent matter."

The young woman set her phone down and picked up the book. Upon eyeing the cover she jumped a little in her chair, then looked me over.

"How can I help you?" she asked in as relaxed a business voice as she could muster.

"I need to speak to someone on your editing staff, a manager if you have one here."

She gave me one last glance, then handed the book back and pressed a button that buzzed me through the door. After a short wait in an empty white room, I was led down a narrow hallway to an office near the back of the building. A woman in neat business attire was standing behind her desk as I entered. She held out her hand and asked me to sit. Her manners were welcoming, but I thought I detected a hint of consternation in her voice.

"Welcome, thank you for coming. We've been looking forward to meeting you."

I shifted in my chair, but only nodded in reply. These were magicians after all, who was I to question whether or not they knew I was coming?

She continued with a forced smile.

"Now, don't misunderstand, we know that Spindlebrock likes to do things in his own particular way, and we want to work with you on that. But we need more consistent contact, and feedback on deadlines."

"Uh huh," I stammered, beginning to understand that there was some confusion as to who I was.

"We hope that you'll provide a better liaison than his last few agents. We're thrilled that you stopped by, we honestly weren't expecting you until—"

She began flipping through her desk calendar to see when Spindlebrock's agent was expected. I took the opportunity to explain myself before things got any more convoluted.

"I'm sorry, I think there's been a mistake. You see, I was looking for information—not only about professor Spindlebrock, but also about magic in general. I came across this book recently—"

I held up my copy of Spindlebrock's book.

"And, well, I was able to perform one of the simple spells. I'm hoping you can answer a few questions, or perhaps point me to where I might find more information."

As I spoke, the woman's face changed from mock politeness to surprise, and then to annoyance.

"So, you're not his agent?"

"No."

"And you say that you came across a book, somehow?"

"Professor Spindlebrock's Little Blue Book of Traveling Spells, yes. I found it in a used book store."

Fearful comprehension finally rested on her face, a welcome change from annoyance but still uncomplimentary. She leaned forward in her chair and spoke very carefully, looking me full in the eyes.

"You say that you read this book, and that you performed magic, yet you come in here asking for general information? What kind of information do you expect me to have for you, Mr... ?"

"Martin. Thomas Martin. I'm really just trying to make a connection, you see, however I can. Professor Spindlebrock and this publishing company are all I have to start with. This is clearly a house that publishes for authors of this type, and —"

"And what type would that be Mr. Martin? I have very little time, please get to the point."

I spoke hurriedly, hoping to get the words out before being shown the door.

"Well, magical books I suppose. Things relating to those who practice magic—it's a traveling book, it references how a magician might get by in various situations, so there must be an audience of people who would buy and use such a—"

The woman became visibly agitated.

"Mr. Martin, to be blunt, I can't help you. I'm not prepared or equipped to offer you any information, or even point you to anyone who could. It's simply not in my realm. I'm a publisher for a very particular clientele, and it doesn't go beyond that. Now, if you'll excuse me, I have business to attend to."

Rising to her feet and making her way around the desk as I stood, she nearly pushed me out of her office, slamming the door in my face and leaving me to find my own way out of the building. I stood there dumbfounded for a few moments. Though I'm not generally clever, a thought occurred to me, and I turned and walked confidently to the receptionist.

"I'm curious," I said to her, mustering as much poise and authority as I could, "whether you have professor Spindlebrock's most current address. He moves around quite frequently. What address are you sending correspondence to?"

I took out a notebook, as if ready to compare. She paused for a moment, confused, then scrambled through a filing cabinet, procured a record, and recited an address. I took quick note as she read it, catching a glimpse of a small photo of Spindlebrock affixed to the file with a paperclip. I affirmed that the address would do until I called again, thanked her, and left the building as quickly as I could.

Wasting no time, I immediately hailed a cab and gave the address to the driver. I found the house in question, but Spindlebrock no longer lived there and the current resident didn't even recognize his name. The idea came to me to make inquiries at the surrounding businesses, where Spindlebrock might have spent time; a coffee shop less than a block away seemed like an excellent place to start.

"Excuse me, I'm looking for an old friend. He used to live near here, and I believe he mentioned your shop a few times," I started, after greeting the young man working behind the counter. It was almost closing time, and with no other customers in the shop he seemed more than willing to help.

"What did he look like?"

I described professor Spindlebrock as best I could, having only seen the small photo at his publisher's office. My meager portrayal didn't seem to spark any memory, and the barista shook his head slowly in the negative.

"He was a writer and a professor, he likely would have come in here with his work," I added in desperation. As I was speaking another young man came out from the back room. His appearance was unique, marked primarily by jet-black hair falling over one side of his face, with bands of bright, rainbow-dyed colors. He seemed to have overheard at least the last part of my conversation with his co-worker.

"What's that? You looking for someone?"

He sized me up in an instant, taking perhaps more interest than a young coffee-shop worker normally would. I repeated my inquiry, adding nonchalantly that it was nothing urgent, and that perhaps I'd try the phone book.

"You won't find him in the phone book," the rainbow-haired barista noted, motioning to my copy of Spindlebrock's book. I looked down at it, and then back at him. His name tag read "Scott." I hastily put the book back in my bag.

"Listen, Scott, can I speak with you for a few moments?"

Wiping his hands on his apron, the barista nodded and motioned for me to head outside. A few moments later he followed. He was quick to speak and sharp with his answers, offering a wealth of useful information. Professor Spindlebrock had in fact been a regular customer at that very coffee shop, always arriving when the shop first opened. Scott often took the first shift and was Spindlebrock's favorite barista, but apparently Spindlebrock wasn't anyone's favorite. He was blunt, demanding, and non-appreciative. Scott seemed convinced, from what he knew of the man, that Spindlebrock must be in some kind of trouble, and that I must be the one pursuing justice.

"A real pill, always flying off the handle if everything wasn't just right. I got used to him, though."

The young man lit up a cigarette and began drawing on it heavily.

"The last time he came in here, he was really upset, looking over his shoulder. Looked like he was in a load of trouble."

Scott gave me a knowing look. I pulled out my notebook, attempting to appear serious and authoritative.

"So I asked him what's wrong, and he mumbles something about me minding my own affairs. Always was telling people off, so I started in on making his drink, but he stopped me. He grabbed my arm, like this."

Scott grabbed my arm in a tight grip and looked into my eyes seriously.

"He says, 'Listen, you know who I am, I remember you from Intro to Magical Scientific Method. If anyone comes in here looking for me, you'll tell them nothing, you hear me? Nothing!' And he lets me go, but not before trying a wandless Admixtus on me. That old man, always going on about wandless magic, thought he could pull an Admixtus on a college student! Thought I couldn't dodge that one, couldn't see it coming? We used to use those on girls at—"

The smile faded from Scott's face as he realized that he was perhaps sharing something that might shift the focus toward him in an unfavorable way.

"Right, anyway, who didn't do stupid stuff in college? Like I was saying, his charm didn't take because I guess I knew a bit too much about it from some harmless pranks me and my friends used to pull. Anyway, I played along like I was confused, and didn't know what was going on, and all that, just like it did take. He seemed convinced alright; he took his drink and relaxed."

I jotted down the word Admixtus and a few other notes while he was speaking.

"Did he mention anything about where he was going?"

"Well, not exactly mentioned, but as I was clearing his table, I did catch sight of something he was writing; part of an address. It stood out to me because when I was a kid I used to have a friend that lived on that street. I'd walk over there nearly every day, and we'd go from his house to the park—"

He would have gone on, but I interrupted. He gave me the name of the street, ground the remnants of his cigarette into the pavement with his heel, and asked if there was anything else. In a moment of boldness, I decided to attempt to play the part of whatever authority figure this young man thought I represented.

"Scott, you've really helped us out, thank you—and Scott, don't discount the power of 'wandless magic' entirely. You never know when it might come in handy."

With the same little flourish and the few words of magic that I had used to repair my luggage, I fixed a fraying and almost broken strap on the young man's apron, right there on the street corner. He was taken aback at first, as if he half expected I was about to do something far worse. Then, he examined his newly repaired apron, chuckled, and turned to head back into the shop.

Chapter 4

Professor Spindlebrock

Perhaps the best way to help the unacquainted paint a mental picture of professor Spindlebrock is for me to simply share, as well as I can remember, the details of the first conversation which took place between us. The sun was setting as the taxi rolled slowly down the long street Scott had named. One house stood out in particular as we passed it; I called for the cab to stop, paid my fare, and got out. Instinct filled me with excitement and conviction, and I was not disappointed. As I started down the walkway, the front door of the house swung open wide, and a man appeared, smiling broadly and placing his hands on his hips.

I recognized him instantly from the picture I had seen at David & Sons. He was taller than I had imagined him, with a grizzled yet full head of hair, and broad shoulders. I judged him to be in his fifties or sixties, and in excellent physical condition. As I advanced down the shady walkway he hailed me by some name that I now forget, and not wishing to be mistaken in identity as I had been with the publisher and the barista, I corrected him immediately.

"Professor Spindlebrock, my name is Thomas Martin."

"Thomas what?" visibly flustered, his demeanor changed from amicable to incredulous in an instant.

"That's not the name they gave me at the agency. Are you a replacement then?"

"I am not, sir."

At this news he straightened his frame and retreated slightly back into the open doorway. His hands hung loosely at his sides, fists opening and closing compulsively.

"Professor, I've been trying like mad to find you, I spoke to your publisher just this morning."

I pulled out his book and held it up. He did not move.

"They didn't have much information, but I was able to locate a coffee shop near your last address and speak to a young man there—"

"Scott?"

"Yes, Scott, that's the one. He gave me this address, an—"

"Gave you this address? And how would he have given you this address?"

I couldn't help thinking about wandless magic as I watched his hands continue to twitch. I rushed to finish my explanation and get to the point of my visit.

"Well, he only gave me the street name, which he had seen on a piece of paper the last time he saw you at the café."

Spindlebrock seemed to consider the possibility.

"Yes, I suppose I can see how that might have happened," he laughed, "Scott was a bright pupil, I should have considered that he might have been a little too advanced for a quick charm, hastily conjured."

He trailed off in thought, his hands finally relaxing at his sides.

"In any case, professor, I took a cab down your street here, and I knew right away that this was your house."

"Really? How?"

I hadn't really considered how I knew.

"Um, I, I don't really know—I mean I didn't actually know it was your house, I just had a feeling—"

"What kind of a feeling?"

At this point the only feeling I was having was that this man was far too easily distracted, and that I might never get to the point of my inquiry. I took a risk and cut immediately to the questions that were burning in my mind.

"Professor Spindlebrock, I want to know about magic, everything you can tell me. My name is Thomas Martin, I'm from a small town in Ohio. I found this book in a used book store, and I know it's the genuine article. I've never seen real magic in my life, but this book has shown me that it is possible, and I want to know more."

Professor Spindlebrock stared at me silently for several long moments. He crossed his arms, glanced down at my book, and then met my gaze directly.

"You mean to tell me that you found that book, never having heard of magic before in your life, then you traveled across your country and into mine and managed to locate my publisher, my favorite café, and my house, with no assistance in any way from any other source?"

I nodded in the affirmative.

"No help? Not sent by anyone, just innocent Mr. Thomas Martin from Ohio, come to get some answers?"

He shook his head and laughed.

"And what about the Curaiv charm?"

"The, cur—what?" I asked in perfect innocence.

He continued to smile as if he were playing along with some kind of game.

"Certainly, how could you know of the Curaiv charm, a charm that has been placed on all authentic books relating to the use of magic, time out of mind. The Curaiv charm would prevent anyone who isn't magically learned from taking even the slightest interest in a magical book; they would find the book disdainful in fact. While on the other hand, the magically learned get the effect of intense interest upon first sight of the book—a rather clever marketing side-effect, which is quite on purpose in modern magical publishing, I think."

His arms dropped once again, his hands at the ready, in what felt more and more like a threatening attitude.

"But not for you, Thomas Martin. You, a man who claims to know nothing of magic, somehow did not recoil from the effects of the Curaiv charm, no indeed. You took the book, and then you actually believed what was written in it, and you magically found your way here."

All at once his countenance changed, as if a dawning comprehension had replaced his suspicious line of thinking.

"You magically found your way here! Hand me that book."

He reached out and caught hold of the book before I could comply with his demand willingly. Flipping open the cover, he located the inscription, which he read aloud absentmindedly. He ran his fingers over the ink of his own signature thoughtfully before almost whispering a word that I did not recognize.

"Conexus—"

He snapped the book shut, quickly glanced around me and surveyed the yard, then looked me once more straight in the eyes.

"Follow me."

Spindlebrock's house was a large, stately affair on a generous plot, and his front entryway was even more luxurious than the exterior of the home implied it would be. It was perfectly clean and devoid of clutter; in fact, the only items to be found in the entry were entirely generic in every sense, like one might see in a stock photo. I walked to the center of the room before the professor shut the door, eliminating much of the already sparse light.

"Now, I want you to listen very closely, Thomas Martin. I'm going to tell you everything that you want to know, if all you really want is what you have already claimed. But first, you're going to have to tell me a few things."

He paused, smiling.

"Well now, let's not waste this opportunity; a thought has occurred to me. Wait here, do not leave this room. I think you would find that the stairs and halls all lead to locked doors in any case."

He disappeared through a side door. I caught a glimpse of a room quite in disarray, in total contrast to the one which I inhabited. After a few moments, professor Spindlebrock returned.

"I have in my hand a potion," he held up a vial of clear liquid before continuing.

"This potion is both colorless and odorless, as most well-formulated and well-made potions are."

He took a few steps toward me and held the bottle out.

"Take it."

I took the potion and examined it carefully. It looked like a vial of water, with no markings or other hints of description.

"Drink it."

"But, what is it? What does it do?"

The professor smiled.

"Ah, now that's the interesting part. This potion will allow me, without fail, to know if your intentions are what you say they are."

I hesitated.

"Is it a truth serum of some sort?"

The professor laughed.

"A potion of truth is a fickle thing, even for an advanced brewer. Its effects are harsh, and many subjects deal poorly with them. No, it is not a potion of truth. Let's call it a potion of trust. I will not tell you what is in it, nor what it does. I will only tell you that in order to get my help, you must drink it. It is a potion of my own invention, without a documented name, made from a recipe I have shared with no one. You will drink it, or I will show you the door."

I almost decided to let the professor keep his secrets, whatever they might be, rather than risk downing an unknown potion from an agitated man who was exhibiting clear signs of paranoia. But my curiosity, which had gotten me this far, led me to recklessness and bravado. I uncorked the potion and drank it in one gulp, without breaking eye contact. As promised, it had no smell and no taste whatsoever.

In an instant, professor Spindlebrock procured a small notepad and a pencil. He flipped the notepad open and began scribbling furiously while bombarding me with questions.

"How do you feel?"

"I feel fine, I guess."

"Are you dizzy at all?"

"No, I—"

"Nauseous?"

"No—"

"How many fingers am I holding up?"

He held up none, but continued to write.

"None, you're just wri—"

"Do you remember how you got here?"

"Yes, of course, I—"

"And Scott, do you remember telling me about him?"

"Yes."

"My contact at the publisher, do you remember her name?"

"She never told—"

"Tell me, in your own words, what exactly happened when you set out to find me."

"Well, I looked for an address in the front matter of your book, but didn't find one. I searched on the internet but could find no trace of you, so I looked to your publisher."

"And how did you find them?"

"Well, it said in your book that they were in Toronto, so I arranged to stay with a friend in Toronto while I looked for them."

"Ah, but their address is not listed, is it?"

"That's true, I just walked around, starting in an indus—"

"Did you bring the book with you?"

"What?"

"When you walked around looking for my publisher, did you have the book with you?"

"Well, yes, I needed to show them—"

"Good, go on. You took the book and walked around until you found them. How long did that take?"

He continued furiously scratching out notes, not looking up as he questioned me.

"As it happened I got lucky, I searched very little and found them in a small office on the harbor."

"Uh huh, and what did they tell you?"

"Nothing, really. I did manage to get an old address."

"And when you visited that address, what did you find there?"

"The person there didn't know a thing about you, I—"

"That sounds right, why should they? And then you found my café, by your previous account. How did you manage that?"

"Well, the thought came to me that perhaps I could check around, see if any local businesses knew you—"

"And the café, it was the first place you checked?"

"As a matter of fact, yes, it was."

"Why did you go there?"

"I don't know, it looked like a good place to start."

"And the book, you had it with you still?"

"Well yes, I thought I would need to maybe show it to a few—"

"Yes, yes. And at the café, you came across Scott. Why did he help you?"

"I don't know, he seemed to think that I was some kind of authority out looking for you, I guess."

"I see. And he revealed the name of the street on which I now live, which is a long street lined with hundreds of houses. You searched for days to find the right one I presume?"

"No, not really. Actually I thought this house in particular looked promising."

"This was the first house you came to?"

"Yes."

"This very one? This one house among hundreds, many built in the same time period, frequently similar in appearance, and yet you chose this one. Why?"

"Well, I don't know, I had a feeling—"

"Precisely! Conexus if I ever heard the tale!"

He looked up at me and snapped his notebook shut.

"We'd better sit you down Thomas," he said with a look of grave concern. He directed me to a chair. After a few moments of observation, turning my head from side to side, pulling my eyelids down and prying my mouth open, and mumbling, "Hmm," and, "I see," the professor stepped back, arms folded and one fist under his chin, and just watched.

Time passed—it felt like an eternity—with the professor just standing there as if he were waiting for something to happen. I became increasingly nervous. Ghost symptoms and hypochondria set in, and I started to feel frantic. Finally, I couldn't bear it any longer.

"What did you give me? I demand to know what is going on! What was in that potion?"

At this professor Spindlebrock laughed heartily, continuing on for much longer than I felt was decorous. I was surprised, and began to feel as if I were the target of an unmerited ridicule.

"I honestly don't find this humorous, sir."

"Oh, of course you don't!" he said, walking over and clapping me on the shoulder. He shook my hand, helping me out of the chair.

"It was water, my friend, just water. Nothing in the bottle at all but some harmless H2O!"

I was speechless.

"A non-brewing of my own invention, designed to test even the stoutest magician's willpower and resolve! Consider, my boy, if you were one of the types that I have no interest in speaking with; a reporter, a college student, or someone of that nature. Why, those who know me, or know of me, would never trust me enough to down one of my potions without knowing exactly what it was, and what it would do! But, if, on the other hand, you were what you said you were—Thomas Martin from Ohio, a man out of place in a world that recently lost much of its context, a man with questions—that man, that Thomas Martin, would be ready and willing to do almost anything. And well, if he wasn't, then he wouldn't be worth my time."

The stunned look on my face seemed to please him. He smiled and continued.

"You see Thomas, when you have as many enemies as I do, you need to be sure of things like this. Now, to more important matters."

He led me to a door opposite the one he had retrieved the fake potion from. It opened into a sitting room, ornately furnished, yet as sterile as the entryway, with no signs of any personal touch. We sat down in two wingback chairs, facing a window which overlooked the front yard.

"As I promised, I will answer all of your questions, but before I do, I think it's important that you take a few facts into consideration. First, the ease with which you found me at my residence. Now, it may not have felt easy to you, traveling about, searching high and low. But at the very least, you accept that you did have several apparent strokes of luck along the way?"

"Yes, that seems fair."

We sat comfortably, but I was not yet comfortable with the man or his methods. Still, he was candid, and his logic was just. He continued.

"And you may not know it, but your stroke of so-called luck at the very end was the most remarkable of them all. Did you take note of the house number as you walked up to my door?"

"No, honestly, I did not."

"That's because there isn't one. There is no marking of any kind on this house. There is no mailbox, no mail slot. The house is not properly identified on any map, nor does it have an address of any kind assigned to it. But that's not all."

He smiled knowingly and continued.

"This house is protected by a charm, and a very powerful one at that. Like the charm on the book, or the simple charm I attempted to attach to Scott which most obviously failed; I have attached a charm of considerable complexity and power to this entire property."

I listened intently, forgetting my apprehension. After a bumpy start, we were finally on the subject that had brought me there in the first place!

"That charm should have made this house the last house you would have wished to try. You most likely would have overlooked it entirely, unless you were paying strict attention and had some level of understanding about these kinds of things, enough to watch out for them. But even then..."

"What are you saying?"

"Only that luck had nothing to do with you finding this house. Every bit of luck and logic—and even magic—was working against you. Everything was working against you, except for this."

He handed back the book that he had taken from my hands earlier.

"This book is a rare book indeed. Oh, it was published and read widely enough, but I only ever signed a single copy. I never sign my books. This one was special."

He leaned back and closed his eyes, touching his fingers together and breathing in deeply, caught up in a memory.

"But what does that have to do with anything?" I asked.

He tapped his fingers on his mouth thoughtfully a few moments before opening his eyes again.

"You see, Thomas, this book was more than just a bound printing of my contrived words. This copy that you found, it has my own writing in it, it was signed by my own hand—

with some amount of thought and emotion, I might add. This book helped lead you to me, Thomas."

"So," I ventured, "this book has a charm, because you wrote in it, and that led me here?"

Spindlebrock shook his head.

"No. No charm did this. Something far more powerful and unique. You, Thomas. You did this. The power is in you."

Chapter 5

A Borrowed Trinket

ur discourse was interrupted by the hired help that Spindlebrock had mistaken me for, who had finally arrived at his front door. Leaving me in the sitting room, he answered the knock and promptly dismissed the young man, apparently an intern of some kind from the university where Spindlebrock taught. I was flattered, at the time, with the idea that I was more interesting than whatever project the young man had been sent to help with.

"You'll stay for dinner, of course?"

The rhetorical question was rattled off abruptly as Spindlebrock peeked his head into the sitting room for an instant before withdrawing again. A few minutes later he re-appeared holding two plates stacked with sandwich materials.

As I ate, professor Spindlebrock explained the power that he had alluded to, a power called Conexus. Since I'm certain that many of my readers are magicians, I will acknowledge up-front that the science of Conexus is rather hotly disputed, and that Spindlebrock himself is perhaps one of the only respected and well-known magicians to find merit in the idea. Nonetheless, I submit to all readers—for the purpose of this recitation—a few scant details on the subject, which were given to me that day.

Conexus is, simply put, a power that an individual may posses that allows that individual to "connect with others through the medium of created works." That is to say, a person with this ability might use a created object to locate, understand, or communicate with the creator of that object. I've learned through my own experiences that this ability is rare in the utmost, and its existence is not widely accepted, even within a group of people accustomed to witnessing fantastic things. The feelings and impressions that I had in relation to my search for professor Spindlebrock were in fact a subtle pulling or drawing, almost like an internal compass. For reasons that he did not share at the time, professor Spindlebrock had a special interest in such a gift.

After we finished dinner, the professor enlightened me with some promised details of the "magical commonality," as he called it. He gave me a very brief glimpse into the modern uses of magic, answered a few of my uneducated questions about the bounds and limits of magic, and introduced me to the very loose organization of the commonality. His description of the distributed nature of the magicians, in terms of governance, was of particular interest to me at the time.

As our discussion wound down, the professor offered me a room for the night. I attempted to refuse, noting that I was staying at a friend's apartment downtown, but Spindlebrock seemed intent on precluding my refusal by arguing that his house was of considerable size and only inhabited by himself, and that he wouldn't be able share more information about magic if I were to leave precipitously.

As he was quite insistent—and out of a strong desire to learn as much as possible, as quickly as possible—I accepted the offer. Spindlebrock arranged to have my luggage picked up and my friend's key returned to his building doorman. Things were arranged quickly and efficiently, and in very little time I was retiring to bed reluctantly, with the promise of having more revealed to me in the morning.

For those who know nothing of professor Spindlebrock —including the majority of his acquaintances who have never known him personally in any meaningful degree—I have offered a brief glimpse into our first meeting as a sort of introduction to his character. He can be hard, exacting, and even threatening at times, but he is ultimately straight-forward, efficient, and not entirely without humor. He is private in the extreme, but hospitable and accommodating when the right occasion presents itself.

I slept so soundly that night that I half wondered if Spindlebrock had put something in the fake potion after all. Waking was surreal. The discussions and events of the previous day flooded my mind as I sat in bed, taking in the morning sun and the sound of the birds through my open window. Those who have woken up the day after their life changed forever will perhaps understand a little of what I felt.

As soon as I was dressed, I followed an amazing aroma down the stairs and into the dining room, where the professor was already seated, eating and reading a paper.

"Good morning, Thomas Martin! Pull up a chair and have a bite!"

I pulled up a chair and surveyed the table. It was covered with an array of appetizing dishes: fresh fruit and cream, several decanters of different juices, and even English muffins, my favorite. Hunger overcame shyness, and I began to serve myself.

"Did you use magic to make all this?"

Professor Spindlebrock set his newspaper down and smiled.

"With magic, my boy, anything is possible."

"Not likely," came a voice from the kitchen, followed by a chuckle from Spindlebrock. Moments later a cheerful woman with auburn hair and a playful smile emerged through a swinging half-door, carrying a small plate with butter and a knife.

"Here you go," she said, setting the plate down in front of me. Instinctively, I stood.

49

"Sit down Thomas, there's no need for all that," Spindlebrock said, picking up his paper again.

"This is Delphine Harris, a colleague of mine at the University. I asked her to help me out this morning, since I had company."

"A pleasure," I said.

Delphine looked to be about the same age as Spindlebrock, with bright and attractive features, and an extremely pleasant disposition. We conversed lightly on various subjects. She seemed surprised to learn that I was not at all connected with magic; she turned several times toward Spindlebrock, looking for an explanation, which he did not give.

When everyone appeared to be done eating and talking, I began to gather dishes to clear the table, but quickly found that my help would not be required—with a wave of her hand, Delphine set the whole table in motion cleaning itself.

"Telekinesis," Spindlebrock explained, "the ability to move things with the mind."

"Can all magicians do it?" I asked, watching in amazement as dishes flew themselves through the open top of the kitchen's half-door, wiped their contents either into the trash bin or into bowls to save for later, and then delivered themselves to the dishwasher.

"Well, most magicians can manage some small display with a great deal of effort, but with her it's an art form."

Delphine seemed to appreciate the compliment, which she returned with a light kiss on Spindlebrock's cheek. After everything was cleaned up we thanked her as she headed out to prepare for a class. As soon as she was out the door, Spindlebrock ran to a nearby window and watched her walk down the street until she was out of view. He then hurriedly motioned for me to follow him into his study, the cluttered room which I had only glimpsed the night before.

While most of his home was an impeccable tribute to good housekeeping, Spindlebrock's study was a perfect garbage heap. We wandered past tables covered in Bunsen burners warming beakers of foul smelling liquids, precariously tall stacks of papers, and contraptions of every description, to a desk in the back of the dimly lit room. There were no windows; the only egress appeared to be the door coming in at the front, and a door marked File Room at the back. The professor pushed aside a pile of clutter on his desk, reached into his pocket, and set down a small silver charm which he began admiring with a magnifying glass.

"What is it?" I asked.

"Have you ever seen a charm so intricate, so beautiful?"

I sheepishly answered that I could not yet detect a magical charm on an object.

"No, no, not magic! Look man, it's from a charm bracelet!"

I examined the tiny silver charm. It was indeed intricate and beautiful.

"I've never seen a charm with so much detail," I said quietly after a few moments study.

"And you never will again. Delphine makes these, but only for her bracelet. It's one of her many talents."

"Did she drop it?"

"No. I took it, while she was leaning over to give me a kiss on the cheek."

I look at him incredulously.

"Slight of hand,"—he made a sweeping motion—"it's a very simple kind of magic, if you will."

He admired the charm for a few more moments before straightening up and turning back to me.

"Now then, I probably don't need to ask, but have you ever been to the University of Magic, Toronto?"

I shook my head. I did not know such a thing even existed.

"Good. We're going to test this Conexus theory out for a second time, Thomas. You found me, let's see if you can dazzle us both by finding Delphine, and the University—which is more hidden and well protected than my home."

Digging through a few of his piles, Spindlebrock produced a small piece of sturdy looking cord, which he threaded through the ring of the charm and tied into a makeshift necklace. He motioned for me to lean forward, and slid it over my head.

"There. Now, don't lose that or she'll eviscerate me, you understand? Good, now here's what we'll do..."

The plan was that professor Spindlebrock would go ahead, and I would follow after some time had passed. I was to use the charm—my instructions were simply to hold it in my hands and follow any impressions that I got—to locate Delphine at the University, and professor Spindlebrock would join up with us at that point. I made some objection to the hastiness of it all, but it was no use; a plan devised by Spindlebrock would be carried out.

He left the house, binding me by an oath that I would not so much as peek out the front window to see which way he turned. I was to wait a full twenty minutes, to avoid any chance that I might see him along the route. I did as instructed, but as I left his front yard I was overcome with that particular variety of fear you feel when you have no idea what you're doing, but you have to do it anyway. My mind raced with a flurry of ridiculous possibilities, which resolved into the realization that I had no notion of how to find a magical place that didn't want to be found. I reached down and fingered the silver charm that hung from my neck when it hit me; an obscure sensation that I should head east. Optimism, hope, and a sense of direction seemed to fill my mind. Confidence still lacked, but I started down the street, resolved to follow every impression that drew or pushed me in any way.

After walking for several blocks I ended up at a bus stop, scanned the schedule and decided to get on the downtown line; a transfer later and I was heading north. As the bus passed between Clairville and Bolton, I had the distinct feeling that I needed to get off. I took the next stop and backtracked to the very spot I had felt the impression, and found a road heading west into a conservation area. A short walk later, the road terminated at a large circular turnaround with a small building in the middle, bordering a forest. A large sign read, "Nature Center," and a smaller sign under it indicated that it was closed for renovations. It didn't look like a university, even by the most humble standards, but somehow I knew that I had arrived.

It was a strange experience, attempting the seemingly impossible with only an ephemeral awareness that something within could aid me in the process. To this day I still can't fully explain the power, but it's as real to me now as my sense of smell or taste. Regardless of the status of Conexus as a power or study within the magical commonality, I personally have no doubts.

I walked around the nature center, looking for any sign of activity, when I spotted a path leading into the woods. It was dark, ill-used, and overgrown. My heart sank despairingly at the thought of exploring it, but something stronger than fear moved my feet onto the path, and before I could think through what I was feeling, I was under the dark canopy of the trees. A black cloud of foreboding swirled in my mind with each step, the sort that you encounter in dreams, when you know that some unknown evil is mere moments from wrapping around your very soul. It took all of my resolve to push forward.

Just as I felt I could bear no more darkness, the trees thinned out and the light of the sun touched my skin. Relief rushed through me in tingles as the woods opened into a great field, flanked by orchards surrounding a cluster of large buildings, the tallest and most central emblazoned with, "University of Magic Toronto." Chuckling softly, I took in the scene. Spindlebrock's test had worked; I had arrived.

The path opened into a wide paved lane, which gave entrance to a commons bustling with students of all ages. Fantastical scenes overwhelmed me as I slowly made my way in the direction of what looked like an administrative building: a group of teens debating levitation with an octogenarian feigning seriousness while slowly floating a few inches into the air; two women chatting as they walked to class, their skin tones morphing dramatically in sun and shade; and a young man doing ridiculously high kick-flips on a skateboard with liquidy rubber wheels, while his friends sat watching nearby, flicking a hacky sack back and forth through the air using only magic wands.

Hardly paying attention to where I was walking, I tripped over the edge of a planter and clipped the arm of a passer-by, upsetting his cup of coffee as I toppled to the ground. After a brief exclamation followed by a long, frustrated sigh, he helped me to my feet.

"You need to be more careful."

I excused myself profusely while dusting off my embarrassment.

"Where are you heading? You look a little lost."

Finally looking up, I found that I had collided with an rather serious and authoritative looking gentleman; a small tag on his sport jacket read simply, "Dr. Patel." I stammered out a nervous half-response.

"Hi, yes, um, I'm looking, um..."

Delphine came to mind, but I choked on her last name. I blurted out the only other name I knew.

"Spindlebrock. Professor Spindlebrock. He asked me to come and see him."

Dr. Patel was visibly taken aback. His shocked expression faded into a smirk as he eyed me up and down.

"You? I can't imagine why. Spindlebrock hardly speaks with faculty, let alone individual students."

He examined me earnestly for a few moments before realizing something was out of place.

"Where's your student ID badge? You're required to wear one at all times on campus."

He started to reach for something on his belt, a wooden handle protruding from a long, narrow leather case, when he caught sight of the charm around my neck.

"And what's this?" He pointed to, then examined the charm.

"Isn't that—"

"This? This is what professor Spindlebrock wanted, actually. I was to return it as soon as possible."

The man looked at me quizzically.

"He loaned it to me for a project. I was to bring it back to him, I think he said it belonged to someone named Delphine."

"Professor Harris—yes, she makes them. Though, I can't imagine her ever loaning them out. What was the project?"

I breathed a sigh of relief as I caught sight of Spindlebrock approaching. He shouted out greetings as he hurried toward us.

"Thomas! Professor Patel! I was just looking for this young man, Patel, what kind of trouble is he giving you?"

Dr. Patel looked confused.

"None, Spindlebrock, none at all. I was just wondering where his badge was."

"Indeed, good eye Patel. I mostly ignore the students and their petty problems, but you tend to pay a lot more attention to even the least meaningful details! Yes, he forgot his badge in my classroom, and thanks to your fastidiousness, he is now late in bringing me back something of great value."

Spindlebrock held his palm outstretched. I removed the charm from around my neck and gave it to him.

"You know, this young man was making a particular study of magically-created artistic relics. He begged me to get professor Harris to loan him this one, and I saw an opportunity. As you know, I hire interns regularly enough— this one I've hired for the low wage of a borrowed trinket!"

Patel, unimpressed by Spindlebrock's swindle and annoyed at his jabs, bid us a brusque, "Good day," before turning and walking away. After watching him until he was out of earshot, Spindlebrock turned toward me, excited.

"So, you did it! And no small feat, Thomas Martin, no small feat at all!" He clapped me on the shoulder and turned to face the campus buildings.

"Impressive, is it not, that such a spot can be hidden right here near the heart of Toronto! It takes a fair amount of work for our freshmen to find this place for the first time, even with instructions."

He began to walk toward the large center building, motioning for me to follow.

"We have an entire city convinced that this area is nothing more than wildlife space. On the technical side of things, we have contacts in various governments around the world, who help ensure satellite imagery doesn't give us away either."

Spindlebrock glanced at me.

"Ah, but all this might be a bit fast. Come, we'll go to my office and settle a few things before I tell you anything more."

He was correct in his observation; despite my great desire to learn about this new world of spells and charms, I hadn't prepared myself for the depth of it, and I was overwhelmed. Though I knew from the very beginning of my adventure that the book I possessed was written by a man who had earned the title of professor, I hadn't considered that he might actually teach at an educational institution entirely dedicated to the learning of magic. I hadn't considered that a thriving community, with hopeful youth and wise leaders might be hiding in plain sight in one of the most populous cities in the world. There were many things that I hadn't considered, and the implications of my naivete were beginning to worry me.

After winding through a maze of hallways, with many students and faculty members giving me empathetic looks that said, "Good luck," and, "Sorry you got caught," we found our way to Spindlebrock's office. It was almost as messy as his home study, but we managed to find two seats that could be made serviceable with only a little cleaning.

"Now, let me tell you that what I said back there about hiring you as my intern was not a joke, but a suggestion. I'm involved in a line of study and work that requires a great deal of—"

Over-enthusiastic, I took a risk and interrupted.

"Wait, just please wait a minute. This is, well, amazing. I had no idea there was a university of magic with such a large population of people like you!"

He peered at me with a quizzical, almost accusing look. I suddenly recalled that he was a published and apparently well-known author.

"OK, yes, I understand—an author has to have an audience. I just didn't expect—"

"That we'd be organized, educated, cohesive?"

"No, it's not that—"

"That we'd have students and teachers, places to meet, security, and beautiful homes?"

"I just—"

"Did you think we'd live in swamps or on mountain tops, with long beards and capes, pointy hats, stooped over iron cauldrons all day and turning visitors into frogs?"

I had no words. Thankfully, Spindlebrock began to laugh. It was several moments before he regained his composure.

"I tell you, Thomas, I haven't had this much fun in a long, long while. The stereotypes are so antiquated, and the connection between magician and modern man so completely severed, that all people really have to draw from are storybook ideas from ages past. Now, if you'll be patient, I'll back up and start from the beginning before putting forth a proposition."

To his credit, and contrary to many things I've heard about the man since, professor Spindlebrock demonstrated a great deal of understanding and patience that day. Because his explanations were so valuable to me then, and because at least some of those who read this will certainly not be acquainted with the magical commonality, I will continue my narrative from memory, and try to capture everything that was shared in as true a recounting as possible.

"First, Thomas, I'll give you a bit more of a foothold in the history of magicians. We don't have all day of course, and you'll be able to delve into written history in your own time, I'm sure, so I'll keep it short and to the point.

"Magicians have been around at least since the start of humanity's earliest remaining records. Like most people of influence and power, Magicians were often mixed up with political and religious affairs, sometimes to their credit and advancement, but more frequently to their detriment and danger. What people call us, and what they think about us, have changed over the years. All in all, we're the same type of people we've always been, as far as talents and capacities are concerned.

"Around AD seven hundred, in a time period humanity in general refers to as the 'Dark Ages,' Magicians faced particular challenges politically. We suffered great persecution, which did not abate until well after colonial American times. Many Magicians simply went into hiding, while others formed societies and groups of various kinds, in an attempt to subdue the rising persecution.

"We had our share of power seekers then—and we still do now—which caused a great deal of havoc for the rest of us. Gain-seeking impostors, of the variety that you read about in the Bible, also took a serious toll. Thankfully, in the late nineteenth century we began to follow a more responsible tack, creating and following our own rules, and working together. We also ceased to be important to the ruling classes, and disentangled ourselves from religion and politics. That's not to say that we're not religious or political, but rather that churches and governments no longer seek to exploit our skills for their own gain.

"In the twentieth century, with the rest of the world, we experienced an explosion of progress. Our scholars turned their efforts toward more disciplined scientific studies, and have indeed contributed to many of the modern advancements that you are unavoidably familiar with. In our own realm we've also enjoyed magical advancements that we haven't been able to share with the general population, for obvious reasons.

"Today we have our own notion of political and organizational ideals. Having learned from the past, we avoid anything akin to a central government, opting instead to rely on tribunals at the local level, and a larger council for affairs that grow beyond a local scope. That larger council is what you might call the ultimate authority in our world; it's known as the Preeminent Council, or the Pre-em, for short.

"We have our own social circles, our own educational systems, et cetera. All of this we call the commonality—not a community, per se, but a group of people with common goals and interests, spread throughout the world's societies."

He paused for a few moments, examining my external response.

"As for me personally, you already know that I'm a professor at this university, the University of Magic, Toronto. This is one branch of a larger set of universities that are located in several important cities around the globe. I have a variety of personal interests and pursuits, but my current focus is primarily on first year magical studies; it's the area where I feel I might have the most influence, and where I might meet the most talented magicians early in their careers.

"Now, you no doubt wonder how it is that you haven't heard of 'real magic' until recently. How could we keep such a thing secret? The question of 'why?' is hopefully obvious— the world has not demonstrated itself capable of knowing such things without being tempted to abuse them roundly. So we'll move on to the 'how' of the matter. First of all, everything we produce in the way of reference material— anything that might lead someone like you to us—we protect with powerful but simple differentiation charms. These charms operate on the minds of those that come into contact with those objects. In point of fact, I believe I explained that much to you previously, did I not?"

"Yes, a little. Like the charm on the book, the curve, um..."

"Curaiv, yes, that is one such charm. Books, of course, have the added cloak that the classification of fiction provides. If a person picks up a book that strays too far outside what they feel are the bounds of reality, they drop it neatly in that category.

"Another way we conceal our existence is through a sort of cloaking charm, very powerful and complex. Such a charm might hide an entire university, or it might simply hide a private meeting or other activity, as needed. These charms also work on principles of differentiation, being able to distinguish between magical and non-magically inclined individuals for example, but other forms are possible. They work through a sort of hypnosis, or if that word offends your sensibilities, call it a redirection. The charms first affect the awareness and render the target prone to suggestion, then suggest that certain things their senses can perceive are in fact something else or simply don't exist at all. As a double precaution, these charms also tend to distract or redirect the targets attention to other things. All of this, of course, brings us to the question of what to do with you."

He sat back in his chair. I shifted uncomfortably in mine.

"You have sought me out to learn more about magic, about magicians, about our ways, and about our communities. Maybe you had no idea of the scope of what you'd find. You took considerable risk, since one who is magical might also be dangerous, in the general world view. Did you not think for a moment that a magician might be affronted by a non-magician finding them out?"

"I, I don't think I thought it through much—"

"Obviously. You most likely understood the fact that you yourself had performed some magic to mean that you had a right to learn more, is that correct?"

"Well, when you frame it like that, yes, I suppose I felt that I deserved at least an explanation of what was going on."

"Precisely so; at the very least an explanation, and then your memory erased."

He reached into his coat and produced a wand. It looked to be just over a foot long, perfectly carved of a rich dark wood, lightly polished. He leveled it at my head. I froze in my chair.

"Generally when someone of your age and from your background—that is to say, someone without any real ties to the magical commonality—stumbles upon us, we lead them on as much as necessary in order to learn what they know, secure the situation, and erase their recent memories."

"Wait—"

"Yes! That is generally what we do Thomas Martin! Unapologetically! You would not be an exception, but..."

A slight smile formed on his lips as he gently rolled his wand between his fingers.

"But for the fact that you did not stumble upon us. You did not, by chance or luck, happen upon magic. It was no accident that led you where you sit today, no indeed. A latent gift, magical in the utmost, and rare to boot, manifested itself in you. That 'Conexus' of which we spoke. Fate gave you the key—the book with my signature—and your gift took you the rest of the way. You finding me is more than fate, it is destiny. Do you believe in destiny Thomas?"

He lowered his wand, but kept it in his hand.

"I don't think I've ever given it much thought."

"And God, do you believe in God?"

"No," I answered him honestly, though my answer would be far more complex if one were to ask me today.

Spindlebrock smiled and shook his head.

"Shame. You can know so much about life, and then in an instant you can have your eyes opened to entirely new worlds of information—anyone can do that, it happens in science all the time—and yet, so many people have a difficult time believing that God could exist."

He studied me for a few moments. I attempted to look calm, but my eyes kept darting to the wand in his hand. His gaze never left my face.

"It is destiny, Thomas Martin, no matter what you believe. I am perhaps one of only a very few magicians alive today that would consider letting you enter our commonality, at your age and in your circumstances. I will, in fact, help you do this to your utmost advantage, and at my own great personal expense and risk. But, you have to do something for me.

"Conexus has a particular value in relation to my research, but also in and of itself. If I am to help you, I will ask that you commit to helping me. The ends will be primarily scientific, though our studies may demand that we venture into a variety of endeavors. I can't possibly delineate the whole of what would be required, so I'm offering you a simple choice here and now. I'll assume half the risk, as I don't know you at all and you may prove to be an utter waste. You'll take the other half of the risk, as you certainly don't know me, and are entering a new world, and a new life."

Spindlebrock, who had been bouncing his wand carelessly on one closed fist, now snapped it to attention and aimed it once more at my face.

"Therefore, here are your choices, Thomas. Either I erase your recent memories right here and right now, including all that you know of magic, and hand you over to the Toronto Police Service as a missing person to hopefully be reconnected with your prior life; or, you commit to the situation that I just described: your help in exchange for mine, an introduction and placement in the magical commonality—I'll even let you stay with me—in exchange for your assistance in my research and work."

He stopped talking and we both sat staring at one another for a few moments. My mouth opened and closed as I pondered on the choice before me. To this day I still recall this as one of the most important moments of my life. I know now that professor Spindlebrock's terms were both generous and duplicitous; the work he had in mind for me was especially downplayed. And yet, I would not change the response I gave for anything, regardless of what it has meant and where it has taken me. Though my reply may sound a bit forced, please recall that a wand was pointed directly at me; I was anxious to make my intentions unmistakably clear.

"I swear to you, in the most unbreakable and enduring way possible, that I'll help with your research in any way that I can, if you'll help me explore and understand all of this. I'll be your servant if I must, but please, let me try to earn your trust. Show me exactly what all of this means."

With my unprompted oath, Spindlebrock lowered and then put away his wand.

"Very well. You do understand, I hope, that once you start down this path you can never go back."

I only nodded in reply.

Chapter 6

Spindlebrock's Plan

Integrating into the magical commonality was easily accomplished with Spindlebrock at the helm. All said, it took only a few weeks to organize things to the degree that I could start attending the University as Spindlebrock's assistant. Obtaining a long-term work visa, which would allow me to remain in Canada, was easy enough; but entering the school as a legitimate student was more complicated. Papers had to be in order for admissions, and a suitable personal history, complete with ties to traceable and well-known families, had to be contrived. In all of this Spindlebrock was adept; my papers were signed by his personal friends—who proved to be very significant connections—and family ties were fabricated that joined me with a well-known yet singularly aloof and reclusive magical family.

In addition to clerical formalities, a certain amount of learning was necessary so that I could pass as a student of magic. Adult initiates are unheard of in the commonality, which meant I needed to learn what most of the students would have learned at home in the course of their childhood. I was eager, and the necessary education in elementary magic was therefore achieved with energetic efficiency.

To this day, much to my amazement, my integration has never been questioned. I have no doubt that my lay origins may be a surprise to those of my readers who might know me by name, and a complete shock to those that know me by my association with Spindlebrock, but I offer no apology. I share these things casually, but I want it known that I am not generally of the viewpoint that people should lie about who they are. In this case, and perhaps in many others, the need seemed to outweigh the transgression. The choice was conscious, and I take full responsibility for it by sharing the details openly here and now; others must account for themselves.

As for my old life, there really wasn't much left to worry about. My remaining family members were already distant to the point of being practically unknown to me, and my few friends understood that I was exploring a variety of possibilities.

Almost as soon as I began to feel at ease in this new path, the real work began. Intolerant of mediocrity and unwilling to enlist my aid unless it truly made his work easier, Spindlebrock took note of my comfort and set himself to the task of disrupting it by accelerating my education in more advanced magic. I am pleased to report to you, reader, that I showed a fair bit of talent for one so new. I was especially gifted in wandless magic—having been introduced to it from the very beginning—which gave Spindlebrock great pleasure.

My previous university studies were also not wasted. I was surprised to learn just how much magicians focus on science, and how they use magic to further their scientific research beyond what non-magicians experience. I was no stranger to a laboratory, and much of my early magical education as furnished by professor Spindlebrock took place in such a setting. When he learned that I had previously studied forensic science, Spindlebrock seemed particularly pleased. I recall his reaction:

"What? Forensics? An incredible coincidence! No, better still, it's destiny Thomas, destiny! The firm hand of destiny has molded you into what you are, starting years before you came to meet me."

Later I would learn what this meant, and why he thought as he did. At this point, I knew simply that that my previous education was potentially useful in Spindlebrock's chosen pursuits.

Spindlebrock personally oversaw my education for the next several months, until he felt I would do well taking classes on my own. I was more than content, but it occurred to me one day that while I was getting everything I wanted out of the bargain we had struck, I was giving almost nothing in return. There were some instances where I was truly useful in the lab, and I helped around the house with the cleaning and cooking as much as I possibly could. Still, I hadn't done anything with the Conexus which Spindlebrock had originally been so interested in; for a time I got quite caught up in my studies and almost forgot all about it.

Then one Saturday morning, as I woke up slowly to the warmth of the first rays of sun on my face, I made up my mind to enjoy a leisurely read in bed before I got up to help with breakfast. Without looking, I stretched and rolled over, reaching for the nearest book on my nightstand. As my fingers made contact with the cover, an overwhelming feeling of urgency and distress gripped me. I snatched up the book and flipped it over in my hands; it was the little blue book of traveling spells. A rush of adrenaline and a sharp breath, and somehow I knew that something was about to happen. I soon found out that something already had happened, and that it had produced a profound impact on professor Spindlebrock.

I dropped the book and rushed out of my room. Before I got to the stairs I saw Spindlebrock starting up hurriedly, head bent down in consternation, his steps heavy. I hailed him, fearing some dreadful unknown.

"What is it? What's wrong?" I asked, obviously disheveled.

He stopped and looked at me, puzzled. Comprehension dawned on his face, and he smiled dimly.

"Yes, that's right. Conexus isn't just for finding people, it's also for understanding them. You've been using your talent again, though I'm guessing it was quite by accident."

I saw a hint of suspicion on his face, but it passed quickly, leaving only consternation.

"Thomas, there has been—that is to say, I have had a shock this morning. The son of an old friend of mine has gone missing. I just learned of it. Their family lives in the States—in Arizona to be precise. He attends university there as a freshmen—actually, universities both magical and non-magical. Last night, he did not come home."

I recall being surprised that there was a university of magic in Arizona, but I was not at all surprised by the idea that a freshman might not come home on a Friday night. Spindlebrock, never one to miss an expression or its meaning, corrected me instantly.

"Do not imagine that this is the mere frenzy of a worried parent whose child has partied more than is reasonable. Understand, Thomas, that this is a most serious student-magician, and of a powerful magician family."

He broke off, distracted. Turning slowly, he started down the stairs before calling back to me.

"Pack your things. Meet me for breakfast as quickly as you can. I have two plane tickets for Phoenix departing in less than three hours from Pearson International. I'll explain everything on the flight."

I did as I was told. Delphine—who had been rather sparse ever since Spindlebrock's theft of her artistic charm —had prepared breakfast. Her face and manners were grave and serious. We ate quickly and in silence. Spindlebrock finished first, then rose and spoke to Delphine.

"I do not expect that we'll be gone for more than a few days. Please watch over the house, invite no one, admit no one. Arrange my excuses at the University, attribute it to some illness—no, just tell them that I'm in a fit of focused study and refuse to leave my lab."

Delphine nodded without comment. Generally she would not accept brusque orders from Spindlebrock, even in jest, but this morning was different. Their whole interaction was altered, brimming with concern.

We parted and made our way to the airport, snaked slowly and silently through security, then boarded the plane and found our seats. Spindlebrock had paid for three, so that we had a portion of an aisle to ourselves, from the row to the window. As we sat, he pulled out his wand and began a series of incantations that I was entirely unfamiliar with. When he finished, he flopped down into his seat relieved.

"Protective charms, powerful ones," he said, recognizing my confusion.

"There are few magicians—and I'm quite certain none on this flight—that would be able to see or hear through them. To all that walk past, these seats will appear empty. Those concerned with the affairs of this flight will feel the seats are meant to be empty, for an excellently logical reason, though they won't quite be able to pinpoint what that reason is."

He folded down his seat tray and removed a small notebook and pen from his jacket pocket. He spoke as he noted a few things in his illegible handwriting.

"No one will take notice of us. We may speak freely, and indeed we will need the time to get you up to speed."

He flipped back through his notes, looking for something as the plane taxied and took flight.

"Here it is; Tera Bedisa of Bakersfield, California. Gone missing five years ago on January fourteenth. Had just graduated from high school the previous fall. Her father taught at the university of magic there. Returned home on her own, three days later, with no memory of what had happened."

Several more pages turned, and he continued.

"Tasia Dorotea of Pula, Croatia. Gone missing five years ago on August twenty-third. Just started her first semester in a university of magic where her mother was the Associate

Head of School. Returned to her dorm on her own, also three days later, with no memory of what had happened."

One, two pages more. He was reading only bits now as he scanned through his notes.

"Charmion Añuli, four years ago, gone three days, prominent connections to a university of magic. Marianna Eulalia, Shashi Ofelia, Avitus Summerfield, Aroldo McCrae, and Peter Althuis, all gone missing about three years ago, gone three days, returned to their homes with no memory of where they had been or why."

Spindlebrock now flipped to a hand-drawn chart of names comprising several pages near the end of his notebook, which he showed me.

"You see, these are the names of all of the prominent leaders and staff members in our university systems around the world, and below each one, the names of their children —only the ones with children are listed."

I saw that several of the names he had mentioned were circled, along with many other names that he had not mentioned.

"Over the past five years, starting with Tera Bedisa, more and more young people, generally around the age when they are getting ready to leave home, have gone missing each year. More and more, until last year."

He paused, then flipped easily to a page that was well worn.

"Lilianne Marie Harris, of Toronto Canada. Gone missing last March, during her final semester at the University of Magic, Toronto. Her mother, Delphine Harris, Research Centre Director and Professor. Returned home on her own, only two days later, with no memory of where she had been."

He tapped his book thoughtfully before closing it.

"I had already been following these disappearances when Lilianne went missing. Two years ago, with a phone call from a friend in Germany, a professor, I became involved in one such case—my first involvement. The son, in this case, was of an incredibly serious nature. He had, for example, already been published in several journals, and was actively involved in his studies, professionally and academically. I flew out immediately to help this dear friend, and his concern was immense. His son, who still lived at home, was never—and I mean never—late or absent without speaking with his father. It was simply the way he did things.

"Admittedly, I was concerned. We magicians aren't without enemies, and the world is by nature a dangerous place. I imagined the worst, but we determined to do all in our power to locate him, and quickly. The local authorities were called out, but missing persons of that age and in those circumstances are common, and our report was not taken seriously. Much of the searching we did on our own. We employed all of our magical abilities, but came up lacking. The few clues we did possess led us to a dead end—we surmised only that he had entered a taxi after completing some laboratory work with a colleague, and that was the end of it.

"Three days later, the son came home. He was a wreck. He looked and smelled as if he had been partying the entire time he was gone. He remembered nothing. Despite his rather narrow and contained behavior as a youth, the father assumed he had been experimenting with another side of adolescence. I might have thought the same thing, but the boy was distraught at the idea, insanely distraught. He truly remembered nothing. No charm or magical device we had access to could get anything out of him, with or without his help."

Spindlebrock sighed and turned to look at the sea of clouds outside his window. Some time passed before he opened his notebook and began speaking again.

"Something about the whole thing bothered me. After I returned home from that trip I began researching missing person cases related to known magician families—that's when I started this notebook. There were abductions more than I thought reasonable, though I confess I did not appeal to hard statistics. I started to notice a pattern: a bulk of the recent disappearances—almost all that I could find in fact—

were primarily late adolescent or young adult children of prominent university staff.

"Now, I don't deny that young people go missing frequently in this disturbing world, often of their own volition, and sometimes in more nefarious schemes. But this was a clear pattern, and I was determined to follow it through until I understood its boundaries, its depth and width. I looked back at as many cases as I could get access to. I have connections enough, and was able to search through police records in various countries relating to the cases that interested me most. Always they were similar in age and circumstance, and always they were missing for three days before returning, unharmed yet with an inexplicable and curiously complete memory loss."

I was enthralled by Spindlebrock's story, and had primarily nodded and listened. But something was nagging at the back of my mind. Finally, it struck me.

"But, Delphine's daughter, you said she returned after only two days?"

Spindlebrock nodded slowly. His gaze was momentarily caught by a steward who was trundling down the aisle with a cart of drinks. Knowing that the crew member would be oblivious of our presence, Spindlebrock reached over and grabbed two sodas before the gentleman moved on. He set one down in front of me before continuing.

"Yes, that's right, Lilianne was a unique case. I'll get to that, but first you need to realize how deep this went. I followed my pattern all the way back to Tera Bedisa of Bakersfield, California. Before hers, there wasn't single case —not one—that matched the pattern. I searched back as far as I could. Tera was the first.

"I visited with Tera's parents, but they had little to offer. Tera herself was away from home when I dropped in, and when we called her on the phone she was unwilling to agree to a meeting. Her parents recalled the disappearance as best they could, but even right after it happened they said that they couldn't get anything out of their daughter, not so much as a fuzzy memory of the incident. They are quite accomplished magicians, and used advanced methods— potions and charms that you won't come across unless you're deadly serious—but in spite of all this, they came up empty handed.

"Thomas, I realize that you have very limited knowledge of these things, but this sort of science is part of my life's work. It is unheard of to have two solid magicians of their skill and experience apply themselves with no results. Even in the worse cases of memory extraction that I have seen, something is always extracted. There is at least a vague memory, a faint picture, a clue. But in the case of Tera, there was nothing. Void. Darkness."

My attention and awe seemed to please Spindlebrock, who went on with a slight look of satisfaction in the effect that his words were producing.

"I attempted to research other cases, with similar results. After I started studying them, several more cases cropped up, and always I immediately became involved. Each and every time, nothing could be done, nothing could be found out. Always the person returned after three days, and upon their return they had absolutely no memory of the events. It was the most infernal affair, and it drove me mad. Never could I find out anything.

"From what you know of me, you probably will not be surprised to learn that I carried out my involvement in these cases with total and complete discretion. Where it was necessary, I even altered the memory of those people who knew me, or knew of me, and might reveal my interest. My goal, throughout, was to find a culprit without first being found out myself. I knew that once I was revealed, whoever was at the heart of this would be a great deal more careful in their activities, and my chances of finding them would be diminished."

At this point a thought began to occur to me, and I voiced it to Spindlebrock without really thinking it through.

"But professor, I don't understand—why did you take such an interest? I mean, the youth were in all cases restored to their families and lives, right? And don't you have enough going on without involving yourself in something as common as missing persons cases? That's the realm of the police."

Spindlebrock nodded.

"Yes, it is their realm, you are right. For the moment, suffice it to say that I had a scientific and personal interest. I don't let those interests go lightly."

He paused, watching to see if his explanation was sufficient, then went on.

"You asked about the case of Lilianne, Delphine's daughter. It was a truncated case of only two days, cut short because whoever was carrying out these abductions had become careless, and did not realize that anyone was on their trail. Delphine has long been a close friend of mine, and when her very upright daughter went missing, I knew exactly what it meant. I poured my whole soul into the effort to find her. I activated every resource at my immediate disposal in Toronto, and I called in every favor owed to me. Beyond just the city, I reached out to the most powerful magical minds around the globe—we were all bent on the problem of finding her. This was my chance. I don't know where it was or who it was, but one of us was close, very close, and the abductor became nervous. In this one case, the abductee returned in only two days instead of three, because the abductor feared being found out.

"Additionally—and again only in this one case—her memory had not be as cleanly and completely destroyed. She was confused and disoriented. She had not returned home, but had been left in a park. The city police had returned her home, after doing a few crude drug tests and finding nothing. But I did my own tests, with Delphine's help. We went to work with the full resources of the University, and my own laboratory. We found traces of the potion she had taken, or was forced to take, still in her system, not fully metabolized. We isolated the compounds involved. While working on this, we also worked on recovering any memories that we could."

"Recovering memories?"

"Yes. It's a complex process that you should learn about at some point, as it comes in extremely handy when you're working with people who have been, we could say mistreated, by a magician. It's squarely in the realm of forensics, you'd enjoy the subject."

I nodded, and he went on.

"In the end we gained two things out of our monumental effort. First, we found chemical traces of what we later perfected into the most powerful Mundus Memoraie serum—that's a memory potion—ever conceived by magicians. And second, we captured a clue, which consisted of a single word."

"A single word?"

"Yes, a faint impression that had not been entirely effaced—like I said, it's a complex process, with complex and fascinating results."

"What was the word?" I asked.

"I can't tell you right now—and, no, I can't even tell you why."

I let the subject drop. He again tapped on his notebook.

"These clues were certainly a break, but they did not amount to very much. I still had—and still have today—no real understanding of what is motivating these abductions. But I do have cause for great concern. Aside from myself and perhaps a handful of other magicians I know, there are no other magicians in the whole of the modern or historical magical world that know as much as I do about potions. Yet this potion, the one that we discovered in Lilianne's veins, is like nothing I've ever even conceived. It is a work of art."

Spindlebrock's gaze drifted once more to the endless sky outside the tiny window. Questions started to crowd my mind, but instinct told me to respect his silence. After a lengthy pause he began again, without taking his eyes off the sky.

"I tried the potion on myself. Under the supervision of Delphine, and in strict laboratory conditions, I recreated and drank this Mundus Memoraie potion. It was risky and Delphine did not approve, but she never could stop me in my work, no matter how foolhardy it was. The potion worked, but was significantly stronger than expected.

"Delphine told me that for an entire month after taking the potion I was almost myself, though more completely honest. It was the honesty that tipped her and me off that the potion was still functional. Toward the end of that month I became listless and disoriented, until I fell suddenly ill. In the course of that brief illness I eventually blacked out, and when I came to, I remembered nothing of the entire month prior. We attempted to recover any memories that we could, but found nothing. We analyzed my blood looking for any remaining sign of the potion, but all trace of it was gone.

"As it turned out, the potion was—once in the body—a volatile compound. After it metabolized fully there would be no trace, nothing left to find. It was by pure chance—no, pure providence—that we were able to recover Lilianne before the compound had disappeared. We surmised through the first experiment on myself that the compound was likely administered at the beginning of the abduction, and did not take full effect until the end. It was relatively simple to re-formulate the potion to increase its volatility; the three day period was an intentional formulation, long enough to accomplish a task, but short enough not to raise too much suspicion or alarm."

Spindlebrock began to flip through his notebook once more. He stopped at his most recent entry.

"This one, in Arizona. My old friend, Edmond Bennett, called me as soon as he suspected something. He knows that I've been working on these sorts of particular cases, as I put him on the alert some months ago. His son, Talbot, went missing last night. Unless something was seriously wrong, he would not have neglected to come home last night for the world; he and his father were to start a trip today that they've been planning for more than a year.

"Whoever is responsible for this has been more cautious since Lilianne. I suspect that my highly visible involvement has something to do with it. There have been no abductions that I've been made aware of, nothing has made it to my ears. But this one—this one proves that there is still an unattained goal, still a reason to take risks."

The story stopped and the notebook closed. The professor turned to me expectantly.

"Why do you think that these abductions only involve people connected to the Universities?" I ventured.

"One can only speculate."

"And, why only younger people?"

"Well, I call them children, because I can't help seeing them that way. They are adolescents to relatively young adults, to be precise. Recall, Lilianne was just finishing university. She was twenty-eight at the time."

"It's a narrow age-range, there must be something they want. Is it some kind of extortion? You said their parents are prominent magicians, right?"

"To date there have never been any demands, no ransoms. If it's extortion, they're doing a very poor job of it."

"But they have to want something. Why kidnap these people, then erase their memories and send them home? Did they want to get information out of them?"

Spindlebrock bore my questions patiently, and answered thoughtfully.

"For information, they might have had better luck kidnapping the parents; a few of which, I know, are privy to some fantastical information. Plus, the targets are too dispersed; they only correlate on age and connections. The pattern doesn't strongly support a search for magical information."

"You said that the potion made you more honest, when you took it?"

"I did."

"They could have given the potion and asked anything?"

"No, Thomas, it wasn't a potion of truth; not even related chemically. Being more honest doesn't imply complete and uncontrolled interrogation. During the time when I tested the potion, I was just more willing to share, and more open perhaps."

88

"What could they do with that?"

"One could only speculate."

"That's it then? There must be more to it, more that went on."

"I agree."

"But what, then?"

"I'd prefer to hear your thoughts on the possibilities, in case I've missed something. What do you think went on?"

I sat quietly for a few moments and attempted to come up with some novel idea, but was frustrated.

"It has to be something. You don't go to all this trouble for no reason. Were there any other clues, on the persons kidnapped I mean? Injuries, abuse, missing items, dirt stains, anything?"

"Nothing notable. In some cases there were what appeared to be fabricated clues; stains to make it look like a youth had been drinking heavily, but no alcohol metabolized in the hair—you studies forensics, so you're familiar with such tests?"

"I am."

"We held every possible clue to rigorous tests of science, and ended up with no real leads, except for the fact that whoever was responsible wanted the disappearances to look like voluntary foibles of the young, on the surface."

"What about the three days? Why three days, specifically, if you could potentially have any amount of time?"

"That, I feel, is the correct reasoning to pursue. Go on."

"Well, I suppose like you said, three days is short enough that the police might not get as involved, depending on the case. The parents might not even call them."

"There is that, yes. What else?"

"I'm not sure. Maybe they needed three days at least? Maybe that was the shortest that the potion could be made to function in?"

"No. The potion could be formulated for a very short stint, if needed, hours even. The three days must therefore have been intentional."

"I guess the next question would be, what did they do during those three days?"

Spindlebrock tapped his temple and pointed at me.

"Exactly what we need to find out. We have, presumably, three days to find Talbot and discover what it is they are working at. That is all that we know of the matter at present."

The steward was making another trip down the aisle to collect trash. Spindlebrock tossed his can into the wastebasket as it passed, then leaned back in his seat and closed his eyes. I couldn't help wondering, in that instant, why he would bring me along. His own skills in a laboratory were exceptional and proven, while mine were only academic. His connections and resources were deep. What could I possibly offer to be of real help.

"Conexus..."

The word escaped from my lips involuntarily as I started to grasp the reason for my inclusion. This was the favor for which Spindlebrock had over-paid me so deliberately. This was the value and purpose that gave him an interest in me, a novice that would otherwise have been nothing but an annoyance.

"Indeed," was Spindlebrock's only response. We flew the rest of the way to Phoenix without further discussion.

Chapter 7

Lewis and the Magic of Technology

Though it may seem trivial considering the growing urgency of the situation I'm relating, I wish to share with you a reality of magic that came to my attention as we stepped out of the Phoenix, Arizona airport that afternoon. In case you're not familiar with the weather in Phoenix, it is one of the hottest metropolitan cities in the world, and possibly the hottest city with a population in the millions. Summer was just starting, but the temperature that day had reached 104F/40C. Not a record heatwave, but still incredibly hot for someone who had recently become accustomed to the climate of Toronto, Canada.

My first instinct, upon feeling the furnace-like blast of hot, dry air on my skin, was to discretely cast a wandless charm that would create a micro-climate immediately around my person; a convenient spell I had picked up while working in a stuffy, cramped lab with Spindlebrock. He must have guessed my intentions, for as we walked into the stifling heat Spindlebrock took hold of my right arm and said under his breath:

"No, save your strength—you're going to need it."

The reality that I want non-magician readers to understand is this: nothing is free, including magic. Magicians are just as subject to the law of conservation of energy as anyone else. Magic is not analogous to the perpetual motion machine that mankind has sought so diligently throughout the ages. After I discovered magic, and fixed my suitcase with some ease, I fantasized that magic was a free pass to a simple, almost exotically work-free life; a metaphorical ticket to lounge on the beach all day while some unknown force did all that I required of it. This is not the case.

Magic requires energy, drawn at least in part from the one performing it. There are incantations that draw power from other sources; sources in the environment, or even from other people or animals, but without exception every incantation requires power on the part of the one casting it. A person who is worn out will not have an easy time performing complex spells. One who is not efficient in their use of magic, as I was not at first, will use more energy than necessary to perform the task at hand. All of this is in line with what science in general comprehends about the conservation of energy; namely, that energy is not created nor is it destroyed, but only converted or conferred.

This fact, I am convinced as I recall the events of the following days in Phoenix, must be clearly understood by the reader, who may or may not have any knowledge of the realities of the magician, and so I have shared it briefly before continuing with my narrative.

A cab transported us from the airport to a less-than-luxurious hotel, where we secured a room. From the moment we stepped off the plane til the door closed behind us at the hotel, Spindlebrock was almost completely silent. He spoke in a whisper as he closed the blinds and started examining the room.

"For more reasons than one, we must be careful in our use of magic while we're here in Phoenix."

We sat down at a small dingy table, part of the scant furnishings in our dull room. Spindlebrock continued, his voice still low.

"Consider what we know. First, that we have one or two solid days to find out as much as we can. Second, that if we don't interfere, Talbot will likely follow the overall pattern of returning home safely after three days time. We're not necessarily trying to rescue Talbot in this case, but rather to observe.

"Now, consider that which we do not know, but which we may surmise. The abductor, or rather abductors—for it is not probable that one person could do this all alone—are nervous. We disrupted their plans in Toronto, and they've waited an entire year before continuing their work. They are probably desperate; there is some part of their plans, which we know nothing of, that requires that they carry out risky, high-profile abductions. They can't get around it, it is the only way, or they wouldn't have attempted it again after having been discovered in Toronto.

"These few facts and assumptions dictate our behavior. We must not let them feel that they are at risk of being caught, as they felt in the case of Lilianne, or they might cut out. We aren't trying to break them here in Phoenix, we're simply using this opportunity to learn more, so that we might eventually get to the bottom of these abductions once and for all."

Our conversation was interrupted by a knock at the door. I was taken aback, but Spindlebrock bounded lightly from his chair to answer it. After glancing through the peep hole, he opened the door just enough to silently admit our visitor, shutting and bolting it after him. The two shook hands heartily, Spindlebrock placing his free hand on the man's shoulder. They spoke quietly.

"Lewis, it is wonderful to see you."

"And you C.C., it's been too long!"

"Yes, far too long. Our work ought to cross more than it does, but who can control such things?"

Recalling me, professor Spindlebrock made a brief introduction. I learned that the visitor's name was Lewis Wright, and that he and the professor had worked together closely on an important project which they left intentionally vague. For my part, the professor simply told Lewis that I was there to assist in our effort, and that he could trust me as he trusted Spindlebrock himself.

"We don't have much time Lewis, show us what you've got."

Lewis had a laptop, which he set on the desk before us. He showed us a map of the Phoenix metro area. It was a heat map—for those unfamiliar with the term, it is simply a map overlaid with colors representing the power or density of a thing. If it were rain, the brighter colors might represent heavier rain, fading to lighter colors or no color where the rain dispersed or stopped. This map, I learned, represented the intensity of magical energy exerted throughout the city.

"As you know, I've been studying this city for some time now. I already had sensors in-place with almost complete coverage."

"Yes, it's perfect, thank you Lewis."

"This map shows the cumulative magical energy over the past twenty-four hours. I can run comparisons showing the change in any given period over the past nine months."

"You've already started looking at the recent data I presume?" inquired Spindlebrock.

"I started right after your call this morning. What I've found is that there really haven't been any significant surges, nothing notable at least."

"What about non-notable?" urged Spindlebrock.

"Well, some slight activity expanding out of a few regions in different directions, but nothing unique; it could indicate movement, but it could just as well be average, normal movement, or it could be data artifacts."

At this point I ventured to interject.

"You mean, you can detect the use of magic? With some kind of electronic sensors?" I asked, quietly.

Lewis responded.

"Yes, and no. I can definitely detect certain magical events, but not all magic, not by a long shot. It's bleeding edge, experimental, and not well tested. Only a few in the commonality even know that I'm working on it. I study here in Phoenix because of the wider geographic distribution of the city compared to most. Fewer subjects stacked on top of one another yet still a population in the millions. Urban sprawl, and plenty of line-of-sight range for radio communication make it ideal."

"Lewis operates in another branch of science," interrupted Spindlebrock, "one that you and I don't work much with: technology."

"Spindlebrock teases me about it, but he's as interested as I am when it comes down to it. As you know, magicians have long been involved in the advancement of humanity, and technology is of course no exception, though it doesn't get the attention it deserves in the commonality."

"Back to the map, Lewis, you can preach later. Can you run a custom report on this data? What I want to see is any movement, even the slightest aberrations from the norm, and I only want to see movement, not totals. Along with that, can you highlight and superimpose any regions without activity, any dead spots? Then one final overlay, one that shows magical activity, any at all, in those normally inactive regions."

"That's technically three reports, C.C.," Lewis said with a smile, "but give me a few minutes and let's see what I can come up with."

While we waited, Spindlebrock brewed and drank some of the cheap coffee that was next to the microwave. I looked curiously over Lewis' shoulder as he tapped away in some kind of programming language for about twenty minutes.

"OK, I've got it," Lewis finally declared, turning the laptop toward us and presenting another map.

"See, right there, the movement is represented with a fade from bright pink to yellow, pink at the start, yellow at the end of the movement trend. Overlaying that, dead zones are in light blue—see, you can see here where some of the movement enters normally dead zones, like you asked. And these tiny spots, green fading outward to white, these are magical activity only within otherwise dead zones."

He sat back, apparently pleased with himself. Not possessing much in the way of technical skills, I was easily impressed by his small, impromptu accomplishment. Spindlebrock studied the map carefully. After several minutes, he presented his hypothesis.

"Since there have been no surges, we can assume that they are using non-magical means to accomplish their ends. And we already know they have access to complex potions—which wouldn't show up on this map, correct Lewis?"

"That's right. The type of energy we're measuring would be expended when a potion is created, not used. I should probably expand my research," Lewis began, but Spindlebrock cut him off.

"These people are experts in potions—quite advanced even by my standards—and we expect they're using them. Lewis, even if they had chosen densely populated areas, we would have been able to detect a general surge, is that right?"

"Most definitely. I can say confidently that magical activity in the area has not changed significantly in the past several months. The latest surge was last year, and it was more perennial in nature, coinciding with a major golf tournament in Scottsdale."

Spindlebrock interrupted again, his attention fixated on the map.

"These green spots, the magical activity in dead zones, they're over what period of time?"

"They're a composite of the past month, the same for the other layers."

"Can you animate the green spots and the movement, so we can see them over time?"

Lewis obliged, the results taking another few minutes.

"Excellent," Spindlebrock said as he watched the looping animation play over and over again.

"You see, right here. Notice anything, Lewis? Over the whole month period, this dead zone has three instances of movement artifacts; and before the last artifacts it has only one or two green dots indicating magical activity. But watch again, after the last movement, the green dots increase. There are at least half a dozen over the past week or so."

Lewis nodded.

"It's not much, but that's our best bet, Lewis. That's our zone."

Spindlebrock paced the room for a few moments before addressing us both.

"Here's the plan. We have this hotel room paid up for a few nights, more than we'll need if everything works out. It will serve as a base for you Lewis, as needed, and as a place for any of us to return to, should something go wrong.

"Thomas and I will leave immediately. We'll need to stop for a few supplies, and I'd like to do a little reconnaissance before we settle down for the evening. Lewis, you stay here for now; we don't want to draw undue attention, if we can avoid it. We'll call you when we're done. You brought us a rental car, right?"

Lewis affirmed that he had rented a car for us in his name, and that he could get back home in a cab when the time came.

"There is one last thing," Spindlebrock said, "and we need to get it out of the way now. Lewis, you're not well known enough to be generally recognized by most magicians in the commonality. Thomas, you're even less known. I, on the other hand, am recognized on sight by many, and I'm something of a controversial figure to boot. I will require a disguise."

With a dramatic flourish Spindlebrock produced a small, brown leather case. He carefully undid the brass clasp to reveal four vials of clear liquid.

"As we discussed, we must be extremely cautious in our use of magic. It might upset Lewis' own tracking and measurements, but we also do not know if our adversaries are capable of detecting magical energy like we are. That leaves either crude theatrical disguises, or potions, which you've already noted are essentially invisible to your equipment, correct?"

Lewis nodded. Spindlebrock removed the first potion from the case, uncorked it, and swilled it in a single gulp. His lips puckered, his eyes snapped shut, and his eyebrows raised, as if it were exceptionally sour. Slowly, his hair started to change color. From the roots to the tips, it changed from the grizzled gray-black mix into a handsome golden, sun-bleached blonde. It grew fuller and longer, finally stopping when it was just covering his ears. He straightened up and smiled, shaking his new head of hair gently.

"Do you like it? Pity it can't last forever."

He removed the second potion from the case and downed it as he had the first. With eyes closed tightly, he stood frozen for a few moments. A look of consternation set on his brow, and his lips began to twitch involuntarily. I watched in horror as bumps began to form under the skin of his face and neck, bumps that moved as if they were alive. Two of them made their way up to his cheekbones, where they rested and slowly evened out. Others stopped near his jaw, and still smaller ones moved I'm not sure where; I began to feel queasy and looked away.

"They're not bones, mind you, but they are sufficient to reshape the face, as long as I'm not examined by a doctor with an x-ray machine."

When I looked again, Spindlebrock's face had been transformed. The bumps seemed to smooth out some of the wrinkles of age, so that he appeared several years younger. His cheekbones were higher and more pronounced, as was his jaw line. His neck appeared more muscular. The effect was amazing.

"Just two more to go." he said, pulling out another vial and drinking its contents, this time slowly. The potion consumed, he dropped the bottle and clenched his fists.

"This one hurts a bit."

His voice trembled and his body began to quiver. We watched his waist shrink; his clothes, which were a bit tight, seemed to slacken all over his body, as if air were being let out of a balloon that had been holding them in place. It was apparent, when the potion had taken full effect, that he had lost quite a few pounds.

"I could be rich, if I could find a way to make that one permanent and market it to the non-magician crowd."

He joked, but you could see in his eyes that Spindlebrock was reluctant to move on to the last vial. He removed it from the case and fiddled with it in his hands before unstopping the cork. He paused before drinking it.

"This one simply makes me a bit taller. You would be surprised at how much humans associate height with identity, subconsciously. I was streaked with gray, and only a little above average in height and build. Now I will be tall and slender, younger, with a head of hair to make anyone my age jealous."

He drained the vial. Immediately his spine arched, his head was thrown back, face to the ceiling. His teeth were bared, and a low growl which he seemed to fight with all his will came from deep within his chest. He looked like the damned, a demon, a werewolf, or some other apparition from an ancient horror story. No matter how hard I tried, I could not tear my eyes away. As he writhed, he did in fact grow visibly in stature. When it was finished he was a good four inches taller, and appeared even more slender. He was pale from the exertion; a drip of sweat or a tear, I don't know which, rolled down his face and fell from his chin.

"I'll pay for that one for months," he said, turning his torso as if to stretch his back muscles. Lewis whistled low, thoroughly impressed.

After several minutes of stretching and rubbing various muscles, Spindlebrock spoke. It was eerie to hear his voice emanating from what now looked like an entirely different person.

"Right, now we'll head out—wait, Lewis, did you get that package from Bennett, the one that I told you about?"

"Yes! I almost forgot."

Lewis produced a very small package—small enough to fit in the palm of his hand. It was wrapped in plain brown paper.

"Here," he said, handing it to Spindlebrock, "I picked it up just like you asked, in the very spot. I'm positive that no one saw me."

"Good. This should have passed through several trusted hands after it left Bennett's house and came to you, I was very clear with Bennett on that point. Everything is settled; we're off."

Chapter 8

The White Rook

As planned, we picked up some food and other supplies at a nearby grocery store. Professor Spindlebrock took to his disguise quite readily, adding to the physical changes a slight modification to his speech pattern as well as a light bounce in his step. All of this made him seem like quite the young man as we strolled through the aisles of the store. He was exceptionally calm, considering our circumstances. I recall feeling like I was shopping with a college roommate; the poor quality of the food he tossed into our cart added to the effect.

Once we were back on the road, Spindlebrock produced the small package Lewis had given him, and passed it to me.

"Open that. Have a look," he said casually.

The tiny package was wrapped in brown paper and neatly sealed. Opening it carefully, I extracted a small wooden chess piece; a white rook, to be precise. Spindlebrock glanced at me as I turned the piece over in my hands.

"Well? What do you think?"

I offered my observations, as slight as they were. It was a white rook, apparently carved from some kind of light colored wood, sanded quite smooth, painted, and finished with a clear lacquer. It had seen some amount of use, as it was dented up. The bit of felt cloth that you normally find on the bottom of such game pieces was conspicuously missing. I experienced a small amount of pride at my astuteness, which was instantly squelched as Spindlebrock broke out in laughter.

"Well thanks for that, man! You're a regular Sherlock, Thomas, with a keen eye!"

I shifted uncomfortably in my seat as Spindlebrock finished his hearty and prolonged chuckle.

"Well, what do you expect me to see in this chess piece, then? What's the big deal—"

I was holding the rook in my hand and looking at it intently, trying to find some little detail I had missed, when it struck me that the piece was most assuredly the property of Talbot Bennett, the missing young man we were trying to find.

"The chess piece—it's his, isn't it? This belongs to Talbot Bennett."

As I spoke a sick feeling came over me, a wave of depression, fear, confusion, and nausea, all comprehended in an instant. I looked out the window to the north—I knew where Talbot was, and I felt some of what he was feeling. With now clammy hands I set the piece down carefully on the dashboard.

"Yes, and not only is it his, but it was taken from a set that he made as a woodworking project. His father helped, but I was assured that Talbot turned this rook on the lathe, and sanded it by hand."

Spindlebrock paused, analyzing my demeanor in a glance.

"Tell me what you know," Spindlebrock said gently, his face grave.

"He's in pain; not physical pain necessarily, but he's afraid—sad as well. I don't know exactly how to describe it. We need to head north from here."

I rubbed my chest. For that moment, as I held the rook, I understood exactly how Talbot Bennett was feeling; not in an abstract or disconnected way, but in a real, tangible way. I was him, I felt what he felt. The raw power of it brought a fresh concern to my mind.

"Professor, will Conexus show up on Lewis' radar map thing? I mean, am I going to mess up his measurements if I keep using it, if I keep picking up that rook?"

"Don't worry about Lewis, he's looking at trends and large sets of data. We can ask him about any unusual spikes, but we can't afford to forgo using your gift. All you need to think about right now is finding Talbot—that's what I told you to save your energy for back at the airport."

He motioned for me to pick up the rook again.

"We're heading north now. I'll need you to help guide us more precisely."

I hesitated for a moment at the idea of diving back into Talbot's bitter emotional well. Compassion for his pain overcame my fear, and I took hold of the chess piece once more. Immediately I was falling, sinking in anguish, but I could not fail him. Tears choked my words as I desperately scanned the roads ahead, calling out turns to Spindlebrock. We passed through a maze of urban sprawl, and some stretches of beautiful open desert, before coming to a large community outside the city to the north, where everything looked like one big master-planned neighborhood.

The house where they were holding Talbot jumped out at me suddenly. It was familiar, as if I had seen it before in a dream. I quickly dropped the rook in a cup holder and inhaled deeply.

"He's in front of us. The light stucco house at the end of the street, on the right."

We drove by without slowing. There were no cars parked in the driveway, nor on the street in front of the house. A For Sale sign from a national Realtor's office was pounded into the dead-looking front lawn.

"You're sure that was it?"

"Absolutely sure. He's in there right now."

Stress and emotion were starting to crack my voice. After driving around the corner and down a few streets, Spindlebrock slowed to a stop and parked, then turned and looked at me for several uncomfortable moments before speaking.

"Maybe we should try it once more, to be doubly sure?"

Spindlebrock was prodding me intentionally, I could hear it in his voice. His tone, and the thought of sinking again was too much to bear.

"No! I told you I'm sure. That's the house."

"OK, Thomas, OK. You astound me; I believe this is the very area on the map that we had singled in on. I know it wasn't easy finding him. Very well done."

Spindlebrock clapped me on the shoulder lightly, then started driving again.

"We'll go back to the hotel, connect with Lewis. We need to see what we can do about getting ourselves installed a little closer to Talbot. You'd better put that in your pocket."

He motioned to the rook. I picked it up and jammed it in my pocket as quickly as I could. It was out of sight, but I couldn't get the thing out of my mind as we drove. We made the trip in silence, which was only broken when we pulled into our parking space and Spindlebrock turned off the engine.

"Lewis doesn't know about your ability, Thomas. It's crucial that we keep it that way, at least for now, do you understand? We'll say that we found some suspicious activity and that we're going back to investigate further. He'll be busy enough with his sensors to think too much about our methods. And it won't hurt to have a second base of operations in any case."

We returned to the hotel room and apprised Lewis of our plans. I made up some excuse about not feeling well, and lied down to rest while Spindlebrock and Lewis arranged everything. The stress of the day caught up with me, and I drifted off to the hushed and hurried voices of my companions.

I awoke to the ding of the microwave, and the smell of a so-called breakfast that never should have been slopped into a divided plastic freezer tray. Lewis had already returned home, Spindlebrock was dressed and ready to leave. It was the second day of Talbot's abduction, the only full day that we figured we would have to learn more about what was going on. Sleep had cemented my determination to help this young man in any way that I could, regardless of the pain or price. I quickly got myself ready for the day ahead.

By mid-morning, the professor and I had established ourselves in a house not far from the one where Talbot was being held. We had a narrow but useful view from a second-story window, where the house was visible between two other houses and a few sparse palm trees. Lewis had provided Spindlebrock with some covert, long-range listening equipment, and a few pairs of binoculars. We continued to avoid the use of magic, for fear that we weren't the only ones with tracking capabilities, and for fear of lessening Lewis' chances of detecting any magical activity from the house we were watching.

We found through our observation that there were at least two people with Talbot at all times, as well as a third person that sometimes left the house. We were not equipped to follow the person that left the house—at least not without being discovered—nor did we get even a glimpse of that person's face or features; even in the hot Phoenix weather they always wore a dark, long-sleeved hoodie. We never got a great view of the two who remained inside either, as they only occasionally passed by slivers of open curtains, with quick and irregular movements. We could not see Talbot, but with our equipment we could hear him, at times arguing bitterly with his captors, and at other times muttering incoherently.

We surmised that Talbot was being forced to consume something at regular intervals—serums or potions, most likely—which he resisted strongly. He would then become complacent, and during those intervals one of the abductors would speak to him in a droning tone. Knowing that his captors were experts in brewing potions of the most powerful variety, we assumed that a regimen had been devised, potentially to increase susceptibility to suggestion. For all of our efforts we gained very little actual knowledge of who or what we were facing.

As the last rays of light faded away late that second evening, I concluded that our operation was more or less a bust. Spindlebrock, who had been mostly silent the entire day, caught me by surprise when he tossed his binoculars aside and started talking.

"Well, what do we do now?"

I thought for a few moments before setting down my binoculars and responding.

"I don't know. I mean, activity has pretty much died down. I guess we could stay up and watch through the night?"

"We could, but based on what we've garnered so far, that might be a waste."

"True. Plus, we'll want our energy for tomorrow, for when Talbot is released."

Spindlebrock began to pace. I started to feel like something was wrong.

"It won't do, Thomas. We didn't come here just to wait them out and get nothing. We need more details."

I sat there in silence, watching him ruminate. He continued.

"There's a problem with Lilianne, something that I just can't place, or prove. Something isn't right, and it must be tied to her disappearance. Whatever they're doing to Talbot down there, they did to her. I need information, badly."

My heart sank.

"Is she in trouble?"

"I believe so. Her case, and all of the others, depend on us getting to the bottom of all this, quickly. I really thought that we'd get more of a hint from our observations, but they're running a really cautious operation. I need access to Talbot before whatever they're using metabolizes. We can't afford to pass up the opportunity."

"What do we do?"

"I need to get in there. I need to get Talbot before they let him go. It's the only way now."

We debated our options. Attempting an ambush in the dark of night was too risky. Our only chance to outmaneuver them would be in the final hour, when they felt they were about to finish their work unimpeded. Spindlebrock insisted that he only needed a brief time with Talbot to learn what he needed to learn. Early the next morning, we determined, would be our mostly likely window.

I recall our attempt quite vividly. It was the morning of the third day. Lewis had joined us in the rental house during the night, and the three of us were watching closely for a sign that we should put our plan into action. The movements of the aggressors changed, and we were convinced that it was time. My job was to take the rental car, go rather faster than the speed limit, and attempt to create a distraction by jumping the curb and hitting a street sign in front of the house where Talbot was being held. Lewis and Spindlebrock would drive around the block from the other direction using Lewis' car, a few moments after my staged accident, and attempt to enter at the back of the house unseen. Presumably those in the house would be focused so much on my escapade in the front yard that they would not notice my companions in the back until it was too late.

As I write it, I realize how comically trite the plan was, but our goal was incredibly simple: distract the captors, disable them, and get to Talbot before whatever they were giving him wore off. The element of surprise, coupled with Spindlebrock's skill, were our two advantages, and we thought they would be enough.

Our miscalculation of the entire situation quickly became evident; as I rounded the corner, one of the individuals in the house rushed out, wand in hand, and cast some kind of repelling charm that forced my car off the road in the opposite direction, and into a cinder block retaining wall in the yard of the house across the street from our target. I instinctively ducked as another charm struck my windshield, shattering it into cubes of safety glass that rained down on me.

Still crouched in my vehicle, I heard Lewis squeal around the corner and screech to a halt, car doors opening and people shouting, then several deep-toned blasts and earsplitting crashes.

I stayed down, hands covering my head, until I heard a pause in the noise followed by Spindlebrock calling out, "Come on!" Peeking out of the empty metal frame that previously held my windshield, I witnessed destruction far worse than I would have imagined possible in such a short confrontation. A corner of the house near the garage was blown out and scattered across the yard; Lewis' car was crumpled, the two side doors facing the house smashed in entirely; broken glass and other debris was scattered across the full width of the street and into the yards of several of the neighboring houses.

At this point we were entirely without a plan. Somehow they knew we were coming, and the element of surprise was gone. Originally I was to stay outside the house, playing the part of an average citizen who was concerned about having hit a street sign. Now it seemed that my presence might be helpful inside. I am not generally a courageous person, even in more ordinary circumstances, but my heart was pierced with the memory of Talbot's pain, and I felt a strong desire to help.

Using whatever cover I could find, I made my way quickly to the front door, which had been blasted in with enough force to remove much of the door jam and all of the door. I picked up a chunk of the splintered wood to use as a cudgel and moved toward the sound of a scuffle inside the house. Just as I was marshaling my courage to spring around a corner, I heard someone behind me scrambling through the rubble of the front door, trying to make an exit. Startled, I whirled around to defend myself, and made eye contact with a man who appeared to be a few years younger than me. He looked even more terrified than I felt. His glance shot to my hands, and seeing no wand, he relaxed just enough to reveal a glimmer of sadness and regret before disappearing out the empty doorway.

Turning my attention back to the scuffle, I heard Spindlebrock shout, "Enough!" just as I jumped around the corner. Lewis was on the floor, apparently knocked out. Talbot was tied to a chair in the middle of the room, his head slumped over, and through a window I could just see the shadow of a person sprinting through the back yard. Another figure was attempting to clamber through a small hole blown in the wall.

I scarcely had time to take all this in—less than a second perhaps, knowing how adrenaline amplifies the body's senses and perception of time—when Spindlebrock arced his wand over his head in two massive, sweeping circles, his movements so wide that his body swayed as he made them, and uttered booming words that I will not share here. A pulse of power seemed to burst forth out of Spindlebrock's very being and undulate through the room; when it hit me, instantly and for a moment I felt my heart stop. After the alarming sensation passed, I realized that I was frozen in place, completely unable to move or even blink, but still able to witness what was about to happen in front of me. I could see the man in the back yard, petrified halfway in his climb over the fence. The man struggling to get through the hole in the wall now dangled in the opening, limbs frigid in a sort of grisly mock rigor mortis.

Still in full control of his own faculties, Spindlebrock quickly surveilled the room, then turned all of his attention to Talbot. He grasped for his wrist—apparently looking for a pulse—while leaning in to feel for his breath. He then burst the ropes with a charm and scooped Talbot from the chair, gently lowering him to the ground before attempting to resuscitate him. My eyes burned with tears that I could not wipe away or hold back as I watched him struggle, alternately performing chest compressions and checking for any sign of life. Lastly, Spindlebrock took several vials from his pockets and poured them carefully into the young man's mouth, but nothing seemed to have any effect. He swore violently and continued the compressions as I stood there, frozen.

The man scrambling over the fence in the back yard—the one furthest from all of this—was the first to break free from Spindlebrock's spell. He fell back into the yard for a moment, then without looking back he made his way over the fence and escaped. The man climbing through the wall was next; I saw a look of absolute horror on his face, as he fell out of the hole, cursing, and made for the fence to follow his cohort. Spindlebrock continued his efforts, oblivious to all that was going on around him. A tingly thaw of self control rushed back into my body in an instant, and I fell to my knees, unable to take my eyes off the scene.

A few moments later Lewis came to and got up from the ground with a groan, rubbing his forehead. As a comprehension of the situation dawned on him, he rushed forward to help; Spindlebrock stumbled back and fell to the ground, still cursing. He broke into convulsions, crying into his hands quietly while Lewis checked on the boy one last time.

Talbot Bennett was dead.

Chapter 9

A Mysterious Letter

part from the moments I have just described, Spindlebrock kept his emotions in close check throughout the rest of the affair. As the initial shock transformed into the beginnings of grief, he composed himself, then fixed his eyes on me.

"Put your education and training to use in collecting clues. Lewis and I need to contain this."

I set to work willingly, while Spindlebrock made a phone call and Lewis went outside to calm the neighbors that were starting to gather. There was very little to be found in the way of clues. A spell revealed that a handful of empty glass vials on the kitchen counter had all been thoroughly cleaned. Remnants of the abductors' holed-up lifestyle— packaged food that required no preparation and no dishes, sleeping bags on the ground, etc.—were plainly evident, but provided no useful insights into either motive or nefarious activity. Most of the rooms in the house were untouched and unused. There were no signs of physical struggle by Talbot; even his wrists indicated that he hadn't fought against the ropes. Magical crime, it appeared, was far more subtle than anything I had been trained for during my studies in forensics.

Within minutes, a police car arrived. To my amazement, the officers went straight to Spindlebrock, who they seemed to know. He summarized the situation in a few words, and assured them that a local tribunal was en route. They began calming and interviewing the small crowd of neighbors, to ascertain whether any memories would need to be erased. Magical crimes are a delicate thing, and must be dealt with by magicians alone. These officers were planted, in effect, for just such a situation as ours.

The local tribunal that Spindlebrock mentioned constituted a panel of investigating judges, selected from a group of prominent and trusted magicians in the area. They arrived together in a large black van, six men and women, all relatively old, or as Spindlebrock would say, "experienced in life." I relayed my version of the events, along with the few forensic findings I had gathered, while they conducted a search of their own. Even with their expanded use of magical detection, no additional evidence was discovered. In the end their conclusion was nothing more than what you've already read here: kidnapping and murder by three unknown assailants, still at large. Cause of death was deemed magical poisoning, even though the evidence was only circumstantial and not medical; no traces of the potion that caused his death were found. Time of death was narrowed down to within an hour before we arrived on the scene.

After everything was sufficiently managed with regards to the crime scene, Spindlebrock and I accompanied the body of Talbot Bennett home to his parents, where Spindlebrock personally related to his friends the entirety of what had happened. News of the sudden and tragic loss was heartrending; Spindlebrock remained with them and personally oversaw all of the arrangements that needed to be made.

For the sake of the reader, I'll omit most of the details of the funeral and its preparation. Funerals for the young are exceedingly painful, and those are the only words that I will give to the memory of the occasion, as they are the words that resound so clearly in my mind and heart when I think of it. After the service, however, something notable happened that you must be informed of. Spindlebrock and I had just offered our condolences to the family, and were getting ready to leave, when a young woman approached us. Apparently crying, she avoided eye contact, held out a crumpled letter for Spindlebrock to take, then rushed away. Upon opening and reading it, but before revealing any information about its contents, Spindlebrock quickly looked up, then dashed about as discreetly as possible searching for the lady. Unable to find any trace of her, he returned and handed me the letter to read. It was beautifully handwritten in dark blue ink, with flourishes that only a fountain or feather pen could have rendered.

Spindlebrock still keeps the letter in his file room, where he keeps a great many items of personal interest to him. With his permission, I share it here with you verbatim:

Most esteemed Dr. Spindlebrock,

It is with a heavy heart that I express my sincere condolences over the loss of your friend's son. Young people of magical aptitude represent the bright future of this world, and it pains me when one is taken before their time.

Please know that it was in no way my intention to allow any harm to befall this young man. Indeed, every provision was made for his safe and healthy return. Had there been no interference in my process, no harm would have come to him.

While it flatters me that you have taken such a personal interest in my activities, I must caution you that further interference will not only agitate me, it will endanger more innocent lives.

How I wish that I could share more! You, of all the magicians that I have known or studied, are of a most peculiar interest to me. In my mind I believe that you would rejoice at the endeavors that I am undertaking. Yet, in my observance of you I realize that you have given too much place for things outside the realm of pure science and reason.

May we meet someday on better terms, and with a better understanding of one another.

Sincerely,

—W. C. Crane

After I finished reading the letter I looked up. Spindlebrock was watching me intently.

"What do you think?" he asked.

"The audacity, to try to blame this on us, is incredible. Just incredible."

Spindlebrock tapped his lips nervously, then took the letter back. In a lowered voice, he continued.

"With the murder of Talbot, the author of this letter made his—or her—first mistake. Now, in giving us this letter, he—or she—has made another."

He looked at the letter thoughtfully before continuing.

"Don't you see? It's handwritten."

Spindlebrock looked at me with raised eyebrows, and I finally caught up with his train of thought. Using my gift, a hand-written letter could be traced.

Chapter 10

Ever Shrinking Circles

My assumption, after the funeral, was that we would set to work using the handwritten letter to find whoever was responsible for Talbot's murder. We had a strong lead, a fresh trail, and the wherewithal to follow it. I readily projected the strength of my conviction, and the simplicity of my understanding, onto Spindlebrock; how could he want anything different from what I wanted? Wasn't this his undertaking, his pursuit? If I, as a mere helper, burned internally for justice, wouldn't he be outwardly ablaze with an even more fervent flame?

To my dismay, there was no evidence of such a pressing flame that I could perceive. On the flight back to Toronto, Spindlebrock wanted only silence and repose; I hardly remarked anything strange in this, as I too desired a rest. After we returned to his home, his detached manners continued for several more days, but I took no offense, since he might very well be expected to have received a greater blow than I, given his closeness and history with the family. I respectfully gave him his distance.

After a week, impatience grew in to irritation. How could he waste any more time? Was his grief greater than his desire to make things right, to avoid future pain for others? I attempted to broach the subject one morning at breakfast.

"So, about that letter?"

My blunt introduction of the subject snapped Spindlebrock visibly from his reverie.

"Yes? What about it."

"What about it? What are we going to do about it, is what I was wondering."

Spindlebrock set his bagel down and eyed me inquiringly while he finished chewing. At length, he spoke.

"Well, I think that's quite clear."

Unsure if he and I were on the same page, I persisted.

"Right, so do I. We take the letter—the handwritten letter— and using Conexus we figure out where they're hiding, then somehow we set a trap. You have connections, we could—"

"No, we wait," he interjected, holding up his hand, "what we need to do is wait."

"Wait?"

Spindlebrock nodded. Then, to my astonishment, he instantly produced the envelope containing the letter, from his pocket.

I glanced at the envelope, then back at him, and at the envelope again before continuing.

"You've been carrying it around with you! You know it's important, why don't we use it? Today! What are we waiting for?"

"You may not realize it Thomas, but you've risen to your feet, and now appear quite menacing. Please, sit down, and we'll talk about the letter."

He was right, I had not realized that I had risen from my chair, leaned forward, and placed two fists on the table. I plopped back into my chair roughly and folded my arms.

"Thank you. Now, if it won't agitate you, let's take a moment to review a few of the facts surrounding this letter."

He paused for an answer, which I did not give.

"Alright. We'll start at the end of the funeral and work our way back as far as we need to, in order to fully grasp the import of this letter. Think and remember. Imagine yourself there again. What do you feel?"

"Pain."

The word broke harshly from my lips before I could consciously form it in my mind. The sound of it, the feeling of it coming out of me, somehow renewed all that I had felt that day, and all that I had felt when I had taken Talbot's rook in my hand. I was already angry with Spindlebrock for

128

his inaction; now, I was furious with him for opening my wound afresh.

He continued.

"Exactly. And it clouds your sight now, as it clouded it then. You think you have more pain than I do? Than his parents do? It consoles me to know someone as compassionate as you, Thomas, but let us set aside our feelings for now, and work this out.

My heart softened at his commiseration. I nodded.

"As everyone was filtering out of the funeral, saying their final goodbyes and offering their condolences, a young woman approach us and handed us a letter, then promptly disappeared as we read it. The letter was handwritten, and its contents are likely still fresh enough in your mind. Distilled, it says simply that we ought not to meddle in the abductions, and that more lives would be lost if we did.

"Mere moments before the letter was handed to us, however, I was in the process of observing each of the people that had gathered at the funeral. In you, I observed sincere suffering and a true desire—no, a longing—to reach out with compassion for the family's loss. Was my observation correct?"

He was indeed correct, and I told him so.

"Apart from yourself, I noted the immediate family, who was still very much in a state of shock. Their intense sadness mingled bitterly with confusion at their sudden loss. They appreciated my efforts, but they couldn't erase anger, outrage, and passion at my failure. I could see it and feel it in the way they acted, though they did their best to shield me from it."

"But, they must have known we did every—"

Spindlebrock would not hear my objection, and continued.

"Take no insult in this thing, Thomas, I know I did not. How could I fault them in their agony? I'm certain I would feel the same way. I count them all the more my friends for their humanity.

"Continuing then, I noted, among the guests, many whom I knew personally and others that I could easily identify as being close friends of the family. Hugs, handshakes, tears, and furtive whispers were exchanged almost universally among these first two groups, namely family and friends. You did see this, did you not?"

Spindlebrock, ever observant, could see that my mind was wandering with thoughts of grief and funerals. It's a continual fault of mine to wander mentally; he often asks me small questions to help keep me focused.

"Yes," I answered, brought back to the present, "I do recall that. It's a normal way to act at a funeral, I think."

"That's right, it is normal. Perfectly normal. So normal, in fact, that anything else would be quite out of the ordinary. Did you see anything else at the funeral, anything out of the ordinary?"

"Well, no, I don't think so. I didn't," I confessed.

"And why would you, Thomas? Most people aren't looking for anything out of the ordinary at a funeral. Even so—perhaps especially so—it is valuable to look for things that are out of the ordinary when no one else would.

"What you didn't notice was that there were two groups, groups that anyone could readily identify at any funeral: friends, and family. They were easy to pick out, but at a funeral you'll invariably find a third group as well: those individuals who knew the family a little but not enough to feel comfortable approaching them, coupled with those who are there because they're connected in some way to one of the first two groups. Are you following me?"

"Yes, I believe I am. You've identified three groups: friends, family, and a third group, not quite friends of the family, but people that knew the family a little."

"Quite right, but remember that the third group includes those who are simply connected, not really known, such as co-workers and schoolmates. The people in this third group exhibit a particular sort of behavior at a funeral. They're lost, not quite known, not quite noticed. When a person feels lost or out of place, they display those feelings in their body language. They avoid standing alone, tagging along instead with the people they feel comfortable with. When they do end up alone for some reason, they tend to busy themselves with something; some trinket in hand, a phone, or a plate of food if such is being served.

"You can observe this, not only at funerals, but in any social situation where people feel out of place. However, I have noted that these behaviors and others are especially marked at funerals, due to the gravity of the event. These things I witnessed plainly in that third group. But, it wasn't the third group I was looking for. It was a fourth group."

As my interest built I had unfolded my arms, and was now leaning forward intently, one elbow on the table, chin in hand. Nothing of this nature would have ever suggested itself to my mind at a funeral, and I wondered at Spindlebrock's method.

"Now, normally, I wouldn't categorize a broad fourth group at a funeral—and by your expression, I can see that you feel I'm perhaps an oddity, categorizing people at a funeral? You think me insensitive, calloused, even heartless maybe?"

I was caught off guard by his accusation.

"I—I'm sorry, I didn't think—that is, I don't think you are any of those things."

"Nonsense; and such feelings on your part might be fair, but consider the ordeal that we had just gone through. Though I mourned, I could not let go of the fact that the entire tragedy was someone's fault, and they were still at large! Knowing a bit about human behavior, I was on the lookout as discreetly as possible for anything amiss. My heart was divided, and I believe rightfully so."

He paused for a brief moment to examine my expression, then continued.

"As I was saying, I was searching for a fourth group, and I found one. An appendage to the third group perhaps, if you want to call it that. I postulated before the funeral that the fourth group, in an attempt to fit in, would naturally try to behave like the third group. A fourth group would have absolutely no place at the funeral, they would have no connections whatsoever. They would not only feel out of place, they would actually be out of place.

"It's a critical distinction, you see, because the behavior would not be the same. A person who is out of place—say a liar for instance—is not only uncomfortable with their surroundings, they're also uncomfortable with themselves. Like the people in the third group, they don't want to stand out. But unlike the people in the third group, their efforts are more conscious than unconscious.

"In the moments before the letter was handed to us, at the end of the funeral, I identified at least seven people that would belong to that fourth group. They stood, each quite alone, but glancing at one another. I say glancing, but it was momentary enough that one might not even observe it unless one was observing them as a group; indeed they were trying not to look at one another, and when they did by chance, they would quickly look away. They had no apparent connection with anyone that was part of the other groups. They looked out of place and uncomfortable, but they tried hard not to look it. They remained on the outskirts of all activity, mingled with no one, and never approached the family."

Spindlebrock, sensing that I had a question, paused.

"So, you're saying that we were being watched at the funeral? That somehow, whoever is behind all of this wanted to see what would happen there? Why?"

"Well, Thomas, the reason was made apparent; they wanted to give us the letter. But we haven't finished our mental exercise. Consider, the letter is connected to the fourth group at the funeral, but it is also connected to the people at the house where Talbot was being held, and eventually to whoever is behind all this, one W.C. Crane. If the people at the house doing the dirty work weren't the organizers—and make no mistake, those slattern thugs were not responsible for the organization of all this—then the fourth group at the funeral wouldn't logically have included the organizer either."

"Why not?"

"Think! If the organizer of all this wasn't even willing to risk being caught in a situation where they could reasonably expect to remain hidden, why would they risk a situation where they most certainly would be exposed? No, whoever is behind all of this is accustomed to having other people do their dirty work."

"But," I ventured, "that doesn't really explain why they would have bothered coming to the funeral. What was the purpose? Why not just mail the letter?"

"That is a good question. It reveals to me what I already knew: that you still don't understand what happened in Phoenix. You think we went to Phoenix to get the jump on someone. Certainly, I led you to believe that. I led Lewis and Edmond Bennett to believe that as well, and hopefully I've led whoever is behind this to the same conclusion. I'm sorry Thomas, I can see that you are hurt by this confession of my actions, but they were unavoidable."

Without waiting for absolution, Spindlebrock went on.

"If I were to draw this all in a diagram, I think it would make more sense. Come with me."

For only the second time since I met the man, Spindlebrock led me to his study. Whether it was more disheveled than before I cannot say, but the scattered equipment, piles of papers, makeshift contraptions, and countless glass containers of putrid chemicals all made a fresh impression on me. The mess, and even the smell, seemed to have no effect whatsoever on the professor; he proceeded to a whiteboard on a far wall, erased a jumble of scrawled formulas, and began to draw. In the middle of the board, he traced a small red circle with three dots in it.

"This represents the three criminals we encountered at the empty house in Phoenix."

He drew a second larger circle in green, encompassing the red circle. In that green circle, he put three dots.

"These represent us, attempting to ensnare the criminals in their hideout. We were closing in on them, metaphorically speaking. It's a simple visual."

I nodded. The drawing made sense.

"In this paradigm, you take for granted that we are the outermost circle. You consider us to be the hunters, and not the hunted."

Spindlebrock then drew an even larger black dotted circle, encompassing both of the others. In it, he added several small question marks.

"What was unseen and unsuspected by you, was that someone was expecting us. They were waiting for us, and watching for us."

Here I interrupted.

"Wait—so the whole thing was a setup, a trap? And you somehow knew this, all the time, and said nothing?"

"I postulated, I did not know. You might have formed a similar hypothesis on the plane to Phoenix, given all the facts that were presented in our discussion."

"I would have shared it if I had."

"That is your personality, yes. My experience has taught me that too much information can paralyze and influence in subversive ways, in spite of the earnestness of the individuals involved. I knew that neither you, nor Lewis, nor Edmond would be able to perform your parts, if you understood the potential scope of the problem. I suspected a trap, but needed to see the inquiry through to the end."

"The end?" I snarled, "The end was horrific! If you thought it was a trap, why did you risk it? Why would you put Talbot's life on the line by interfering?"

"Now you're quoting Crane's letter, which isn't fair or objective at all. We didn't interfere, as you well know, we only came in at the very end. What's more, I had no reason to believe that there was any risk of Talbot dying. The patterns of all the prior abductions did not suggest that outcome. On the contrary, great pains seemed to have been taken to not hurt a single abducted subject."

"But you said that you expected a trap. If Talbot wasn't at risk, what was the trap supposed to be for?"

"To kill me."

I was stunned at his revelation. After a long pause, Spindlebrock continued.

"In flexing my influence and resources during Lilianne's abduction, I proved that I am a real nuisance, and a considerable threat. Of course, they could have made an attempt on my life at any time. I knew this, and have been on the lookout; but I'm not an easy person to find in the first place, and I'm not an easy person to reckon with either.

"They held off on the abductions for a while, then for whatever reason, recommenced, but without addressing the problem of me. That is what made this abduction feel like a trap."

"So, you just walked right into it? Why? What was so important that it would cause you to do that?"

"Information. That, and perhaps a sense of moral obligation. I knew what was going on, and was therefore obligated to help. Certainly you can understand, in light of these facts, that if I had mentioned any of this to you or the others, there's a good chance you would have all acted quite differently."

"I can't argue with that, certainly. We probably would have tried to stop you."

"Quite so. But to me it was worth the risk, if I could find out more about what was going on with these abductions. I figured that I was gambling with my own life, not Talbot's. But something went wrong; they were shaken. We moved too quickly throughout the whole affair, gained too much ground. They did not suppose that things would go that way, and their plans changed. We forced that change.

"Their adaptation is where our new opportunity was created. The letter at the funeral was this black dotted line closing in on us, with a new, revised plan, based on new information, or at least new guesswork, on their part. Do you know what they guessed at?"

"I do not."

"Conexus."

My stomach sank at the word. A fearful, nauseous dread, that somehow I was responsible for Talbot's death, overwhelmed me. Spindlebrock noticed. His fist came down hard on the table, jolting me to attention.

"Don't blame yourself, Thomas! Nothing we could have done differently would have saved him. I'm convinced of that point. Yes, they were watching us, and they guessed that you, an unknown magician that they had never encountered and certainly not a magician of apparent talent or ability that I'd normally have with me on this kind of task—no offense, of course, but that is what they likely thought—you must have some particular skill set. Conexus is not a well-known magical ability, and so the low-level thugs would not have thought of it. But, whoever organized all of this, that person would. That person who brews potions that most magicians would only dream of, they would know about Conexus. They would covet it, suspect it, and fear it.

"You see, whoever is behind all this wants more than anything to carry out all of their plans, every single one, and to stop anyone who gets in their way. When they heard of our progress, they had to know how it was done. It must have burned them up. They postulated that Conexus could be involved, and the funeral is the proof of that postulation."

"How is that?"

"To the one who is orchestrating all of this, the idea that they could be found at any time terrifies them, and therefore even the possibility of Conexus terrifies them. Abandoning their original plans to destroy me, they instead devised a scheme to present us with the handwritten letter. If you were capable of Conexus—they must have reasoned —then we would follow the note. If not, then nothing was really lost to them, and they could at least worry less."

"But, why would they give us a note that would lead right to them, at any time? We could hold on to it and use it later, make it look like we found them through some other clue. They would have given themselves away, without really finding out anything for sure about Conexus!"

"You say 'at any time' but you yourself don't feel that way. You're impacted, emotionally. You could hardly take time to grieve, or give me time to grieve. I'm sure they assumed, rather carelessly, that I would have a similar response. Their thugs likely reported my emotional behavior and efforts to save Talbot; they probably thought that I would be driven by my own personal involvement. Perhaps they thought that their insulting insinuation that I shared any of the blame would enrage me. Certainly, we could hold onto the note and use it any time, but why would we? The trail was fresh, as you said. But, the trail is false.

"More than anything, whoever is behind this wants a definite answer on the question of Conexus, I'm convinced of that now. Their plan is to draw us out, and detect our pursuit of the writer of this letter. What could be easier? They could be anywhere; this would lead us right to them, and they'd certainly see us coming. If we followed the trail then we'd be tipping our hand outright, as far as your talent is concerned. This is my theory, and I believe it is correct.

"Our plan, therefore, must be to do nothing until they give us something else to act on. They cannot know for sure that Conexus is involved; but even suspecting it, they'll be far more careful. We must make them believe that the only tools available to us are of the common variety. I propose that we wait, as long as it takes, until they make a move."

He paused, examining his drawing on the whiteboard.

"Besides, I recognize the distinct handwriting of the person who penned this letter, and their name is not W.C. Crane."

Chapter 11

Guardian Stones

Spindlebrock's proposition—that we wait to act—was more informing than it was consensus seeking. Over the next few days I sought opportunities to debate the point, thinking we might somehow use the letter to our advantage, but his resolution was clear: we would do absolutely nothing relating to the matter of the abductions until our adversaries gave us some new reason to act. He retained possession of the letter, so that no temptation would lead me to act on my own.

With time on my hands, I resolved to load up on my courses at the University of Magic, Toronto. My decision was made all the more readily when I learned that my old student loans would slip into repayment if I didn't recommence my schooling in a more serious way, and that the University was well equipped to help me defer them while I studied. My instructors, many of whom I knew through my affiliation as Spindlebrock's assistant, seemed pleased to have me in their classes. Even Dr. Patel was amenable; though my enrollment in his notably dry class on fourteenth century magical philosophy was more of Spindlebrock's idea than my own.

In addition to classes, I began devouring every fascinating book on magic that I could get my hands on, both in Spindlebrock's home, and in the University library. As an exercise, and motivated by a strange sort of admiration for both the book and the author, I decided to master all of the incantations found in my very first book of magic: Professor Spindlebrock's Little Blue Book of Traveling Spells. I told myself that they might come in useful, if the onerous business of the abductions were to recommence.

Of all the things that I recall from that period, deeply studying that small book is the one thing that stands out most clearly and distinctly in my mind. Though the spells were simple and practical, there was a certain quality to the writing that I had never before encountered. Spindlebrock, who is generally not highly communicative, can come across as reserved and even standoffish in person. In the classroom one might judge him to be pompous, arrogant, self-aggrandizing, and smug. In a public social setting, their opinion would not be much improved. Even in private, Spindlebrock tends toward egotism more than intimacy. I say all this without reservation; Spindlebrock himself uses these very words, from time to time, to describe his character.

But in his writing, a whole other side of him appears. He is frank, forthright, and open. He shares his knowledge as if he wishes nothing more than to imbue the reader with every gram of information and understanding that he possesses. His writing is unreserved, unpretentious, and genuinely gracious.

In the book—as I call it; it standing apart from all other books in my mind—I discovered an unlikely foundation of magical knowledge. Spindlebrock touches on magical history (some of which I've shared) in a very succinct way, and connects that history to a treatment on the laws, rules, and governance of magic in the modern world. He informs on the relationship and influence of magic and global culture, with a concise analysis of how magic is treated by the non-magical in various regions. All of this is covered, with references and suggested further reading for each topic, in the preface alone.

In the body of his book, Spindlebrock manages to use simple incantations and methods as vehicles for delivering in-depth truths and concepts relating to important aspects of magic. There is the section on wandless magic that I've already mentioned, which encourages the reader to learn and practice all spells, in and out of the book, with and without a wand. He covers things a magician should always pack when traveling, charms to cast before leaving home, and much more.

What I learned through my study of this little volume helped me to feel confident in my magical abilities more quickly than I believe any other teaching could have. On campus this was incredibly important, since I often felt like an impostor in a strange world. I'm certain that in the literary world of magicians, the book is almost universally overlooked. Still, for me, it served as my bedrock and guide, and helped ease what felt like a new life of continual revelation, an explosion of unimaginable new experiences.

Readers unfamiliar with magic might be surprised at how mind-blowing even the simplest things can become when you mix in a spell or two. The cafeteria, for example, appears a veritable madhouse to the magically uninitiated. Food and dishes moving about on their own; selections made and served with the wave of a hand or wand; tables bused by freshmen already loaded with a mountain of dishes carefully balanced on their heads. In the halls between classes one finds an equally chaotic, but highly controlled scene. The classroom alone is calm; everywhere else, magic is in such high use, one can't help but be amazed.

Reminiscing on these days spent studying has brought to mind another fascination that I wish, and ought, to share with you. The first time that I located the University, it was through the help of a borrowed trinket, a charm of the physical type. That help was necessary because the campus is protected by a powerful charm of the magical type. The school is invisible to the outside world—an entire campus, hidden in plain sight. After some time on campus, I became aware of an observance that many of the students and faculty participated in as they entered and left the school grounds each day. They would stop at one of two large stones placed by the pathway leading to the school and utter a few soft words under their breath, accompanied by a flourish of either their hand or their wand. It seemed as if almost everyone would do this, every time they arrived at or departed from the grounds.

Curiosity worked its particular brand of magic, and while Delphine was visiting for breakfast one day, I inquired of her as to what all this meant. She glanced at Spindlebrock, as if to allow him time to answer if he would, but he was engrossed in his hash browns, so she responded.

"It is an old and powerful magic, Thomas, and one that I'm not really an expert in. I believe it's classified as a protective charm, but not like the shifty ones that you've probably encountered while kicking around with this guy."

She shot a glimpse in Spindlebrock's direction, but the jab seemed to glance off the newspaper that he had picked up. I got the faint impression that she was uncomfortable explaining more, and I was prepared to let the subject drop. Curiosity had not been satiated, however, so I was grateful when she continued of her own volition.

"It's kind of a multi-part enchantment I suppose you could say. The charms you've mostly seen or heard of are cast once, and generally last a certain amount of time, or until something or someone breaks them. I've seen such charms used to keep a conversation secret, or to skirt past a

146

crowd without being seen. There are related protective charms on this house, for example."

She shot another look at the professor, who cleared his throat and reached for his juice. Delphine waited a few moments before continuing.

"The charm that protects the University, and other magical centers, is quite different from all of those. An initial charm is cast by a few advanced magicians, quite in secret, and generally before construction even begins. Well, I should say, it's usually cast before an announcement is even made that a place will be constructed. Then, after the initial charm, incantations are cast by those who use the grounds, generally when they arrive or leave. These aren't protective charms on their own, not really. They simply amplify, or magnify the charm that is already there. The more connection you have to a place—the more important and meaningful it is to you—the more powerful your amplification charm is to the original charm."

This new idea that Delphine had shared left a significant impression on my mind. It is a cold, distant thing to have a place that is protected by some powerful unknown force, but quite another thing to be on ground that is hallowed and protected by the hearts and minds of those that care about it most. As the University had become more personally meaningful to me during this period, I asked Delphine if she would teach me the simple incantation so that I might be a part of what I felt around me. She seemed delighted that I had such an interest, and taught me willingly. The words are unique to that particular place and those particular stones. They are beautiful, simple, and poetic; I wish that I could share them here, however, they may only be learned by those who are intimately connected to the University. To this day, I never pass those two stones, which I call Guardian Stones— a name that I gave them, as they had no common name that I could discover—without speaking the words and adding my voice to the unknown masses of magicians that came before me.

Chapter 12

Paranoia and Powerful Potions

Months passed, and no further evidence of abductions was manifested. The magical world was, by and large, quiet and peaceful. Had I not known that there was a scheming, murderous criminal planning their next move, I may have found more peace and solace in my studies. But, as hard as I tried to distract myself, I could not stop churning the abduction and murder of Talbot over and over in my thoughts.

Even more disconcerting to me was the fact that Spindlebrock seemed to have completely put the abductions out of his mind. He was, in all appearances, back to his usual self. He spent almost all of his free time in his private study or at the University. His teaching style and manners were unchanged. If anything, he was more easily distracted by triviality, and more prone to arguments with his colleagues over minutia. In a judgmental moment I wondered if he was too crestfallen from his failure in Phoenix to want to face the reality of what most certainly lied ahead. I am positive that if I had asked anyone other than Delphine if Spindlebrock cared at all about the events in Phoenix—which many people had become cognizant of

—they would have responded with a unqualified and contemptuous no.

Eventually I discovered that my assumptions and judgments were incorrect; an error which I am all too happy to admit. It had been almost a full year since the funeral, and my pain and worry had finally softened. Summer had faded into fall, fall into winter, and winter had given way to a bright and colorful spring, which almost erased the hurt entirely. I had, in truth, taken to reveling in the gorgeous Toronto "printemps," without a care in the world.

It was nearly June, and the University campus was surrounded by flowerbeds and cherry trees which had made themselves into an exposition of life and blossom that none could ignore. On one particularly fine afternoon, I skipped the class that I normally attended (I recall it was a class on magical accounting, a subject which to this day entirely baffles me, though the blend seems quite appropriate and careers apparently abound) opting instead to find a quiet bench near a third story window of the same building, where the view of the cherry blossoms was phenomenal and the people-watching was equally good. Most of the foot traffic was near the courtyard, off the main path. As I watched the distant and miniature-looking humans moving about, I noticed three individuals—a man, a woman, and a young lady—who broke away from the crowds to walk through the flower-laden thickets.

At first I was amused, and just a little envious of their amicable association; my introversion made it difficult for me to make friends, even in a sea of people. Then I recognized the forms: Spindlebrock, Delphine, and Lilianne, Delphine's daughter. A tinge of jealousy and loneliness welled up in me, buried feelings that I hadn't realized were on the point of brimming over. I rose to my feet to get closer to the glass, watching them intently.

The trio made their way through the orchard, pausing to chat from time to time, meandering in their path. There were a few others that had strayed into the trees as well, drawn by the glory of the show, but these eventually dwindled as classes started. When they were at last the only three in sight, the behavior of my associates changed. They slipped furtively to the threshold of the woods surrounding the campus, then huddled together in conversation for a few minutes, their heads rising occasionally to cast about anxious glances.

Without warning, Spindlebrock stepped quickly back from the group; I thought I could just make out his signature wandless flourish, when the three suddenly disappeared from view. I started in shock, but kept my eyes glued to the spot where they had been, and where I was sure they now stood cloaked from view. The charm which had worked so instantly on my sight, started to affect my mind. As I stood watching, I felt something foreign in my consciousness, strongly suggesting that the particular spot I was starting at was of no interest at all. It was subtle enough that I would not have recognized and fought against it, had I not been so acutely interested in what was going on there. I wrestled against the power of the charm, but even the memory of my reasons for struggling was starting to slip through my desperate hold.

Just as my will was about to falter, a spell from the professor's book popped into my mind. Without wasting a moment to consider whether or not it would work, I sprung up and cast the charm intended to "help the weary traveler bolster their memory, so as not to forget anything that they might need to pack for their trip." My mind snapped back to a remembrance of the three people I was watching. With eyes willfully glued to the spot where I last saw them, I witnessed as the brush of the surrounding woods parted itself broadly to create an opening wide enough for the group to pass through. Moments later the opening closed, and the effect of Spindlebrock's charm broke entirely. I had vanquished, witnessed what was meant to be hidden, and kept my memory of the events intact.

Until that day, I had taken it for granted that the main path between the guardian stones was the only way people could pass in and out of the University campus. The stones seemed to be infallible protectors, powered and renewed daily by those whom they protected. Seeing three people I trusted walk unhindered through their bulwark pierced my heart and trust.

Jealousy and shock turned to anger and indignation. Over the past several months that I had spent living in Spindlebrock's home and attending the University of Magic, I had grown close to Delphine, and as close as one can to Spindlebrock. I had even formed a casual connection with Lilianne, in spite of her constantly being overloaded with her studies. Had I not proven myself worthy of their trust and friendship? Something in me knew that the three were headed back to Spindlebrock's home, to work on the problem of the abductions. I can't explain how I knew it, but I knew it beyond a doubt, and my exclusion was agonizing.

In a brief moment of anomalous creativity, I planned out exactly what I would do. First, I would immediately rush down and call a cab; Spindlebrock often took the bus—to avoid dealing with an unknown individual who might recognize him then, or remember him later—and a cab would buy me some time. I would pay the driver double to get me there quickly, buying even more time. Instead of going to the house, where Spindlebrock would surely discover me, I would set myself up inconspicuously near the bus stop where Spindlebrock and the others were sure to disembark, and cast a simple charm that would let me go unnoticed. I had, and still have no confidence that I could manage to cast a charm of the sort that would protect me from Spindlebrock's gaze if he were the least bit determined to find me, but I was hopeful that at the bus stop he would suspect very little.

From the bus stop I could watch them until they rounded the corner on Spindlebrock's street. There was no way that I could actually see them go further or enter into his house, without risking detection, but it would be enough. If they were headed that way, my instincts insisted that they were working on something related to the abductions in Spindlebrock's personal lab. I would simply have to confront them about it when the time was right.

I carried out the plan, though I immediately started to feel that I was irresponsible for attempting it, irrational for feeling as jealous as I did, and insane in my delusions of being left out. Still, the plan worked quite well, and I did in fact discover that they were heading to Spindlebrock's home with a great deal of haste, and some apparent concern. Looking back, I realize that it was more than concern. I saw it especially in Lilianne's eyes; it was an urgent look of impending terror.

That look haunted me over the next few days, and thwarted me in my attempts to build up the courage to confront Spindlebrock about the events. I continued to skip my accounting class, so I could see if the three were leaving the campus on a regular basis. I discovered that they left every day that week. To my dismay, they sometimes took Dr. Patel with them—whom I thought Spindlebrock disdained—or one other professor that I did not recognize. My anger and frustration grew. How could he exclude me, after all that he had already put me through? I felt like I deserved to be included, but in my fear (and, now, guilt for my spying) there was really nothing that I was willing to do to find out more than what I could observe from a distance.

That Saturday, Delphine joined us for breakfast, as she frequently did on the weekends. Spindlebrock, perhaps sensing that I was out of sorts, uncharacteristically left his newspaper folded on the table and attempted to converse.

"So, Thomas, you've been studying quite hard it appears. I hear from several of the other professors that you're very adept in their subjects."

I nodded, but had nothing to say in reply. Spindlebrock didn't really wait long enough for a reply anyway.

"Professor Patel says you are taking a particular interest in folk healers and heresy, and the reign of James the First."

At this comment I didn't even nod; I had barely been listening in Patel's class, and certainly hadn't expressed any level of interest. Spindlebrock shrugged and continued.

"I must say, though, that this past week you've been quite out of sorts. Is something going on?"

Our eyes met and I encountered in his gaze a firm resolution to find out what was bothering me. I was nervous; I had chased them down, invaded their privacy. Could he know? Why else would he bring up speaking with Dr. Patel? Was I simply afraid to find out what was going on, to know for sure that I was being excluded? To this day I can't exactly recall what I was feeling, because of what happened next. Smiling warmly, Spindlebrock reached over and poured me a tall glass of cranberry juice.

"Here you go," he said cordially, pushing the glass toward me.

I gulped the drink down quickly in an attempt to parch my nervous, dry throat. It was notably bitter, even for cranberry juice. For a brief instant the thought occurred to me that it was odd that we were having cranberry juice that morning; normally we had orange juice, Spindlebrock's favorite. I didn't have long to think about it, as the thought was followed by an immediate sense of disorientation and nausea. I wanted to get up and run to the restroom, but I felt as if I were rooted to my chair.

Thankfully, the nausea was only momentary. After it passed, I was still stuck in my chair, unable to speak or move, yet fully aware of my surroundings. I noticed that Delphine and Spindlebrock were watching me intently, and I was about to ask for their aid, when Spindlebrock broke the silence.

"I'm truly sorry to have done it Thomas, but I've spiked your juice this morning. In my defense, it was out of necessity."

I swore at him. Generally I am reserved, and attempt to keep my speech controlled and professional at all times, but my thoughts seemed to burst out of my mouth. He chuckled, but I could see that he was still watching me intently, with a look of concern.

"That is one of the initial effects, and I won't hold it against you. The juice was laced with a truth potion and an immobilizing potion. The truth part kicks in right away, but the immobilizing part works its way from your feet up, ending at the mouth. The combination is a little hard on the stomach, and a little bitter. The cranberry helps with both side effects, I've found."

For a moment I relished the unbridled expletives that I thought were coming, but I was suddenly altogether unable to speak, even at will. My mind struggled to make my mouth move, but it would not budge.

"This particular potion, once it's fully active, has the effect not only of preventing your movement, but also of preventing your speech—that is, unless you're questioned. Do you understand?"

"Yes."

The response came out involuntarily.

"Good. Our business with this potion won't take long. You see, for the past week or so, you've been acting rather peculiar. Just yesterday, I checked in with your professors, and found that you've been skipping one of your classes pretty regularly. Is that the case?"

"Yes."

"Which class?"

"The class on magical accounting."

Spindlebrock smiled.

"To be honest, I think I would skip that class as well. But even so, it is a little odd that you would skip it so consistently. Normally, you're a very attentive pupil, even when the material is dry."

He helped himself to some of the quiche that Delphine had placed on the table. Delphine's eyes darted from me to Spindlebrock. They were filled with the same concern, and a measure of the terror that I had seen in Lilianne's eyes.

"Delphine wanted me to just ask you outright, to pull you into our confidence without precaution; but as you know Thomas, we're dealing with some very dark characters right now. We're still fairly new acquaintances, in the grand scheme of things, and I wanted to be absolutely certain."

The comment caught me off guard and filled my head with questions that I literally could not ask. Most especially, I thought it was odd that he referred to our dealings with the abductions in the present tense, considering that he seemed to have all but forgotten them.

"Where did you go when you skipped class yesterday?"

"I went to the third floor of the North Building, to look at the cherry blossoms."

My lips felt like they were filled with Novocaine, and my voice sound foreign and hollow. It was surreal to hear my voice coming out involuntarily.

Spindlebrock chewed his food carefully before continuing his inquiry.

"And nowhere else?"

"That's correct."

"What about the day before that?"

"I did the same thing."

"And what about all of the other days when you skipped Mme. Vidal's Magical Principles of Economics? Did you do anything but look at the blossoms?"

"Yes. On the first day that I skipped, I followed you, Delphine, and Lilianne."

Spindlebrock put his fork down and wiped his mouth.

"Why?"

"I saw you in the orchard. I wanted to know what you were doing."

"Did anyone ask you to follow us?"

"No."

"Tell me how you followed us."

I explained the whole affair to him. He looked dutifully impressed as I recounted my effort to overcome his cloaking charm using his own traveler's memory charm.

"And you had no other motive for following us, no one else was involved? No one put you up to it?"

"That is correct."

My answers were uncharacteristically succinct. In a way, I could understand why Spindlebrock wanted to do it the way he did.

"And have you told anyone else about what you discovered? That you followed us here to my home?"

"No."

Spindlebrock looked relieved. Delphine wore a distinct look of, "I told you so," as she glared at him.

"Can we please give him the antidote now, C.C.?"

Without waiting for a reply, Delphine produced a small bottle and held it to my lips. In an instant I felt released, completely free. Just as I was about to turn on Spindlebrock and demand an explanation, I passed out.

Chapter 13

Self, Revealed

The events at the breakfast table came back to my mind all at once, and I was annoyed at being deprived of a large part of my morning just to placate Spindlebrock's paranoia. The feeling passed as I mused on the professor's reasons for moving me into his private study. Glancing around, I jumped when I saw Spindlebrock at his desk. His head was resting on his arm; he had apparently fallen asleep at his work.

I took the opportunity to nose around a bit, feeling somewhat entitled in light of the earlier escapades at my expense. The first thing that stood out to me was Spindlebrock's whiteboard. It had been—the few times I had seen it—covered with a chaotic smattering of apparently disconnected ideas, written in even more chaotic handwriting. The entire mess had been wiped clean, and the board was now covered in carefully written notes, organized into sections by color and subject. The handwriting was too neat to be Spindlebrock's; the thought came to me that it might easily be Delphine's.

I studied the board for a few moments, unable to comprehend most of the chemistry and math it contained. Meandering over to the door marked File Room, I tried the handle, but found it locked. Noiselessly, I wandered around to see what else I could discover. The usual mess prevailed, but along one wall a workbench had been cleared, its contents neatly stacked on the floor at one end. As I approached, I noted that the pile was not just neatly stacked, it was methodically puzzle-pieced together in such a way that only Delphine could manage, with her penchant for telekinesis. The workbench was now in perfect order, with Bunsen burners, graduated cylinders and other miscellany arranged on its surface. A small open notepad held more chemistry and math, this time in Spindlebrock's unintelligible scrawl.

I glanced around the room while I pondered what they might have been working on. When I looked at the couch, something clicked. The couch, like the workbench, had been previously covered in a terrible mess of bric-a-brac. It was now perfectly clean, with a carefully puzzle-pieced pile next to it, much like the pile near the workbench. I couldn't believe that it had been cleared off in that careful manner just for me. I examined the pile of items, and noted that it was topped with a thin layer of dust, telling me that the couch had been cleared of its contents for some time. The sanctuary had been breached; Delphine, and likely her daughter as well as the other professors, had most certainly been here working with Spindlebrock.

I might have discovered more but for a soft click of the door's lock behind me. I turned and plopped down hastily on the couch as Delphine opened the door and peered in. She smiled upon seeing me awake.

"Oh good, you're up."

She motioned for me to follow. As I walked out of the windowless chamber and into the grand entryway, I was confused to see that it was dark outside.

"It's late. You've slept the day away, Thomas."

There was a natural and effortless hint of lightness and laughter in her voice, which she flattened into seriousness as she continued.

"That is to say, Spindlebrock's potion and antidote have caused you to need quite a bit of rest. I'm sure he'll have an apology ready when he comes out."

Delphine was always quite conscious of Spindlebrock's weaknesses and failings in the realm of interpersonal relationships, but in spite of her knowledge of the man, she always expected more of him than he was inclined to give. This made her a true friend. I pondered on this as I followed her into the kitchen.

"I've made a late dinner, nothing heavy. Come in and sit down."

She sat down at the table with me, and without looking away or making any noticeable movement she put that amazing part of her mind to work bringing in dishes and cups of food and drink, all while conversing with me about the events of the morning.

"You're probably wondering why he gave you that potion, right Thomas?"

I had already made up my mind that Spindlebrock's potion was the result of an overly paranoid mind, but since I was eager to hear Delphine's side of the story I nodded as I bit into a chicken salad croissant.

"C.C. worries too much. We've been working on a project together, one of particular importance, you see? Just the other day he told me that you had been quite distant—"

Delphine must have noticed the vague look of surprise on my face. In the months that preceded this day I had felt that Spindlebrock had lost all interest in me. I thought, at that time, that perhaps he only kept me around for those particular talents that he might find useful for his research and efforts. That he could detect my emotional distance, and that he might care, was a shock.

"He really is quite fond of you. You're a breath of fresh air in his life. He's been distant himself, and not just with you. There's a lot going on right now that has been taking his mind elsewhere."

She paused to catch a teapot that was floating in from the kitchen.

"You saw us coming here to the house, so you already know that we've been working together."

At this comment I interjected.

"You, Spindlebrock, and Lilianne? I did see all three of you leave the school and come here, right? And sometimes Dr. Patel and another?"

Delphine seemed a little unsettled at the mention of her daughter.

"Well, yes."

She paused for a few moments, looking around as if she would find her next words in the room somewhere.

"I can't tell you everything, Thomas. Not right now at least. Not because I don't trust you; in fact, it was all C.C.'s idea to use the truth potion. He made inquiries with your other teachers, as he already told you, and he was suspicious. He likes you, but his experiences in life cause him to doubt almost everyone and everything. He's a wonderful scientist because of them, but not the easiest kind of friend."

A beautifully arranged plate of fruit and a croissant set themselves down in front of Delphine, who took a moment to eat a few small bites before continuing. I was too lost in thought to add anything to the conversation. I appreciated Spindlebrock, and I viewed him as a friend, but the idea that he might hold me in any kind of real regard had not occurred to me.

"In any case, he decided to use the potion, because he needed to be sure," Delphine continued.

"Our work is critical, and with everything that is going on with the abductions, C.C. thought we needed to know for sure that you were on our side in all of this. You did originally come to us in a very unusual way, after all."

I nodded, laughing a little at the memory of how I had come to be a part of the magical commonality. Delphine seemed relieved at my entire response. I don't know for certain, but I've always suspected that in addition to her telekinesis Delphine also has a hint of telepathy. She seemed to truly believe that I was in fact a good friend worthy of trust, though we had spoken very little up to that point.

It was this feeling of trust, and this notion that Delphine could somehow peer into my thoughts, that led me to share with her what I am about to share with you. My motivations at the start of all this had been morphing, very slowly, into something more than curiosity. A realization of purpose, a deeply rooted sense of obligation that I hadn't quite grasped until that night. These nagging thoughts in the back of my mind finally came to the forefront as I opened up.

"Delphine, you probably think I'm crazy. Sometimes I think that I am. After Phoenix—I mean after it really settled

—I thought I was. I've never been really brave, and Phoenix showed me the kind of people we're up against."

"The very worst kind," she acknowledged.

"Yes, and that's just it. I've always thought of myself as someone who would investigate after-the-fact. Well, not always, but for a long time anyway. I didn't feel like I had the courage or strength to be the kind that runs toward danger."

I paused, formulating my thoughts. Something was breaking out of my mind, and I could feel it. To be honest, I was searching for a way to not share what was on the tip of my tongue.

"But you have changed, haven't you?"

"Yes. I mean, I think so. It's Lilianne—"

For some reason, I choked on the name.

"Go on."

"In Phoenix, Spindlebrock said she was in trouble. Something snapped, or, just changed. I wanted to help, more than I've wanted anything in a long, long time.

"Then, when I saw you three coming here, I felt compelled to be a part of what you were working on. I knew it was for her."

Delphine smiled faintly.

"It's not her, I mean, not like that. It's more than that. When I was a kid, I—this is really hard. I've never told this to anyone who didn't already know about it. When I was thirteen, I lost my sister."

"Thomas, I'm so sorry."

Her voice was sincere. I swallowed hard; the pain was still fresh, in spite of time.

"She had been sick, a flu or something. It was bad, it lasted most of the summer. By August, she was getting better, just a lingering cough. She was so tired of being cooped up in the house.

"We used to swim together. We did everything together —we were twins."

Delphine breathed in sharply. Her eyes started to water, and my nerve was fading, so I plowed on.

"Our house was next to a sort of park, a nature area. It was just a thin sliver of woods that separated us from the Miami River—Great Miami, or whatever you want to call it. The river was wide there; there was a small dam that pooled it up. We would jump in off a small dock and have races across. She always beat me."

Delphine touched my hand.

"What was her name?"

"Sarah. Her name was Sarah."

She closed her eyes, thoughtful.

"She wanted to race again, she was worried that I had gotten ahead while she was sick. I was excited—I hate to say it now—that I might actually win for once.

"It had been a particularly wet summer, and the river was swollen. When I saw it flowing fast over the low dam, I thought maybe we should just go back home, but she dared me. I don't know why that dare was worth anything, but it was, somehow. We counted to three and jumped in, just like we had so many times before.

"As my arms pounded the water, I was oblivious to everything but that desire to win. I had never been in the lead before, I didn't even know what it felt like. I touched the other side and doubled back without thinking or looking.

"When I reached the dock, I turned around to shout out my victory, but she wasn't there. I looked around and found her, struggling against the current.

"I dove in without thinking. I wanted to get to her so bad. I thought I had poured everything in to that race; maybe it was pure adrenaline at that point. But she went over the dam before I could get to her. I swam to the edge and ran around to the lower part, and dived back in. I couldn't see her.

"I'm not sure how I found her, or how I got her out. I just remember being on the shore and turning her over and patting her on the back. She spat out water and coughed. I was so relieved, but I couldn't stop shaking.

"We walked back to the house. When we got there, our parents were fighting. She was tired—she kept saying she wanted to lie down—so Sarah went to her room, and I went to mine.

"It was me—I found her hours later. I was the first one to see her. My dad was a police officer, so he heard the call, and when the ambulance came, he was right behind it.

"The doctors tried to explain that it was a complication from the flu, that she already had water in her lungs, but that the partial drowning had gotten it to a point where she died because of a lack of oxygen. But my dad blamed me. He blamed me for letting her race, for not telling them about what had happened right away.

"I blamed myself, too. Growing up, I always wanted to be just like my dad. He was a hero, the one people called when they were in real danger. I can't even remember how many times I was a police officer for Halloween before that year. Then everything changed. I never thought, after that, that I could ever save anyone.

"I guess, when Spindlebrock mentioned that Lilianne was in trouble, something in me snapped. I didn't want to sit there and do nothing. I've always thought that if I had done something differently—"

Delphine's hand had been resting on mine the whole time I had been speaking. She squeezed my hand gently and spoke kind words of comfort which I will always treasure.

"You're a good man, Thomas Martin, always remember that. Thank you for caring about my Lilianne as much as you cared about your Sarah."

It was enough; we ate in silence for a few moments. The window over the sink was open, admitting the soft sound of crickets which reverberated off the walls of the kitchen. It felt to me like a surreal morning in the middle of the night. My heart felt light, as if a massive weight had been lifted.

"I'm glad you're alright now, Thomas. Many of C.C.'s potions are quite powerful, more so than you would find almost anywhere else. He's known the world over for them, really. The potion he gave you can have grave effects—well, it can be very dangerous in any case."

Indignation started to creep back into my heart. Delphine seemed to notice, and hastened to continue her explanation.

"With C.C. to look after you, there was of course no real danger. After you fainted, he carried you into his study. He watched over and cared for you all day. There really was no danger."

My opinion of the humanity of C.C. Spindlebrock is constantly re-arranging itself, and it changed again in that moment. He had administered a potion in a moment of exigency, so he thought, and he had accepted responsibility for the care I required afterward. I did not appreciate the risk he took with my life, but I understood why he did it. I truly understood. It's amazing to me how we construct ideas about people based on the way they act and interact externally, and we cling to these ideas as if they truly defined a person throughout. Then, in moments of revelation, all of our notions and judgments evaporate as we realize that we can never really have the full picture of a person's heart and mind.

You, reader, don't know me, yet I don't wish to hide myself from you. I hope that through what I write you will know me—and my friends—better.

Chapter 14

A Mistlethorpe Wand

The very next morning, Spindlebrock was up early preparing breakfast for the two of us. Where his cooking lacked, his warmth and friendliness made up for it. As we ate, we conversed about my course of study, touched on the various challenges the University faced, and brainstormed ideas for Spindlebrock to reinvigorate his own classes, which he felt had been lacking due to distraction on his part. We talked about the few people that we both knew: Delphine, a handful of professors, and a few faculty staff. When I started to bring up my previous night's discussion with Delphine, he interrupted me with this gentle reassurance:

"I'm treading very lightly for Delphine's sake, Thomas. Her daughter is tied up in all of this, and it has her worried sick. I don't have all the answers yet, and Delphine wants to keep things under wraps for the time being. I promise, when the time is right, you'll know everything."

For the next several weeks, professor Spindlebrock proved that his thoughtfulness that morning was not a fleeting caprice. It seemed to me that he took a greater and more sincere interest in me than he had previously taken.

We spent a good deal of time together, working on my magical skills. He was tickled that I had taken to learning from his book of traveling spells, and he took the time to help me through some of the spells that I was struggling with. We covered the section on "What to Pack and How to Pack It," which I was excited to tackle mainly because of the inclusion of a simple telekinesis spell. Spindlebrock insisted on going over the section titled, "Magic in Public Places," which wasn't particularly interesting, but did have some good tips for staying out of trouble with non-magical folk. The section on "Dealing With Trouble," seemed like a fascinating look at magical street smarts, and I would have loved some help understanding it, but Spindlebrock seemed displeased with the quality of the content that he had written, and flatly refused to go over it.

After class one afternoon, Spindlebrock informed me that it was high time I had a decent wand. He had previously given me a wand, for my classes, but it always felt like it was in the way, rather than an aid. He was thrilled that I had done so much with wandless magic, but, as he said, there were things I could do with a good wand that just weren't possible without one. He had also found, through his own philosophizing on the subject, that "to entirely ignore the merits of a wand was just as bad as ignoring the merits of wandless magic."

We started our search for a wand by looking online. You may be surprised to learn that one might purchase a legitimate wand online, but such is the case if you know where to look. We browsed through several collections of extravagantly ornate wands, created by master wand makers around the globe. They were beautiful, well made, and expensive. When he could see that I was beginning to take a particular interest in a few of these online wands, Spindlebrock closed the browser window abruptly and turned to me.

"Now that you've seen what you might have, let's talk about what you ought to have. Come, we'll have a look in the campus library," he said with a smile.

As we walked across the campus, Spindlebrock commented on how enjoyable it was to watch spring change into summer. I knew that he sincerely meant it, when he breathed in deeply and tilted his head up to feel the full warmth of the sun on his face. In rare moments, when he isn't entirely absorbed in work or when he is so absorbed that he needs a break, he has the capacity to take in the world with a true and deep appreciation.

Once we were inside the library, he located a dusty old volume and carried it to a quiet corner. The title read, "Mistlethorpe's Wands, Volume III." It was a somewhat large book, at least eight centimeters thick, with a binding that spoke of very little use.

"I have the entire set as a gift from Mistlethorpe herself, back in my file room. The library here only has the first four volumes. She even shared a few things with me that you won't find in any of the volumes, before she passed away."

This last sentence he spoke gravely, his hand running thoughtfully over the cover. An instant later, the gaiety and lightness came back to his voice.

"I mean to say, I spoke with the grand-daughter of the great Agatha Mistlethorpe, one Agnus Mistlethorpe. It's curious, you know, the Mistlethorpe family—they only have female children, and though they marry, they always keep the Mistlethorpe name. I'd say they always have names that start with the letter A, but I don't think that's quite true. It seems to me there was a Bonneville Mistlethorpe at one point, though I can't recall if she was much of a magician or not."

Spindlebrock smiled broadly, then opened the book and flipped easily to a chapter on wand selection. We read about different types of wood, cutting and carving methods, and several variations on the traditional wand shape. He went through many aspects of "the perfect wand for the wielder," including particular instructions on choosing a tree to harvest wood from, drying and curing freshly cut wood, and the finishing process. My head was swimming with what felt like minutia, but I remember the conclusion that he arrived at for my perfect wand: birch wood, straight, thirty centimeters in length, cut in the first month of summer from the highest branch of a tree approximately as old as I was, finished by hand.

When he finished reading and set the book down, I imagined that we were about to embark on a woodsman-esque adventure, complete with plaid shirts and axes. But to my great surprise, he produced, on the spot, a small wooden shaft of light colored birch, unfinished but dried, roughly carved, and cut to the proper length, clearly meant to become a wand.

"This is the perfect piece of wood for you to fashion your wand from, Thomas, and only the work that may be effectively completed by someone other than the wielder, has been done. You must finish the wand, in order for it to be entirely yours."

He handed me the wand. I was speechless, but he seemed to know what I would have asked.

"I didn't carve it myself, Thomas, nor did I seek out the perfect birch. I enjoy the woods, but I don't often have time for them. No, instead I contacted Amanda Mistlethorpe, the oldest living decedent of Agatha, and a close personal friend. She is used to my odd requests, and has a close-knit group of assistants and apprentices who are quite adept at locating and starting the perfect wands—for magicians who still believe in that sort of thing."

"Thank you, this is—I mean, this is really wonderful and thoughtful—"

"It's nothing really, I just pulled a few strings is all. Now, we'll turn a few more pages in this volume, and you'll learn to finish that wand properly."

He again instructed me, in the brusque and abbreviated language of one who has a deep well of vast experience. With the proper methods rehearsed and repeated to Spindlebrock's satisfaction, I set out over the next several days to finish my wand's overall shape and design. Without Spindlebrock's knowledge—fearing perhaps he might think me either too inept or too cowardly—I purchased a few bits of spare wood to experiment and practice on. Using some small hand tools (wands must be finished by hand), I got a feel for the work and the wood, and came up with a carved pattern in the spare wood which I then repeated on my actual Mistlethorpe wand. After some reading online about how to do such a thing, I worked the birch to a smooth, even finish by both dry-sanding and wet-sanding.

I had been instructed not to stain or varnish the wood in any way, with the exception of a coat of linseed oil, which I could re-apply by hand as needed. This I did, and when I was finished, I took the wand to Spindlebrock for inspection. After turning the wand over several times, and eyeing it carefully from several angles, he burst out suddenly with the words of an enchantment that sent sparks flying across the room. He admitted that he was impressed, and confessed that he had almost ordered a second one in case I had troubles with the carving.

"This wand," he said, handing it back to me, "is perfect for you."

He asked me to hold the wand out, my arm extended, then he stepped back a few paces. Chin in hand and one arm folded, he examined my posture. In a flash, he produced his wand, uttered a charm, and knocked me to the floor. He leaped forward and caught my wand before it hit the ground.

Before I had time to register an emotional response, Spindlebrock helped me to my feet and began dusting off my shirt.

"There now, no harm done," he said, looking me over. He smiled into my dazed face, supporting my arms while I regained my equilibrium.

"Now that you have a proper wand, you'll need to learn how to use it. You may be surprised to learn that many magicians have almost no skill at efficiently producing and wielding the fancy, lacquered wands they carry. They treat them like a pen, or a phone, or some other inconsequential thing to pack around nonchalantly for convenience."

He placed the wand in my hand, making sure that I had a firm grip, and stepped back a few paces once more. Instinctively, I took a more defensive pose, with my body turned away from Spindlebrock at an angle, my wand raised to eye level.

"Good! You see, you already know what to do when trouble is expected. Now, if you can get it into your head that trouble is always expected, you'll soon learn how to appear calm while consistently remaining on your guard!"

He waited a moment, motionless and inert, a smug smile frozen on his face. I dropped my wand hand to my side in frustration.

"Look, I know we're going to do this your way, but I'd prefer not to end up on the floor again," I ventured. "If you would please tell me what I need to know, I'd be more than happy to practice it diligently."

Spindlebrock nodded, the smile still there.

"Yes, Thomas, if I could tell you in words everything you need to know, that would certainly be easier—"

As he finished his sentence, he somehow produced his wand and knocked me to the floor with an incantation so quickly that I didn't have time to even think about how I might react. This time, instead of helping me up, he stood above me menacingly until I regained my senses.

"I could have killed you just as easily, Thomas," he said seriously.

"You see, a wand is not at all like a pen. It is not like a cell phone, or a wallet, or anything else you might carry around to make your life easier. It is more like a gun; a loaded weapon ready to strike in an instant. With practice, a wand may be produced from the most concealed place on your person, in a matter of mere moments."

All this he said in the most serious tone, his wand pointed directly at my face as he leaned in closer and closer until its tip almost touched my nose. He stopped short and smiled, then put his wand away and helped me up.

"I promise that will be the last time—today at least—that I lay you out on the floor like that. I just wanted you to understand that a wand, and indeed magic itself, is not a toy. It is a tool, which can be used for good or evil. It can heal, it can help, and it can hurt. Most magicians that you encounter will have no intention, nor need, for hurting anyone. Unfortunately, in light of our particular pursuits of late, we won't be mingling with the most common garden-variety magicians."

Spindlebrock proceeded to teach me how to hold, hide, and produce a wand from concealment. Being from the States I had some experience with firearms, and the lesson felt strangely similar to one you might take when getting a license to carry. When we were finished, Spindlebrock gave me what I felt at the time were utterly ridiculous instructions on what to do next.

"Now, when you get home this evening, and every evening before you retire, or whenever you have some time alone, I want you to find a mirror; I want you to practice producing your wand, without incantation, from any place you might decide to carry it on your person. Produce your wand, hold it at the ready, and then conceal it again. Repeat this process one hundred times each day, or more if you have the patience and time."

Then, as if to drive the point home, Spindlebrock produced his wand in a flash, pointed it at my face, and cast a charm that blew a harmless puff of air in my eyes. He really was phenomenally quick.

"Practice diligently, Thomas, as you said you would, and I promise that in time you'll be as quick as I am. Most magicians completely overlook this aspect of their craft; be one that doesn't overlook it, and you'll always have the advantage. You never know when you might need it."

Chapter 15

A Short Flight Across the Globe

ooking back, part of me wishes that this peaceful learning period could have gone on forever. While I had enjoyed my studies in a regular university, the early time I spent at the University of Magic in Toronto was beyond compare. More than just learning facts and information, I was learning about a whole universe of thought and experience that I hadn't realized existed. I felt what I believe the earliest scientists and astronomers must have felt, learning things that were entirely unknown and undiscovered.

However, fate, it so happened, had plans for us beyond education; Spindlebrock in consequence of his life and learning and position, and me simply by association.

It was near the end of summer that our peace was interrupted with the news of another abduction. Rather than hearing directly from the parents (details of Talbot Bennett's death had spread far and wide, and people were more afraid of Spindlebrock than ever), Spindlebrock caught wind of this latest abduction from a magician close to the family.

The abducted youth fit the profile neatly: early twenties, enrolled in a magical university, with parents of prominence in the magical commonality, and a child that normally did not get into any trouble to speak of. Her name was Toba Karademir (similar to the ice skater, but no relation), and she was attending school near her home, in Adana, Turkey.

I was eating breakfast alone when Spindlebrock burst out of his study with the news. After all that had happened in Phoenix, I wasn't sure what he would propose that we do. If we interfered, we risked serious consequences, while if we did nothing, there would be little or no chance of ever understanding what was going on. The business was deadly serious, that much was clear, but the correct course of action did not seem as evident.

"What should we do?" I asked, trying to look unfazed as I ate another bite of my cereal. Spindlebrock stood there looking bright but serious, both hands on his hips. He smiled.

"Why, we head over to Turkey, that's what!"

I set my spoon down in the bowl and picked up my napkin to wipe my mouth. My mind raced with good reasons why I didn't want to go to Turkey: I had never been in the region, nor had I ever traveled that far; I did not know the language; there might be dire consequences if we got involved, and I wasn't ready to deal with that kind of pain a second time around. All of these thoughts and more weighed down on me in the few moments it took to dab my mouth.

Spindlebrock spoke again before I could formulate my concerns into words. He paced around the room as he began his monologue.

"We won't get involved directly. No, that might bring down more trouble than the family could bear. Besides, the family didn't contact me directly for help, so it would be an intrusion."

He turned sharply on one heel and headed in the other direction, hardly pausing for breath.

"We'll stay far enough away from direct involvement to warrant any concern. Our movements will certainly be watched—no dotted black line this time—so we won't attempt to conceal them. We'll make it clear, by our actions, that we simply wish to be near the events, not involved in them. They'll understand why."

This last bit he said while turning and gesturing in my direction, as if to drive home a point.

"If my theory is viable, they'll be looking for us to use Conexus. More than that, they'll be attempting to draw us out. But, we'll show them that we're apprehensive—fearful almost—about getting involved. We'll stay out of their way entirely, visibly, purposefully.

"They'll be forced to conclude that we're only interested in the aftermath of the whole affair; that we want to be there when it's finished, to search for clues, information, anything to feel like we're making a difference. That's what they'll assume. That's what we'll lead them to believe."

He smiled and looked at the ceiling as he began to pace again.

"Yes, they'll be expecting us, without a doubt. To not go would raise even more suspicion and concern. We must go."

Without giving me any opportunity to respond, Spindlebrock walked out of the room. I sat there confounded for a few moments before he popped his head around the corner for one final outburst.

"I'm packing now. I expect you can pack up and be ready to go within the hour."

If you're not accustomed to travel, it may interest you to learn that the things you need to pack for a trip to Turkey are quite the same as the things you need to pack for a trip anywhere else in the world. As Spindlebrock suggested, I was indeed packed and ready within the hour. We walked to the end of his street, where a cab was waiting near the bus stop, having apparently been called in advance. We drove to the airport, but we didn't make our way to the normal terminal. Instead, we stopped at an aviation center off of Derry, where we unloaded our things and started walking toward what appeared to be a commercial complex.

Spindlebrock didn't wait for my questions; as we walked, he spoke.

"Time is of the essence, Thomas, that much you know. I suspect that the distant location of this abduction—at least in relation to us—was intentional. It would test our seriousness. A commercial flight would have to leave on a schedule, forcing us to wait, and would have at best one stop, which likely would waste even more time. That, and a large jet is somewhat limited in speed."

We stopped in front of an unmarked building. The glass on the door was tinted dark enough that I could not see inside. Spindlebrock rapped brusquely, then turned to me.

"A Gulfstream G650, on the other hand, has more than enough range to make the approximately nine thousand kilometer trip without any stops, and is the fastest thing a civilian can hope to charter. It so happens that I have a friend who owns one—Lucas Brevig, a recluse who currently resides somewhere in Norway. He doesn't use the jet much; I make sure it's properly maintained and magically secured, and I employ an unquestionably trustworthy pilot for him. In exchange, he let's me use it at my discretion. He's a famous collector, by the way, you might have heard of him in your book collecting circles. Anyway, the jet is fueled and waiting for us now."

Without the hassle of airport security, lines, and everything else that accompanies a normal commercial flight, we were airborne before we knew it. The plane itself was exceptional, though I realize that it's hardly relevant. Still, it was nice to make the long flight comfortably, with low stress, and with some amount of privacy. Spindlebrock didn't bother casting any protective charms as we conversed. We talked a bit about Turkey, which he had apparently visited many times, and about Toba and her family. The conversation was light, especially considering the task we were embarking on, and the risks involved.

Even though we were there on very serious business, I recall experiencing a certain fascination with Adana. We landed very early in the morning, local time, then drove to a hotel near the center of the bustling city. Our drive took us past the most beautiful, towering mosque, encircled with lush green gardens and flanked by a calm, wide river. I found myself wishing that I had made the effort to be there for more personal and relaxing reasons.

Our hotel—called Bardo's by magicians, but known under quite another name by its more typical tourist visitors —was beautifully adorned. Spindlebrock chatted with the staff at the front desk much longer than was necessary. He seemed determined to converse on as wide a variety of subjects as possible, including the history of the city, things to do there, and places of particular interest. During the course of their conversation—which I was not really a part of—I let my gaze wander around the luxurious building.

The decor was very modern, and perhaps just a little ostentatious, but it was a wonder to behold.

Bored, I started to meander, primarily to separate myself from the din of Spindlebrock's chatter. The lobby was large and spacious, almost in the style of an open court or atrium. Luscious plants and fine sculptures crowded the perimeter, with several crystal water fountains adorning the center of the room. The open space vaulted upward through all the levels of the building, with suspended walkways wrapping around at each floor, connecting a network of halls and rooms. At the pinnacle, the roof was composed of glass panels which invited the warm, filtered daylight, and cast it gently down to the floor. Various plush chairs, couches, and benches were scattered about, some sitting in the open and others nestled in shaded corners.

As I took in the scene, the circles Spindlebrock had drawn to describe the people at the funeral came to my mind inexplicably, and I had the wild notion that I might try my hand at sleuthing out the bustling room. I looked around again with new eyes, trying to surmise any details I might glean about the people around me. Most were going about their business in a very purposeful manner, rapidly moving from door to desk to elevator. These people almost seemed to be background noise, entirely unimportant; a first group. A second group presented itself in the individuals who, like me, were engrossed in the beauty of the lobby. They didn't need to rush off anywhere; perhaps

189

they were already checked in, or perhaps they were waiting for someone as I was. Maybe they were lucky enough to just have time for nothing in particular. This second group was slightly more interesting than the first, but still unimportant, and easy enough to identify.

Then I saw a third group of people, sparsely sprinkled around the lobby in the most peculiar places, lingering. They didn't seem to have anywhere to go, nor did they seem particularly interested in the beauty of their surroundings. I wondered what they were about, and for a brief moment the thought of picking out Spindlebrock's "Fourth Group" of truly out-of-place individuals crossed my mind; but, paranoia caught hold of me and I became suddenly and acutely aware of my own behavior. I looked down, trying not to appear like I was staring. If a fourth group was there, I didn't want to raise suspicion. I took to examining a sculpture nearby, so as not to draw attention to myself.

At that moment, Spindlebrock, who had finished his reveling at the front desk, came up and slapped me on the shoulder, announcing in a loud voice that we had checked into a pleasant room on the third floor, with a view of the river. We made our way to the room, and once inside, we both flopped down in the comfortable armchairs near the open curtains.

I half expected Spindlebrock, who had been acting like a lighthearted and enamored tourist, to strike up a lively conversation about the hotel or the city, but he just sat their looking tired and serious, gazing out the window. After a few moments he spoke, but not really to me.

"We're here. Any time now," he said, resting his elbows on his knees and leaning forward.

I waited to see if he would finish this undirected thought. He did not, so I ventured a few comments on the hotel lobby. I was hoping to share my observations about the different groups of people, thinking that he would be pleased that I had remembered what he had taught me. He interrupted before I could get to the point.

"Yes, the hotel is amazing, I quite agree. And I think we made a sufficiently public entrance. Now," he paused and looked as his watch, "we've used most of the first day in travel. According to pattern, we'll have two more days to wait before we can safely do anything in direct connection with the abduction."

Spindlebrock glanced around the room. He was nodding and bouncing lightly on his chair, with apparent impatience.

"I think at any moment we shall get a ring on the telephone over there. It must be thus, or I'm entirely mistaken in my thoughts."

Spindlebrock, owing perhaps to his methodical and forward-thinking mind, often tends to appear prophetic.

191

This was one of those moments. As he was finishing the last word in his sentence, and before he had dropped his wristwatch from view, the phone rang. It was the front desk, with a call holding for professor Spindlebrock. He took it. I heard his side of the conversation, which was cryptic, abbreviated, and generally useless, along with the hurried mumbles of a female caller on the other end. I thought I recognized the voice as Delphine's. It turned out that I was right.

"That was Delphine," Spindlebrock affirmed as he hung up the handset. A slight smile flitted across his lips, and his hands involuntarily rubbed together in anticipation.

"There's been another abduction."

Chapter 16

All I Had to Do Was Stay Inside

Spindlebrock rummaged through his suitcase as he explained the situation. The second abduction had taken place in Belarus, a young man named Paavo Mand. He had apparently gone missing about a day prior to Spindlebrock's contacts being informed, which meant his abduction had been around the same time as Toba's.

Without inquiring as to my thoughts on the matter, Spindlebrock declared definitively that he would travel to Belarus to ascertain what he could about the situation, while I remained in Turkey. Lewis, who had already hopped on a commercial flight from Phoenix to Turkey, would alter his travel plans and meet up with Spindlebrock in Belarus instead.

"Ah ha! Here it is."

From his disheveled belongings, Spindlebrock finally produced the object of his excavation: a crumpled envelope, the letter from Phoenix.

"I want you to do a few things for me, Thomas. First, I want you to stay inside the hotel until I return. I promised Delphine that I'd keep you safe—she tends to worry, you know—and that is the best way to do it. It's a large and interesting hotel, there's a nice gift shop and wonderful lobby, and a very pleasant restaurant. In any case, there isn't much you can accomplish on your own here, at least not until Toba finds her way home in a couple days."

Spindlebrock removed the letter from the envelope.

"Second, here is the letter from W.C. Crane. I mentioned to you before that it wasn't written in the handwriting of the supposed signer, and that I knew whose hand it was in. There was a young woman at the University, who was only there for a semester before traveling abroad. Her name was Olivia."

"She was the one that handed you the letter that day?" I ventured.

"Not at all. I've not seen her since she left Toronto. She was a most talented magician, and very upright in her thinking for the most part, which I appreciated. She worked hard, and was serious about her progress; she had a particular talent in elemental magic which could have taken her far, if it wasn't for a few distracting interests."

He turned the paper over, examining it carefully from every angle.

"Before she left, Olivia changed. Her focus took a slight turn; a turn that likely went unnoticed by all around her, but not by me. I knew her raw talents and I had hopes for how they would develop, so I was actively observing her educational path. I saw a marked difference in the books she read while in the library, the books she took home, and in her lines of questioning in my classes. These things, along with offhand remarks from other professors, led me to believe that she had started to study darker subjects."

Spindlebrock replaced the letter in its envelope and set it down on the bed. He began to re-pack his suitcase—which was now too ruffled to close properly—then paused and looked me in the eye.

"I've told you that I'm a somewhat religious man. We've not spoken about a darker side of magic, but you aren't naive enough to believe that there is any light without corresponding darkness sulking off in some corner. The battle between light and darkness is eternal, I'm quite sure of that fact. It will be important for you to understand that darkness is real, and that magic is not all science and learning and light. There are those that would use magic for more sinister things, and their pursuits differ quite radically from the mainstream.

"Olivia was not evil, she was just curious. I'm guessing she grew up in a home where such things as darkness and light were not well understood. Such is the case in many homes today. And so, when she began to realize that there were aspects of magic that were unexplored, she became inquisitive. There is no evil in that, and there was—at first— no evil in her.

"But darkness has a way of parasitically clinging to a person, especially a young and curious one. Olivia changed. The thing that always bothered me about her transformation was how dramatic and rapid it was. I did not understand then, but I believe I understand now, why that was.

"The letter is in Olivia's handwriting. I never said anything to her about it, but her handwriting always annoyed me. It's a particularity of mine that I don't often mention to people. I've made a deliberate study of handwriting over the years, and am acutely aware that handwriting is as unique, almost, as a person's fingerprint. Some handwriting is lovely, a pleasure to peruse. But hers always set me on edge. The slant of her 'E' was quite peculiar, her 'Y' with the inverted tail, and a mixture of open and wide letters with others that were sharp and tight; the whole combination made for a hand that was obfuscated and on the whole unpleasant, squarish and mechanical.

"As I said, I never mentioned it to her, nor to anyone else for that matter. In this thing I tend to keep my opinion to myself, though that may come as a shock to you. I found, long ago, that attempting to correct a person's handwriting only served to make them self-conscious and nervous, which generally made the handwriting worse."

I laughed involuntarily, breaking Spindlebrock's train of thought. The idea that he would forgo the opportunity to correct his pupils simply because the correction would be inefficient in producing the desired behavior was entirely like him, but the comment was unexpected. A normal person might simply realize that they were being overly particular, and let the subject of other people's handwriting drop. Spindlebrock, however, had no such realization, which amused me in that moment, and still amuses me now.

Confused by my merriment, he paused to see if I was distracted by something outside his monologue. Finding nothing amiss in the room or out the window, he continued.

"In any case, the letter is most obviously in her handwriting. My suspicion is that Olivia was abducted at some point. We don't know everything that happens during one of these abductions; it's possible that additional potions or other things are in play, beyond what we know for certain. I've long thought this was probable, and I've made additional study with Lilianne to that end, as you're partially aware. I think I've found an answer that would explain Olivia's situation at least, and perhaps all of the abductions at best, but I need to be sure."

After much fiddling, compressing, and repacking, the latch finally snapped shut on his suitcase. Spindlebrock picked up the letter and held it out to me. As I reached for it, he pulled it back.

"I want you to take this letter and keep it safe, for now. Keep it with you, in your pocket, everywhere you go. With your gift, it will eventually reveal to you the location of Olivia. She is tied up in all of this, and it would seem she is quite close with this W.C. Crane character. She may be another victim. We will have to find out."

He placed the letter in my hands.

"Before you put it away, take the letter out of the envelope, hold it in your hands, and tell me what you feel.

Nodding, I complied. At first, I didn't get any strong impressions about the writer as a person, nor did I feel drawn to them as I had been with previous objects. With Talbot's chess piece, for example, I had an extremely strong and urgent sense that he wanted to be found. As that memory crossed my mind, another impression struck me: whoever wrote this letter did not want to be found. What at first seemed like an absence of any feeling connected to the letter, morphed into the impression that someone was hiding; it was almost as if I could hear them breathing, crouched behind a wall, but I could not discover their hiding place.

Those were my feelings, and I shared them with Spindlebrock in a free-flowing stream of consciousness, as they came to me. I had, without realizing it, closed my eyes to focus. When I opened them, Spindlebrock was standing with his suitcases in-hand, ready to depart.

"Concealment is a gift of the darkness, and an art that its purveyors cherish above all others. Already you've broken her spell of concealment, Thomas, but neither she nor you really knows it yet. You've detected her, when she is most certainly doing everything she can to avoid detection.

"Keep the letter with you, on your person, but don't open the envelope again until I tell you to. The next time you do, you will see her, and she will know it. She is waiting and watching. We have to be ready for that moment, and all that it will bring."

Spindlebrock promised to be available by phone if I needed anything, and to keep me updated on his findings. His departure was so abrupt that I didn't have time to be upset, a sentiment that tried to take hold when I thought about how I had been abandoned in a country that was entirely new to me, and confined to a hotel. I fought the feeling back; after all, we couldn't risk meddling with the abductions, and the fact that multiple situations had arisen wasn't the professor's fault. I determined that I would make the most of things.

I set out to explore the hotel, which was indeed large and interesting, just as Spindlebrock had mentioned. The lobby I've already described from the vantage point of the ground floor, but it was even more breathtaking when viewed from the suspended walkway, just down the hall from our room. After enjoying the architectural splendor for a bit, I took the elevator back downstairs. At the back of the lobby was a large seating area, which opened up to reveal the restaurant. Peering inside, I could see that the tables overlooked the river through large floor-to-ceiling glass panes. Across the river I could see the beautiful mosque we had passed on our drive into town.

Doubling back I inspected two hallways, one on either side of the lobby. They were lined with conference rooms and banquet halls, mostly empty and unlocked. I took my time drifting through them, imagining the large parties and elegant guests they could accommodate. From there I found my way to the pool, the exercise room, and the gift shop. My exploring concluded with a leisurely stroll in the open courtyard behind the building, and a return to the lobby, where I had determined to sit and people-watch before retiring to my room.

It was only mid-day, but the initial charm of the trip was wearing off, and the time difference was catching up with me. I took up residence in a cozy wingback chair, tucked away in the shadow of a large, squat sort of palm, near one of the back hallways. From that vantage point, I had determined, I could see the front entrance, the restaurant, and all of the lobby with the exception of the front desk. My hope was that I would be able to pick up where I left off in my exercise of finding circles, perhaps re-identifying some of those out-of-place individuals I had seen earlier.

Unfortunately, movement in the lobby had died down considerably from the morning bustle. A few people were leisurely chatting, while one or two made their way to and from their rooms, baggage in tow. Activity, it seemed, had slowed to a crawl, and whether because of my drowsiness or because it was actually so, I saw nothing interesting in the guests. Indeed, my tired mind couldn't categorize them at all, and after a few minutes I decided to lean back and rest.

The blinking of my eyes was just starting to linger more slowly, and my head was just starting to nod, when I saw her. The large glass panels of the automatic front entry had slid gracefully open for a stunningly beautiful young woman, neatly dressed in a dark business skirt-suit. Her deep-colored hair glimmered, refracting elusive bursts of fiery red. She looked rather taller than she actually was, her natural height amplified by very high heels, with striking facial features. Especially distinct—almost anachronistic— was the small black hat that she wore slightly offset on one side of her fascinating hair.

I inadvertently leaned forward in my chair. Standing in the still-open doorway, she examined the lobby, and a smile of fresh delight settled easily on her lips. She produced a piece of paper from a small handbag, and read it earnestly for a moment before starting toward the front desk. In less than two strides her heel buckled, and she stumbled badly. It wasn't a fall, but she did lose grip of the paper in her hands; it floated gently for a brief moment before being sucked out the closing glass doors by a mischievous wind.

The young woman took several moments to regain her balance and composure, but I had already risen reflexively and started across the lobby to help. After straightening her suit, she turned to look for the dropped paper, and noticing that it had blown outside she moved to go after it. I was walking briskly, determined to help her reclaim her lost document and perhaps introduce myself, and was able to catch up before the door closed behind her.

"Allow me," I said generically as I nodded to the confused looking lady, stepping past to pursue her paper.

The wind had already carried it across the drive and was holding it menacingly against the trunk of a tree at the edge of the hotel property. I jogged lightly over, expecting to have an easy time of saving the errant document, when a gust of wind from another direction took it from the tree and blew it across the busy street, finally pasting it against the window of a small shop. After waiting for a gap in the traffic, I ran across the street to the shop, only to be disappointed by another gust that carried the paper into a nearby alley.

Without really meaning to, I had left the hotel, contrary to Spindlebrock's instructions. I was more concerned with impressing an anonymous lady than I was with my own safety. At the time, I couldn't see any danger in a jog across the street, to render a simple service. In my pursuit, I entered the alley without a second thought.

There was the paper, at the back of the dead-end alley, resting motionless on the ground with nowhere further to go. It was mine to capture. I walked over, picked it up, and turned around to head immediately back. The silly smile of success that I wore quickly faded as I found that my way out of the alley was barred by a rough looking young man.

Startled, I did nothing but stand there and stare at the man for several long moments. From his clothing I initially took him for a vagabond or panhandler, but something did not line up in that supposition. He looked to be in his late twenties, with a closely trimmed beard and jet-black hair, and a clean, smooth face that obviously had not been subjected to the harsh elements of street life. The more I examined him, the less rough he began to appear. It finally struck me that what was coarse about him was exclusively on the inside, and it shined through in his countenance.

My examination made the man nervous. He reached into his coat and produced a wand, which he flicked to create a draft that pulled the paper from my hands. It fluttered through the air obediently, right into his fist. A smile formed on his lips as he crumpled it up and tossed it aside. He aimed his wand at me. I lifted my hands slightly in the air and away from my body involuntarily.

"I really thought it would be a lot harder to get you out of there. If you let yourself fall for every pretty woman that walks your way, you might not be as smart as he thinks you are."

My mind raced. I decided that I had better keep the conversation going until I could think of a way out.

"I don't know what you mean," I lied, flatly.

The young man took the bait.

"Right you don't, right. Now, if you don't mind, you're coming with me."

"No really, I don't want any trouble," I said as earnestly as I could, a loose plan forming in my mind. "And how did you do that thing with the paper?"

I pointed to his wand, and glanced at the paper on the ground.

The young man looked genuinely confused. He stood up straighter and leveled his wand, then eyed me with his head atilt.

"You're Thomas Martin, and you know perfectly well why I'm—"

"Look, you've got me confused with someone else. If you want my wallet, take it. I don't want any trouble."

Suddenly I heard a voice from overhead.

"Check it."

I stole an upward glance to see two more young men standing on the edge of either building flanking the alley, both with wands extended. The one giving the orders was heavy-set and unfaltering, the other was short, thin, and extremely nervous. A third figure on the rooftop slunk back into the shadows just as I looked up. I thought I caught a glimpse of rainbow-colored hair, but I didn't have time to process what that might mean.

"Check it, we've got him covered," the large man repeated.

"Guys, really, I don't want any trouble, I've got cash—"

"Shut up!" the man in front of me said, as he put his wand under his arm and dug into his pocket. In a few moments he had produced a photo. He studied it, glancing up at me and then back at the photo again several times.

"I don't know," he said slowly to his companions on the rooftops.

"It's hard to see, this isn't a great photo. Let's just take him—"

"We can't afford any mistakes on this."

The man on the roof was getting impatient, and I knew my window of opportunity was closing. Having practiced endlessly, I could produce my wand in a heartbeat, but I had very little experience in the way of combative magic. Most of my study had been centered around academics and science, with the exception of my fascination with the little book of traveling spells.

Something clicked in my mind. In Professor Spindlebrock's Little Blue Book of Traveling Spells, the section on packing had taught me one telekinesis spell! It was really only enough to fold clothes, and I wasn't particularly good at it (I hadn't even used it to pack for this trip), but the principle involved might be my brightest hope.

I glanced up again at the two men on the rooftops. The brick ledges they were standing on were old and crumbling. With a telekinesis spell, I might be able to loosen the bricks right under their feet just enough...

The man in front of me seemed to give up on his photo, stuffing it back into his pocket.

"That's it. It's him guys, I'm doing it."

My time was up; I acted. In an instant, I produced my wand and jumped to one side, rotating my body in the air so as to be facing upward. The man in front of me bellowed out a charm which overshot me by mere inches, and at the same moment I managed to cast a telekinesis spell aimed at the bricks on the ledge supporting the larger fellow. Time seemed to stand still and I thought I saw the bricks start to move, but I was jolted back to reality as my body hit the wall of the alley. There was a bright flash and loud explosion as several of the bricks on the ledge were pulverized, sending the larger man careening down onto the man in the alley below.

I came to my senses quickly. The small, thin man had vanished, and the other two were in a heap. I hardly expected that my plan would work at all, and I could scarcely believe it had worked so well. I leaped over the assailants and ran, almost getting hit by a car as I raced recklessly across the street and back to the hotel.

I don't exactly remember how I got back to my room; the lobby, the elevator—everything was a blur. Once inside I bolted the door with all three available locks, and collapsed on the bed.

I lied there for several minutes, breathing hard. As the adrenaline wore off, I started to notice a pain in my arm and knee. Forcing myself up, I went into the bathroom to have a look in the mirror. My clothes were dirty, and I had torn a hole in my shirt. There was a bruise and a scrape on my arm, and my side was tender, but I was not seriously injured.

As I changed and washed up, I realized that all thoughts of sleep had left my mind. I needed to call Spindlebrock; a commercial flight from Turkey to Belarus would have taken only a few hours, and in the private jet it would have been even faster. He should have been well settled by then. He needed to know what was going on.

"Hello, yes?" was his greeting.

"Spindlebrock, it's me, Thomas."

"Well, what is it?"

Spindlebrock was even more abbreviated on the phone than he was in person. I started to relate the story of the woman dropping her paper, and me following it out the front door of the hotel, but he cut me off before I could tell him more.

"You left the hotel?" he demanded, obviously flustered.

"Well, yes—" I began.

"I only asked you to do two things. The first was to stay in the hotel, where you would be safe."

I had no ready response that would satisfy Spindlebrock, so I said nothing.

"Perhaps I should have explained myself further, Thomas, but time was of the essence. It sounds like you're safe now, and that's ultimately what matters. However, to rectify my oversight, I'll call down to Bardo—the owner of the hotel—and have him explain things to you a little more fully."

Before I could say another word, Spindlebrock informed me that he could not waste another moment, and hung up. Within a minute—much sooner than I had expected—I received a call from the front desk informing me that the hotel's owner hoped to join me for dinner in the restaurant. My evening, it seemed, was all planned out for me.

Chapter 17

The Back Booth at Bardo's

"Welcome to Bardo's!"

The friendly greeting issued forth from the host with surprising warmth and volume as I approached the entrance to the restaurant. I nodded my acknowledgment to the sharply dressed young man standing behind a dark wooden podium. He looked down at a schedule book, a broad smile laced with amusement and joy continually shaping his cheeks and brow.

"Do you have a reservation this evening, or are you here for the bar?"

"No, I'm supposed to be meeting with Bardo."

A splitting headache was wedging its way into my skull, and I'm afraid my voice reflected my mood rather more harshly than I intended.

He looked up, an expression of surprise penetrating his air of determined pleasantry for the briefest instant.

"Of course. You must be Thomas?"

"Yes, Thomas Martin," I motioned to his book, hoping he would check it again; his permanent grin was beginning to disquiet me. Without looking down, he stepped out from behind the podium and motioned for me to follow.

"Right away Mr. Martin, follow me. Bardo is expecting you."

He led me through a maze of tables to a private alcove in the back. I could not help but notice as we wound our way through the crowded restaurant, that all of the patrons—without exception—seemed to be having a most enjoyable and boisterous time. Their frivolous conversations were peppered with outbursts of outrageous laughter, the clinking of glasses, and a general gaiety that is more often associated with youth-filled university establishments during the post-finals holiday.

"I'll go and let Bardo know that you're here, Mr. Martin."

Bardo must have been anxiously expecting me; as the young man turned, he immediately caught sight of his boss and motioned for him to come, but Bardo was already on a beeline to our table. His smile was just as broad as the one the young man wore, but far more warm and sincere. He greeted me with a firm handshake.

"Mr. Thomas Martin, it is a pleasure! My name is Isemberto, but everyone here calls me Bardo. Welcome to my restaurant!"

He took the seat across the table.

"Thank you very much," I offered blandly. My nerves were frayed, and the din of the room was grating harshly on my ears. Bardo seemed to sense something was wrong, and as any exceptional and experienced host is prone to do, he accurately and immediately deduced the source of my distress.

"It is rather loud in here at times—no, it is rather loud in here all the time, actually. Allow me, please."

Rising from his seat, Bardo reached for a curtain that appeared to be designed to shield our alcove from general view. While muttering a few words that I guessed to be a charm, he drew it slowly closed. The drapery was delicately woven from lustrously gossamer, deep-crimson threads, and was thin enough that one sitting in the booth could see through it quite well. Though meager, it somehow transformed the raucous clamor of the establishment into a murmur of muted whispers the moment it was drawn. The dim lighting in our booth assured that while we could see out, others could not see in.

"You'll forgive me for not thinking about it right away. C.C. told me that you've had quite a rough trip so far, I'm sure you're on edge a bit, huh?"

Bardo spoke with a more-than-slight Italian accent, though his English was quite good.

"Yes, I'm sorry, things have been a little intense."

"Any friend of professor Spindlebrock is a trusted friend of mine. I'm sure you feel the same way."

He looked at me knowingly. I nodded. It seemed to be that no matter where I was in the world, professor Spindlebrock was a known and respected figure, and my acquaintance with him was a passport to every imaginable magical connection.

"For instance, this booth," Bardo continued, "is especially for close and personal friends. It is the only place in the restaurant where one can see things for what they truly are —anyone but me, of course, I don't need this cloth."

His gaze had wandered to the gossamer curtain and the guests beyond. My gaze followed, and we watched the patrons for a few moments before I realized that not only had their volume changed, but their very demeanor had transformed as well. Whereas every patron that I had seen upon entering the restaurant was in a sort of playful and partying mood, they were now all eating quietly and speaking in furtive whispers. My mouth must have dropped open as I watched; Bardo, who was now observing me, chuckled.

"This is your first time at Bardo's, eh Thomas? And in the country, as C.C. has told me."

I closed my mouth tightly and nodded, turning back to Bardo.

"I will explain everything to you, like C.C. promised I would. When I opened this restaurant, I wanted to give it a name that meant 'Joy and Laughter' in Turkish. My friends at the time convinced me to name it after myself, as was more customary, but the original name would have matched my purposes better."

I looked at him blankly and nodded slowly. He motioned to the curtain.

"This is an Adclaro curtain. When properly charmed—no small feat, you know—it reveals the truth of all things to the one looking through it."

He pulled the curtain back for moment. The scene behind it instantly exploded into the raucous and noisy restaurant that I had witnessed previously. He let the curtain drop, and peace was restored.

"The entire establishment is under a strong charm, and has been since the day I opened the doors. To every observer outside of each individual table, it is a fun, lighthearted place, full of people who want to eat, and drink, and be merry. To those sitting at any particular table, their conversation and behavior can be anything they wish; to everyone else, it will just look like they are partying."

His gaze had turned again to the other patrons.

"They can talk and interact in utter privacy. It is loud, yes, but the magicians who come here have ways of drowning out the noise they don't want to hear, so they can have their little chats."

He prodded the curtain and turned back to me.

"Not ways like this one here, though! You won't find that almost anywhere else, I think."

The peace and quiet afforded by the dimly lit booth and the Adclaro curtain made my head feel more clear, and I ventured a question.

"Did you start this restaurant with that goal then? To give people a place to talk freely?"

"Yeah, sure. It's just another benefit of the Hotel, really— a necessary one because of our type of guests."

"What do you mean?"

"This is most important, Thomas," Bardo leaned forward and crossed his hands as he spoke, "it's really what C.C. wanted me to explain to you. He would have explained it to you himself if he had time. I'm sure he would have."

Bardo nodded slowly as he spoke. His air was somber, but the warm smile that made you trust him completely refused to be overwhelmed by even the most serious of topics.

"You can see that this restaurant has a particular purpose, that's clear enough from where we sit. The hotel also has a very particular purpose. Most of the magicians who come here already know this—it's why they come."

With a deliberate pause in his speech, Bardo looked around slowly and scooted his chair closer to mine. He leaned in and continued in a whisper.

"To you I can say this. C.C. assured me that I could tell you everything. Most magicians come here for some of the well-known qualities of the hotel and restaurant. The hotel offers protection, thanks to some ancient charms on this little plot of ground, and also thanks to some newer charms on this building that sits on it. It was built especially to be a place of safety and refuge, you know? Guests can come here and rest—actually get some real rest—from any cares or concerns they might have, without fear. But, this hotel is more than that."

He continued gravely, nervousness finally overwhelming his gentle composure.

"I have never uttered these words to anyone, Thomas. Those who might need to know this generally already know it when they come here. I'm not usually in the business of educating."

"You can trust me Bardo, that I can guarantee," I interjected. He smiled again, warmth flushing visibly through his features.

"I know it, for sure! Here is the thing: in this Hotel, a magician can be safe. Many of the darker forms of magic don't work here. Evil charms, and spells, the kind people usually use to hide things or hurt other people, they all melt away when one walks through the front doors."

"That's why he wanted me to stay in the hotel?" I interrupted.

"Yes, that's right. You will be safe here until C.C. returns, that is what he was most concerned with. But that protection isn't all that you'll find here. Everyone already knows about the protection in this hotel—forgive me, those who are acquainted with it, of course. They also know that at Bardo's restaurant they can come to speak freely, for even among the magical guests here, they may not feel entirely at ease. Here, they can discuss anything, and to everyone else it will only appear as if they've had one too many glasses of wine."

Bardo chuckled. Through the curtain I could see serious faces in serious discussions. This was clearly a place for business, and not for pleasure as it first appeared.

"So, like I said Thomas, the hotel, the restaurant, that is all good and fine, you know, but that isn't all. C.C. would want me to tell you, this place is sacred."

He paused, and I leaned back in my chair.

"What do you mean?" I asked after a few moments.

"You know, it's holy ground. Before the hotel was here, there was a great white holy building—I won't say it was a mosque or a cathedral, because it came before all those things—it was just a holy building."

I folded my arms. At this point in my life I was still not religious, though professor Spindlebrock had broached the subject with me a few times. Bardo sensed my apprehension.

"It's OK, not everyone sees things that way. Let's just say that this was a particularly special spot; from ancient times to modern times, it is unchanged. The protective powers here come from the history of this place. There are things you can do here, and only here. Very few know about this; C.C. is one of the only ones that I know of that still comes around for those purposes. I guess only a handful of people in the whole world even know."

As I wondered at the purposes that Bardo eluded to, a waiter came and stood outside the curtain. He coughed lightly, apparently in an effort to get Bardo's attention, but he did not touch the curtain.

"Excuse me for a minute, Thomas."

Bardo rose and left the alcove. The waiter, who was speaking too quietly for me to hear, motioned to the entrance of the restaurant. My eyes naturally followed his movement; there, standing at the entrance, was the red-haired woman that had dropped the paper earlier that afternoon.

Chapter 18

The Lady from the Lobby

Shock and curiosity surged through me as I stood up to get a better view of the lady. Her appearance was unchanged, but her manners were more agitated than when she had first entered the hotel. Her gaze flashed around the restaurant, then fixed nervously on Bardo as he approached the spot where she waited. The two exchanged a few brief words before Bardo turned abruptly and headed back to our booth.

"Thomas, sit down please."

As we both sat down, Bardo pointed to the woman.

"Do you see this woman who is standing at the entrance, about to be seated by my host?"

"Yes, she came into the hotel earlier today."

"That's right, I saw her earlier too, as I was at the front desk helping a new associate to learn the ropes."

We observed intently as the young host hailed a waiter, who led her to a table. She was alone.

"You don't know her, do you Thomas?" Bardo asked.

"No. No, I don't."

Bardo looked disappointed.

"Neither do I, but I do know something about her that you might not know. I have lived long enough to have seen just about everything come through those front doors. Like I said before, evil charms melt off when they come in, this much you already know. But mostly that is something that happens and no one is the wiser. People don't see it happen. Most magicians, they don't see it. But I do."

The woman was seated. I turned my attention toward Bardo, who was staring me full in the face.

"I can see it, Thomas. I can see when the evil melts off a person, when all their tricks and plotting and hatred are stripped away. Spindlebrock knows. I don't like to talk about it; it's not a pretty sight."

He turned and scrutinized the woman again for a few moments before continuing.

"I've seen the worst sort of people imaginable try to come in here. They're usually pretty powerful, and they think that they have come up with a way to beat the system. They walk on in here and learn that just like everyone else, their magic isn't strong enough. Usually they turn around and walk right out again without saying a word.

"Many years ago they used to try it frequently," Bardo continued, "some upstart magician who thought that his new charm or her new spell was going to change things.

They would try to bring their filthy black magic in here, but always, always it would melt away. I used to laugh, but then it just got sad to watch, you know what I mean?"

I nodded, though in my inexperience I couldn't exactly picture such scenes as Bardo was describing.

"But her," he nudged his chin in the direction of the woman, "I haven't seen anyone bother with that sort of silliness in a long time; until today. She walked in, and I saw what she had on her, and it melted away just like that stuff does when it comes in here. She didn't even flinch. It was like she didn't know it was there, like she couldn't tell that it had gone. But it wasn't all gone, either. That's what really gets me. Something was left, but I couldn't quite see what. Maybe it wasn't quite black magic, I don't know, but it was something that shouldn't be there."

Bardo leaned back in his chair and entwined his fingers behind his head.

"Maybe it doesn't matter, Thomas, but he told me to tell you everything, you know? Anyway, most of the time these people would walk in and that stuff would melt off and they'd be left exposed, and they would know it. They would feel it, and there would be this sort of shame and embarrassment and fear, and they'd scoot on back out the door they came in by.

"But not this lady. I saw that filth melt away. It was there, but it can't last in this place, you know? But she didn't seem to care one little bit. That's not normal, I've never seen that before. And whatever else was still there, that's not normal either. Something made it past the door, something not good. I won't say it was black magic; I just don't know. I could be losing my touch, maybe I'm just dreaming things up?"

Bardo sat up and folded his arms.

"Anyway, I didn't have to get involved. She didn't stick around, she went right back out the door after you, and that paper she dropped. I planned on telling C.C. all about it when he came back; I tried to tell him when he called me, but he didn't have time. But now here she is again, bold as brass, sitting in my restaurant alone, and asking for you."

"For me?"

"Yeah, by name. She knows you, she said."

I shifted in my seat.

"She knows me, but I don't know her. Her friends were waiting outside, they had my picture."

Bardo nodded thoughtfully.

"Don't worry, there's not much she can do here. She wouldn't even try, unless she was completely nuts. Maybe she is a great magician, but so are my team members, and many of my guests too. And no one that would come around here is the least bit interested in putting up with anything corrupt. Why would she come here alone, anyway?"

His last question was clearly rhetorical, but I reflexively ventured a guess.

"Maybe she wants to finish what she started."

Bardo looked at me contemplatively for a few moments, and then back at the woman.

"Well anyway, there she is, so what do you say, huh? You going to go and talk to her? We have your back, you know?"

I had already decided that this opportunity was too good to pass up. Knowing full well that this woman had been a party to the earlier attempt against me, and knowing that I would probably not have further opportunities to help Spindlebrock outside the bounds of the hotel, I had made up my mind the moment she appeared.

Without a word I stood up. Bardo stood as well, and pulled back the curtain. The woman—who now appeared to be laughing in concert with the veil of revelry all around her —saw me. She waved playfully and motioned for me to come over, a frolicking smile on her lips. The illusory laughter and playfulness lasted only as long as it took to wind through the restaurant and take my place across from her. As soon as I was seated, the spell of the table was fractured, and the truth of her character was revealed in a stern, forceful, and unyielding countenance.

223

Looking directly into my eyes, the woman uttered a simple and well-known charm of privacy. The noise around us faded.

"Thank you for coming, Thomas."

"Certainly. And who, may I ask, do I have the pleasure of speaking with?"

"What would you like to call me?"

Her eyes had dropped to her purse, which she rifled through to produce a cigarette and lighter. Her hand trembled as she flicked the wheel. I grew up in a place where smoking in restaurants was outlawed (and I've since learned that it is also illegal in Turkey), so I found her behavior strange, but I made an effort not to show it.

"I'd prefer to call you by your name."

"Well, we don't always get what we want, Thomas," she replied after a long drag. She let out a large puff of smoke which engulfed our table. Some kind of force restricted the noxious cloud to a perfectly shaped sphere around us.

I cleared my throat and continued.

"All your men combined didn't get what they wanted this afternoon. Why bother coming back alone?"

She smoked and thought for a few moments, her eyes surveying the room.

"Let's get one thing straight first; those were not my men. Those men and I work with the same individual."

"W.C. Crane?" I ventured.

She took another drag on her cigarette, without flinching.

"Perhaps. In any case, I came here to offer you an opportunity, that's all."

She dropped the cigarette into her glass of water. I waited for her to continue. She moved very little, and as I examined her face, I noted that she seemed to be straining as if to mask some hidden discomfort.

"Failure was not an option for us today, Thomas. We were given a simple task. We were to collect you, and bring you in. We were told that outside this hotel you would be quite incapable of defending yourself. The job seemed simple enough, but since you were traveling with Spindlebrock, we took extra precautions. Still, in spite of the absolute reliability of our information, and our over-preparation, you eluded us."

The woman's eyes closed involuntarily and she coughed without opening her mouth. Her body shuddered as if she were in pain. Her eyes opened again and she scanned the table in front of her, reached for her napkin and dabbed at her mouth. I glimpsed a smear of blood on the white cloth before she dropped it in her lap.

"The opportunity I'm offering is for you to come with me willingly. Avoid the unpleasant ramifications of your actions, and the unimaginable anguish that must certainly accompany them. Come with me now and unravel the mystery, Thomas, that is what I'm offering you. Do this, and I can promise the best outcome. Or, stay here and watch in horror as it unfolds to the worst possible end."

"I don't believe you," I said coolly. "Why in the world would you care about me in the first place, and why in the world would I come with you? Spindlebrock and I are here to observe, not to interfere. We've been warned, and we're not idiots. We're letting you do whatever it is you do, just as Crane required in the letter, and when you're done we'll help these poor souls get back to their lives."

The woman observed me as she considered what I said. I had the strangest sensation that she wasn't the only one looking at me, and I scanned the room involuntarily. In my discomfort, I changed the subject.

"You're bleeding," I noted, nodding toward the napkin she was now clutching in her lap. For the first time in our conversation, the woman seemed taken aback. I grew bold.

"When you came in the door, you changed. I saw it," I lied.

"Some of the evil that was over you faded away, but not all. I can see it even now. It is inside you, and it's not letting go. It's tearing you up."

Extrapolating from what I could see in front of me and interpreting it through the lens of what Bardo had shared, I fabricated what I thought a plausible tale. I must have hit close to the mark; the woman sat back in her chain, stunned. I carried on with my fabrication.

"You spoke of the absolute reliability of your information concerning me, madame, yet I think you may have been deceived. Tell me, why do you trust in people that you cannot see, and who use you to their own ends—who use you up, til there is nothing left of you at all?"

I was taking a risk with my masquerade of understanding, but in the safety of the hotel, with Bardo and his staff close at hand, there was no real power that she could exert against me. It was clear that she was acting in desperation. Having failed in her assigned task, she was trying to pick up the pieces. I guessed at her situation: she was a lackey, a thug, a subordinate taking orders. The worst she could do would be to laugh in my face and walk away. But she did not. Instead, I saw a moment of dawning comprehension, followed by a wince of pain.

The woman stood up, called me some obscenities, and turned as if to head for the door. Wanting to draw more information out of her, I grabbed her wrist. As soon as I touched her skin a searing pain shot through my fingers, up my arm, and toward my skull. I recoiled instantly, stumbling and falling from my chair. I saw the woman turn and look at me, an expression of absolute horror on her face, and then I blacked out.

When I came to, I was on the floor next to the table, still in the restaurant. Bardo was hovering over me, vexed and concerned, shouting orders in Italian to his servers. Relief washed over him when he saw that I was awake.

"Oh, good! Thomas, you gave us a scare—you, bring that here!"

Bardo motioned frantically at a busboy who was rushing over with some warm washcloths.

"Take this, put it on your forehead. You're OK, see? Everything is going to be just fine."

As Bardo pressed the warm cloth against my head, I recalled the woman. Testing my strength and finding it adequate, I rose and started to scan the room for her.

"She's gone, Thomas—sit, sit down."

I obliged. While I felt well enough in body, my mind was still considerably agitated.

"We saw her trying to leave, and you tried to stop her, but then something happened. It was all pretty quick, you know? After, you seemed to take some kind of shock, and she bolted for the door. My men went to stop her, but just outside in front of the hotel she had a few guys waiting— and, anyway, I called off my guys for now, so we could tend to you."

228

I nodded my head and patted Bardo on the arm.

"It's OK, Bardo, it's for the best. We don't need to let this get any more out of hand."

Bardo seemed relieved. He took a seat and pulled it close to mine, checked me over to make sure I wasn't hurt, then leaned back and let out a sigh.

"It's good, you know? You're alright, everything's alright."

He breathed deeply for a few moments, then leaned in with a sly grin.

"And what did you find out, eh? Anything interesting from the mystery lady?"

Bardo nudged my arm a bit. He was waiting in anticipation, and although I knew Spindlebrock had instructed him to trust me implicitly, I had no idea if he was cognizant of the problem that Spindlebrock and I were working on. I looked toward the doorway one last time, half expecting to catch a glimpse of the now long-gone woman. Apart from a few impressions, I hadn't learned much.

"Unfortunately, no. She was trying to get something out of me, but she wasn't about to answer any of my questions. She wouldn't even tell me her name."

Bardo looked momentarily crestfallen, but he quickly recovered.

"Ah well! All is well that ends up well, so they say to me. I think maybe I could tell you a bit more about this place, like C.C. wanted me to, but you're probably a little worn out, yes?"

Without waiting for me to answer, he continued.

"How about this: it's getting late, and you haven't had any proper rest yet. That jet lag is going to catch up with you, you know, so why not get some sleep and we can chat more tomorrow, OK?"

I agreed, thanking Bardo earnestly for his hospitality and attention. He insisted on accompanying me to my room, which I appreciated. We started immediately—Bardo, myself, and two of the hotel's security staff who appeared seemingly out of nowhere at the snap of Bardo's fingers.

We took a service elevator to my floor, then followed the two guards down a back hallway which I hadn't yet explored. As we arrived at the door to my room, the two guards stopped abruptly, barring our path. I glanced around their wide frames and noticed that the door was slightly ajar. Before I could say or do anything, one of the guards was leading Bardo and me back down the hallway as he radioed for assistance, while the other guard stood watch.

"Maybe I dropped my key somewhere," I began to whisper quietly to Bardo as I patted my pockets.

"No, it would not matter Thomas," he replied in the same hushed voice. We were now in the back hallway, still within sight of my room. At a safe distance, we stopped and watched.

"Your door had a special charm on it, you see, and only you and C.C. could open it, no matter about who had the key."

Two more guards approached my door from the opposite hall. All three drew their wands and stood back, as the first guard gently pushed open the door. His body angled away from the doorway, he leaned forward cautiously and examined what he could, then in an instant they rushed the room together. After a few moments, one of the three came out and motioned for us to come.

The chaos in the room was complete. My suitcase was beyond the aid of any repair spell; the outer shell was burst at the hinges, the lining ripped out and shredded, my clothes scattered across the floor. A large dressing mirror had been smashed, covering all of my garments with broken glass—which acted like blades as they trampled the whole jumble in to unrecognizable tatters. My travel papers, and copy of Spindlebrock's book, had been shoved off the nightstand. The furniture was overturned, drawers yanked out, and the mattress was on its side with a large gash. The bathroom was an upheaval, and the little in-room safe—which neither Spindlebrock nor myself had used—was missing.

"This won't do," Bardo muttered. His face was, for the first time since I met him, entirely devoid of any levity. He snapped his fingers and blurted out some terse instructions in Italian. The guards bolted from the room hastily.

"I am quite used to having guests with, let's say, special security needs. I'm even accustomed to having attempted break-ins. But this is like nothing I've ever seen. How did they get in? What did they want?"

He turned to me and waited, but I was in more shock than he was. Before I could say anything, a weak smile formed on Bardo's lips. He let his head hang down as he shook it.

"No, I don't suppose you could tell me, Thomas. I don't suppose you should."

In an instant, his usual cheerful persona was back. He clapped his hands together and surveyed the room again.

"Well! I'll give you a few minutes to see if anything important is missing—"

I held up my hand and stopped him mid-sentence.

"No, Bardo, that won't be necessary. There was nothing in this room worth all this, really. I'm sorry about the mess."

"Sorry? No need my friend, no need!"

Bardo seemed relieved that I wasn't more upset. He was, perhaps, also relieved that nothing important had been at risk.

"We'll deal with all this, you leave it to me. If we can get anything from the cameras in the hall and lobby we'll let you know, and we'll see if there are any other clues in here, OK? Did you want to take anything with you to your new room?"

We both glanced at the mess. Apart from my papers and book, there was nothing even remotely salvageable. I instinctively felt for the letter in my pocket, the only other thing of real value that I had; it was safe.

"No, I think I'll have to—well, I guess I'll have to get some new things," I stuttered, unsure how I would manage without leaving the hotel.

"Tell you what, friend. I'll get you moved to another room, one with a little higher security, OK? C.C. told me you need to stay inside, it's important right? So, I'll send one of my boys out to get you some new clothes and suitcases and things. We'll get you all settled in just fine!"

Since this first visit to Bardo's hotel, I've had the occasion to make several additional visits for both business and pleasure. My positive first impressions have been verified several times over: Bardo is one of the most accommodating and hospitable people you may ever have the pleasure to meet, who will stop at nothing to ensure your comfort. After the incident with the break-in, Bardo relocated me to a beautiful upper-level accommodation. One of the particular features of this hotel is a wide, terraced roof line. The suites follow that line, each one with its own over-sized balcony and courtyard. It was into one such suite that Bardo had me moved.

The suite was noticeably more secure than my original room; it featured a double doorway, with a security-screened second entrance. One could pass through the first door with a room key, but when that door closed behind them they were faced with a second door, a camera and a screen. The second door only opened after one of the staff confirmed that the visitor was legitimate. If you were in your room, the staff rang you up on a video phone inside the room, and let you see the person in the entry before admitting them.

There were other security features that I can't recall clearly now, but the entry stood out to me in particular. A consequence of the entry's complexity was that the guest in the room also couldn't leave the room without an ordeal. Bardo assured me that it was for the best; he had apparently spoken with professor Spindlebrock while my new room was being prepared, and the two had settled on confining me to these expanded chambers, with room service and Bardo's staff at my disposal for anything I might need, rather than to risk my getting into any more scuffles.

I was annoyed, but not at the confinement; the room was, after all, lavishly extravagant, and I had everything I needed, including a courtyard for fresh air, an astounding view of the river and the city, and a host of servants at my beck and call. My discontent was with the fact that Bardo had felt the need to contact Spindlebrock. It seemed that on this first day in Turkey, I was destined to prove to Spindlebrock that I could not manage myself in the least without his constant aid. This last incident with the woman in the restaurant and the ransacking of my room was jarring, granted, but I had not planned on pestering Spindlebrock with the details until he contacted me first. Thinking on it now, Bardo was probably wise to make the phone call, but at the time I found it intrusive and frustrating.

Fortunately, I was too tired that night to worry much about my wounded pride. Bardo's staff obtained some very nice clothing in the correct sizes, and everything else I might need to be comfortable. I prepared hastily, then crashed into my plush, over-stuffed bed.

Chapter 19

Sucker for a Damsel in Distress

The next morning I awoke to a text message from professor Spindlebrock, notifying me that he was heading for a small city called Pau, in the south of France. There had been a third abduction, and at the time that was all I knew. I later learned that Lewis had met up with Spindlebrock in Belarus, and had been asked to remain there, with the same instructions that I had received: to stay out of trouble, to not interfere, and to locate and restore the abducted youth after—and only after—the terrible business with these latest abductions was finished. Spindlebrock presumably would be ready and waiting in Pau, to restore the unfortunate victim that had been the target there.

This news brought the total abductions to three. Though we learned about them at different times, they all seemed to have happened on the same day. If the three day pattern held true, that meant that all of these most recent abductions would resolve at the same time. I never did find out for certain, but early on I suspected that the number of youth abducted correlated with the fact that Spindlebrock, Lewis, and myself, had worked together in Phoenix. My guess was that the abductors knew that our working together had led to their discovery, and they hoped that by creating three situations, they could separate us, weakening us and dividing our resources in hopes that we would be less likely to cause them problems.

Let me also add that, as far as I ever heard, no efforts were made in Belarus nor in France to accost or confront either Lewis or Spindlebrock; the two were able to do their parts in peace, while I struggled with nearly constant torments, which I have yet to communicate entirely. Spindlebrock, I will say, did have his hands full with an undertaking which I'll shortly reveal; but first, I'll conclude the rest of my adventures in Adana.

It was now the second day. After ruminating a bit on Spindlebrock's text message about the abduction in Pau, I phoned room service and ordered a luxurious breakfast—if I was to be stuck in my room, I was going to make the most of it. Once I polished off my somewhat over-indulgent meal, I determined to spend some time seriously pondering my situation. On the hotel stationary, I drew up a mind map of my life to date—that is to say, I attempted to generally summarize the events of my life that had somehow culminated in my current outlandish circumstances. At times I had found the exercise to be helpful in determining if I was on the desired course, and so I set upon it once more.

After spending some time in that existential pondering, I turned my attention to the abductions, jotting down every bit of information that I could wrestle from my somewhat uncooperative gray cells. As best I could, I retraced Spindlebrock's notes on the history of the first abductions, his research on Lilianne, and everything I could recall about the case in Phoenix. Writing and reading and re-reading, I attempted to make sense of it all; but I knew full well that I did not hold enough of the pieces of this puzzle which I wanted so desperately to solve.

Frustrated, I pushed my notes aside and started on a fresh sheet of paper. I scribbled out everything I knew about my involvement and connection with the affair—from the little book of spells, to the University, and the abductions. This was the most painful part of my musings, for it became obvious that I had played only the most minuscule role in the events which felt so crucially important to me. I had wholeheartedly adopted a cause for which I had very little understanding and even less real influence. To make things worse, I had jumped into all of this with a selfish desire to glean as much as possible about a fascinating new world of magic, and with a willingness to hawk my own talents off in the service of a man that I barely knew.

I speak plainly, reader, of how I felt that day. After my mind scouring and note taking were through, I obliterated the pages that I had written, using a violent little charm that I uttered with much satisfaction. My part in all of this—in my own mind at least— had been greatly exaggerated. From this point on I would simply wait in my room, as relaxed as I could manage to be, while those with more investment and more expertise determined what ought to be done. Nothing else would draw my attention to the particulars of the cases in Turkey, Belarus, or France. I could not control the outcome in the least, and I refused to be weighed down with additional stress.

It was now just after the normal lunch hour. My appetite, which had been absent in my mental exertions, was returning, so I ordered lunch. I ate in my private courtyard, at a small table set in the shade of the overhang from the courtyard above. The view was only slightly obstructed by a few large planters made of smooth concrete, which had been designed and placed in such a way as to capture runoff rainwater. Beyond those planters was a small garden extending out some twenty or thirty feet, which was surrounded by a short concrete ledge topped with a glass barrier, so that you could look out over the whole of the city in its breathtaking splendor. Each suite's courtyard looked down on the one below it at the far edge, but the sides of each courtyard extended to match the full width of the building, so that the adventurous—at least those not suffering from vertigo—could look straight down, for an unimpeded view of the miniature-looking scene below.

Listening to the distant sounds of the bustling city, I sat and devoured everything that I had ordered. The weight of the meal started to hit me before I was through eating, and I resolved to relax in one of the lounge chairs that were placed nearby, and take a short nap in the afternoon sun. This I did after calling room service from the balcony phone, to request that they come and take my empty dishes away. By the time they arrived, I was already fast asleep.

My body's clock being off due to the travel and other stresses, I slept for longer than I had intended. When I awoke it was early evening. As I broke from my dream and opened my eyes, I drew in a long slow breath and looked out at the skyline. If ever you wish to fall in love with a place, make absolutely sure that you appraise it in the dusky twilight; the view enchanted me as I stretched and yawned into existence.

Curious about how the river and mosque would look in this luxurious fading glow, I rose and approached the glass-topped barrier wall at the end of my courtyard. No sooner had I reached the edge when I heard a shriek rising above the din of the city. I searched around, unable to tell where it had come from. Again the sound came, this time more clearly—it was a woman crying out frantically for help, in English. I squinted down the line of courtyards that stretched out below mine. Three balconies below I saw a woman, reaching over the glass barrier on the side of her courtyard, clutching something. I strained to see what was just beyond the glass, and barely made out that she was holding the arm of a small child. Horror chilled me to the core as I realized that the child was not danging over the short drop to the next balcony below, but over the sheer side that dropped straight down the full height of the building.

Without a thought I flew into action, yelling for the woman to, "Hold on!" while I turned and started for my room. Before I reached the sliding glass door I remembered my confinement- Bardo's staff wasn't going to let me out, and even if I could convince them, there was no way I could locate the woman's room and gain entrance in time. But, they could help her. I picked up the balcony phone and called the front desk, hastily explaining the dire situation. They assured me that they would dispatch security immediately, and started to insist that I lock myself in my room, but I had dropped the handset and rushed back to the ledge.

Again I yelled for the woman to hold on; she emphatically screeched back that she was trying her best. Her voice, choked with tears, seemed to crack as with the strain of extreme effort. I knew that she wouldn't last. Stupid bravado being a forte of mine, it seems, I schemed that if I dropped from the end of my courtyard into the planters of the one below me, subtracting the height of the planters and my own height from the total fall, I should be able to get to the woman quite quickly and without injury. There was no time to review the soundness of either the facts or the plan. It was crazy, and I therefore set myself to it immediately.

The drops were minimally painful, though my arms were scraping rather harshly across the concrete ledges as I fell from courtyard to courtyard and down to the woman. It must have taken very little time, though the exercise seemed to draw out unreasonably with her desperate cries urging me on in the background. I finally reached her courtyard, and dashing across the garden I lunged to her side and reached over to help pull the child to safety.

My hands, instead of gripping the struggling arm of a child, touched on the hard, cool plastic arm of a mannequin, whose body was apparently elsewhere.

I recoiled, not yet sure of what had happened. In an instant, the woman had pulled the plastic arm up and over the glass, swinging it in an arc as she spun around, and pummeled me over the head. I had just enough reaction time to partially raise one arm in an attempt to block the attack. That, coupled with the adrenaline which was still coursing through my system, helped me withstand the rather heavy blow.

The woman backed up a short distance while I stood there staggering. With a furious scream, she started running directly at me, and before I could even consider my options, she ran into me full force, sending us both careening over the sheer edge of the building.

If you have never been skydiving or bungee jumping, it would perhaps do little good to attempt to explain to you what it felt like to tumble off the edge of a very high rooftop. With no cord on my ankles, and no pack on my back, the sensation was exponentially more gut-wrenching. My heart was in my stomach, an involuntary scream issued from my gaping mouth.

The woman turned out to be a man in disguise; his wig had toppled off in the fall, his build and arm strength were definitively masculine. He gripped me firmly with one arm as we plummeted, while reaching for a concealed wand with his free hand. Just before we landed in a large dumpster on the side of the hotel, my captor belted out a charm meant to slow our descent.

The dumpster was full of cardboard boxes and kitchen scraps, which combined with the charm to reduce our impact more significantly than seemed possible. Even with these advantages our landing was hard, loud, painful, and chaotic; it knocked the wind out of me, leaving me dazed. In no time at all, it seemed to me, my captor had scooped me up under one massive arm and jumped nimbly out of the dumpster as if nothing had happened. I got a good look as he adjusted his hold, and I recognized his face: it was the large man from the alleyway rooftop.

"You're coming with me," he said. His voice, which he had apparently altered magically, was still the high-pitched and feminine voice of the distressed mother from the rooftop. Looking around first to see if anyone was coming, he started hastily in the direction of the river.

Instinctively, I groped for the wand which I had concealed in my shirt. It wasn't there. Feeling me squirm, my captor tightened his grip around my body. He held up his free hand and displayed two wands.

"I grabbed it on the way down," he revealed in his tender and pleading womanly voice, "can't have any repeats of what happened the last time."

We neared a wall at the edge of the building, which had concealed us from the courtyard and pool areas behind the hotel. The man set me down roughly, immediately jabbing the back of my neck with the point of his wand.

"We're going to walk straight from here to the water's edge—the river, not the pool. You've caused us enough trouble already, so if you cause any more, I won't regret relieving you of your lungs."

With a push, we started forward, the wand burrowed solidly between my scapulae.

"What exactly do you want from me?" I ventured in a whisper.

He stabbed the tip of his wand into my back even harder in reply.

We passed the courtyard and pool fence, then turned to square up with the river. A busy boardwalk and a small bit of landscaping was all that stood between us and an impressive motorboat bobbing up and down at the quay; a hooded figure stood motionless at the helm. The man grabbed me by the arm, stopping us both in the cover of a tree.

"Wait."

I heard a scuffle of voices and the heavy fall of feet coming from around the side of the building where we had landed in the dumpster. The grip on my arm tightened just as I was considering making a break for it.

"I said wait."

My captor was fixed intently on the pilot of the boat, as if he were looking for a signal. The hooded figure stared ahead into empty space, motionless and seemingly oblivious. A commotion of hotel security staff noisily exiting the building came from near the pools. Somewhere in the mix I thought I could hear Bardo's voice.

"C'mon, what are you waiting for!" my captor exclaimed urgently, staring desperately at the boat. The man at the helm still did not move.

A shout came from behind us some way off.

"Over there!"

Unwilling to delay any longer, my large unwanted escort grabbed me around the waist and lifted me off the ground once more. I would have had nothing to lose in crying out for help, but the man had taken the precaution of covering my mouth tightly with his hand, his wand digging into my cheek as he held me with a fiercely determined grip. He rushed out from the cover of the tree and made for the quay. As soon as he took his first step, I heard the boat's large engines roar to life.

The wide boardwalk was covered with tourists, which the large man bowled through mercilessly and without excuse. Pandemonium increased and drew nearer behind us as we bolted, and I heard the telltale sounds of attack charms ricocheting off the concrete nearby. People were collectively scattering to clear the way before us, except for one man. He squared up with my captor, barring our way as the rest of the crowd fled. We drew closer and I recognized his face; it was Dr. Patel, resolute, wand at the ready.

In that instant, a surge of courage and a simple thought hit me. I bit hard on the hand that was over my mouth; so hard, in fact, that I tore through the flesh of the man's finger. He cried out in pain, dropping both me and his wand. A blast came from Patel, striking the man on the shoulder, and another blast came from behind us, striking him on the leg. He toppled to the ground with a rather embarrassing high-pitched squeak. I heard the boat start to pull away in the background.

I struggled to my feet, but the large man proved to be more robust than his false voice belied; he spun around on the ground, staying very low, and grabbed my ankle, pulling me down to the ground with him. We both clamored for the wand which now lay on the cement, but another blast from Patel knocked it out of reach. The man cursed, then a dawning comprehension flashed across his face. He reached into his pocket and drew out my wand, instantly sending a blow across the boardwalk and knocking Patel on his back.

With Bardo and his security staff now only a moment or two behind us, I thought in my heart that this attempt on my person would fail like the last one, and that we would be lucky enough this time to have won a captive to interrogate. But to my sheer amazement—and as a tribute to this strong man's ingenuity—my captor pointed my wand behind him and cast a most unlikely charm. It was a simple bit of magic that groundskeepers use to clear leaves and debris in the fall; I had heard it used on campus by students who did landscaping jobs to help pay for tuition. Having never performed it myself, I had no idea how powerful it could be. The force of the wind that came from that wand was enough to lift us both up off the ground and send us careening toward the river. As we soared overhead, I saw Dr. Patel's face reflecting the horror that I now felt. We breezed past the small patch of grass, cleared the gap of water that lay between us and the now moving vessel, and landed on the boat's deck with a tumultuous thud.

The man at the helm threw off his hood, revealing a colorful swath of rainbow-dyed hair.

"I thought you weren't going to make it," he said brightly, pushing the throttle forward full. Charms from the shore were bouncing off some kind of barrier around the boat.

"Bardo had more help that I figured he would. You should have helped out when you saw them," my captor said, rolling over on the deck and massaging his shoulder. His voice was quickly deepening as the charm that had changed it wore off.

The man at the helm spun around. His face was deadly serious, but I at once recognized him as the barista that I had met in Toronto. His name escaped me for a moment as I stared agape, then it came back to me all at once and I couldn't help exclaiming:

"Scott!"

Ignoring me, he stared down my captor with an intense and vehement gaze. He voice, unlike his glare, was flat, calm, and collected.

"You dare to question me? You dare to question my methods, when you know full well were I get my commands?"

He took a step toward my captor, who had stopped rubbing his shoulder and was struggling to stand up.

"I was just saying—"

"No," Scott interrupted, reaching out a hand to help the man up. He took it, reluctantly, and rose to his feet.

"You were not just saying anything. You were apologizing."

Scott brushed the dust off the man as he looked him up and down. He stepped back and cocked his head to one side as the man shifted uncomfortably.

"I'm sorry, you're right," the man said a moment later. He sounded sincere.

Looking over the edge of the boat I saw the riverbank zipping by at a considerable rate. The hotel was now lost behind the layers of buildings that lined the shores. I lifted myself slowly in to one of the seats on the deck.

"So, where are we going?" I asked eagerly, trying to mask my concern.

Scott, apparently satisfied, abandoned his intimidation of the other fellow and turned his attention to me. His face looked cheerful.

"Glad to see you again!" he responded. His pleasant attitude did not change as he snapped his fingers, received a bit of rope from his cohort, and bound my hands and feet. While he tied me up, we conversed.

"You're a difficult man to get a hold of, Thomas Martin."

"I do my best."

"You know, I didn't make the connection when he first sent me after you. I thought I recognized your picture, but I couldn't quite recall from where."

"It was your hair that I recognized," I answered truthfully.

Scott ran his fingers through his hair.

"Yeah, I'm surprised he let me keep it like this. I've always liked it, it's a little more interesting."

"So, who's this 'he' that you keep mentioning, and what does he want with me?"

Scott ignored my question and carried on with his knot tying.

"When Chaz over there flew you across the water and landed you on the deck of my boat, it was then that I remembered where I had seen you."

"Yeah, it was at the coffee shop in Toronto, you helped me out."

Scott finished his knots and sat down next to me. Chaz had taken control at the helm.

"I did help you out, as I recall, in locating an old professor of mine."

Scott looked up as Chaz turned the boat into some kind of narrow canal. A rusty iron gate, which was being held open by a ratty looking young fellow on the shore, closed behind us as we cruised slowly through.

"And that's just what's bothering me now."

Scott looked at me, the humor fleeing from his face.

"You see, I didn't remember that incident until just now. My employer would find that irritating. I'd prefer that you not mention it."

"That won't be a problem," I assured him politely, "but tell me, Scott, who is your employer?"

Again no answer. Scott balanced himself as Chaz brought the boat up to the edge of the canal, where a small group of people were waiting. As we approached I recognized the woman with the red hair and the other two men from the alley, along with three more that I did not know. Scott threw out two ropes. The now idling boat was pulled to the water's edge, where the entire group boarded.

"My team, specially selected for this mission in Turkey," Scott said with a swooping gesture.

I nodded to the woman from the restaurant. Scott looked everyone over, then addressed the three that I did not recognize.

"Did you have any trouble?"

"None at all. We set her free not ten minutes ago. Everything went perfectly."

Scott patted the one giving the report approvingly on the shoulder, then turned to me.

"You see, unharmed. He's a man of his word, always. You stayed out of the way, and she walked free."

I understood that he meant Toba Karademir, the abducted youth. He continued, turning to the woman with red hair.

"And as you can see, Evalyn, Chaz and I have finished your part for you. We left them awestruck back at the hotel."

She nodded coldly.

"Now, all that is left is to meet at the confluence and get out of the country."

Scott motioned for everyone to sit. Those that were able to find one took an actual seat, while the others sat on the deck and held on to whatever they could. Chaz started the boat slowly back in to motion down the narrow passage, the hull scraping dryly against the walls and canal floor at intervals as it wound its way through a dirty and cramped part of the city.

As we rounded a curve that passed between two tall apartment buildings, Chaz stood up at the helm. An instant later he cut the throttle and yelled out an obscenity. From a bridge ahead, three men had just pushed a car over the edge and into the canal. It came down with a violent splash and settled slowly into the shallow water before touching the ground, blocking our passage. The boat cruised to a stop slowly in the now choppy water; there was no room to turn around. As we glided nearer, I recognized the three people on the bridge as Dr. Patel, Bardo, and Spindlebrock—the appearance of the last was a total shock, though it didn't completely register in those stressful moments—all three with wands drawn. Bardo's security detail was positioned on either side of the river, likewise armed.

Scott searched around furiously for a possible escape. Finding none, he seemed to resign himself to capture. He let out a deep sigh and shrugged his shoulders.

"Well, that's it then. You keep surprising me, Thomas. But it doesn't matter, he'll have his way in the end."

For good measure, I ventured to ask who "he" was one last time. Oblivious, Scott reached into his pocket and produced a vial. Each of his cohorts followed his lead.

"Wait!" I cried as they unstopped and lifted the bottles to their mouths.

"It doesn't have to be like that. We can help you!"

They looked at me puzzled for an instant, then Scott let out a melancholy chuckle.

"It's nothing that dramatic, just a sort of Mundus potion."

Without another word, the crew emptied the vials, then fell unconscious where they stood or sat. Far from a surrender, this seemingly sapless act at once protected the henchman and the employer. It was the only and final effective strategy to which they could resort.

Chapter 20

Tourist Attractions and Gravel

Back at Bardo's restaurant—and at Bardo's insistence—a celebration of our victory commenced, with such general enjoyment from the hotel security staff that the enchanted tables appeared exactly as they were in reality: boisterous, genial, lively and full of spirit. Bardo, Patel, Spindlebrock, and I sat in the booth behind the Adclaro curtain, shielded from the din. We had much to be thankful for: the three abducted youth had all been located and were safe, we had escaped the ordeal unharmed, and at least some of the criminals involved had been peaceably apprehended.

Yet in spite of these successes, I didn't feel settled enough to celebrate. While the others laughed and talked and ate, I chatted and listened only superficially, making every effort to conceal the frustration and anxiety I felt in relation to the events of the last few days. Thoughts of W.C. Crane, Olivia's letter, and the real cause of the abductions all simmered obstinately in my mind. My patient hope was that all of my questions would be answered, and that I'd soon have my opportunity to talk with Spindlebrock one-on-one.

254

The conversation was not dull, at least, meandering as it did from subject to subject. I learned how and why Dr. Patel —who as I understood it at the time, thought very little of professor Spindlebrock—came to be in Turkey. After the events in the alley on the first day, he was sent for personally by Spindlebrock in anticipation of further trouble. He apparently owed the professor an "undeniable favor," which is an interesting but unrelated story in and of itself. Patel was to remain unannounced and entirely anonymous until he was needed. His job was to patrol the perimeter of the hotel; he had been walking up and down the boardwalk when the boat stationed itself at the river, and had even heard the muffled screams of Chaz with his female voice charm. Preparation, patience, and a bit of providence, all allowed him to be in the right place at the right time, in the effort to stop my abduction.

We conversed about Spindlebrock's uncanny luck in arriving from France just in time to help locate me and the criminals. His fortune was such, he told us, that he was able to spot a suspicious collection of non-Turkish youths near the canal, while being taken for a fool by a local taxi driver who drove him on an unnecessarily circuitous route from the airport to the hotel. Upon learning that I had been taken by boat, he was immediately convinced that the route the boat would take must certainly pass by the spot where those youth had been waiting, and was able to meet up with Patel and Bardo to head us off at the bridge.

Bardo laughed heartily about the unfortunate role his car was forced to play in my rescue. I was confused at how lightly he seemed to speak about the affair, and expressed my concern, but he reassured me that with a bit of magic and some cleaning by his crew, his car would be as good as new. I'm certain he understated the damage—flooding a vehicle with canal water isn't something that can be easily undone, even with magic. In retrospect I can see that Bardo's good nature and generosity are of the variety that would never let his friends feel the least bit of distress or responsibility because of his acts of service, irregardless of the personal cost he had to bear.

When the subject of the security breaches at the hotel came up, Bardo got more serious.

"You know, guys, that I take security very seriously here at the hotel. The man who jumped off the building with Thomas, he checked in over a week ago. I was working in the restaurant when he came in, and never heard a thing about him, everything was in order it seems. He left some clothes in there, but that's all."

"What about his voice? I thought dark magic—the kind that conceals—didn't work here?" I asked.

"Well, you know, to change your voice isn't really a dark thing. That's not something that would normally be a big problem, you know?"

Patel chimed in at this point, with a scholarly explanation of the functioning of a simple compression charm which, when correctly placed, would work on the vocal cords in such a way as to make a man sound distinctly feminine. Spindlebrock interrupted him as he finished.

"Yes, that's all good and fine, Patel. The thug in the upper-level suite was just carefully placed muscle, we know that. What concerns me is the break-in that happened in our first room. I helped you place the protective charm on that door before I left, Bardo. How do you figure they got past it?"

"Your guess is as good as mine, friend! The door was not damaged, that's the thing. They opened it, they didn't break it down. Someone with some serious skills opened that door, and they didn't use any of the usual tricks, you know. Those wouldn't have worked here."

"My thoughts as well. It's probably time to re-evaluate some of the security measures, and some of the old charms as well."

At these suggestions, Bardo straightened his back and threw out his chest just a bit.

"Security is always improving at Bardo's! The more they try to break it, the more layers I add. I'm already thinking about new door jambs and locks. Magic or no magic, those doors will open only for their guests, you can be sure of it."

Spindlebrock laughed heartily at Bardo's pomp and conviction, and we eventually all joined in.

Though he appeared to converse freely, Spindlebrock was surprisingly reserved in the actual information he shared with our small group. He told stories and embellished details, but he didn't reveal anything new. He neglected any mention of the letter, the woman named Olivia who penned it, or anything relating to my abilities and the presumed reason for my abduction. It was clear that he did not intend for Patel or Bardo to know more than what was already visible on the surface.

Throughout the raucous evening I kept my most pressing questions and frustrations to myself. I could see by his subtle expressions that Spindlebrock appreciated my discretion. At the time, after such jolting experiences, I didn't feel he deserved my thoughtfulness; I'm embarrassed to admit that I was only reserved because I knew that being otherwise would accomplish nothing with one as hard-headed as Spindlebrock.

After our celebration wrapped up, we all retired for the night with the exception of Spindlebrock, who expressed regret at having to take yet another jet in order to help Lewis wrap things up in Belarus. Dr. Patel was to take a commercial flight home early the next morning; his only frustration was that he had missed giving a lecture on gender discrimination between witches and warlocks in the Malleus Maleficarum, just to help out with our little adventure. As I would be alone again, Bardo was instructed to look after me. I was urged most emphatically to stay in the hotel—no matter who was falling from the balconies—until Spindlebrock returned.

Before departing, Spindlebrock promised that when he returned to Turkey he would take me on a splendid tour of the city and give me a "world-class, bona fide tourist experience." I gladly accepted his offer, knowing full well that it was not negotiable, and feeling that it would give me the opportunity I desired to finally give him a piece of my mind. For the prescribed time I stayed inside the hotel, with neither trepidation nor temptation to leave, safe in the knowledge that my assailants were well in hand and that the lives of the abducted youth no longer hung in the balance. I gave myself permission, after all that had happened, to put off my questions and frustrations until Spindlebrock returned.

For once in what seemed like a very long time, I was well rested and at ease. Spindlebrock returned as promised, the morning of the second day after he left. He insisted on paying Bardo extra for all of the trouble we had caused, an offer which Bardo emphatically refused. Spindlebrock, in one of his usual displays of stubbornness, left all of the money he intended to leave with the front desk. I was melancholy and a bit apprehensive as we walked through the automatic glass doors and into the wide world. I had come to understand the value of a protected place such as Bardo's hotel.

As the sun and morning air touched my face, my anxiety eased, and I began to actually look forward to changing gears and playing the role of tourist. There was no need to hail a taxi; several were parked in front of the hotel waiting for customers. Spindlebrock leaned in the window of the car at the front of the line and asked the driver if we could engage him for the whole day, a proposition that seemed to enliven the weary man. We loaded our bags into the trunk and began our tour.

The busy markets were calm in comparison to recent events, and the peaceful mosques were rejuvenating. We ate the most wonderful kebabs for lunch, and walked across the oldest continuously used bridge in the world. Spindlebrock, who was minutely knowledgeable about the layout of the city, directed the dutifully impressed driver to obscure vantage points from which we enjoyed the history and architecture of Adana to its fullest. He even indulged my interest in the used book stores that were scattered around the city, where I located several interesting volumes.

Late in the afternoon, Spindlebrock thanked the driver and rattled off an address where he could drop us off. The man was more than a bit astonished at hearing that our final destination wasn't the airport or hotel. After asking a few times if we were sure we knew where we were headed, the driver proceeded to thread his car through a series of narrow side streets fraught with dead ends and sharply angled, unmarked intersections. Though they generally shared walls, the tightly packed houses were of a wide variety of sizes, colors, and ages. Some were painted vibrantly, others looked like they hadn't been painted in decades. An occasional fig or olive tree climbed out of the various cramped courtyards, secret gardens hidden from the street by block walls of new or ancient stone, covered with peeling plaster.

At first the streets were clean, bustling with people walking, and bystanders sitting and watching as cars drove by. After a number of blocks we passed into an older, darker, and quieter quarter of the city, where the buildings appeared abandoned and derelict, and the people became sparse. The drab envrion had a depressing effect, which cast my mind back to the tumultuous events surrounding the abductions, and lowered my mood back to one of frustration.

At a particularly desolate street corner, the taxi came to an abrupt stop. The driver glanced out his window uncomfortably as he slid the shifter into park; even he, it seemed, felt the disquiet exuded by this cheerless part of town. He was paid and tipped generously before leaving us and our baggage. Spindlebrock stooped over and fiddled with his luggage until the cab drove out of sight, then stood upright and stretched his back and arms. He turned to me with a beaming smile that looked unnaturally out of place given our surroundings.

"Thank you, Thomas, for a most enjoyable day! There is something wonderful and invigorating about sharing a place you love with someone who has never seen it before."

His voice was bright and sincere. I returned his thanks, expressing a few feeble words of appreciation for his tour of the city, but my heart was not really in my reply. Something about our present situation was gnawing at me. Why were we standing on this street corner? Where was this friend that we were supposed to meet, and would they really be able to accommodate us with any degree of comfort in this run-down part of town? More questions, and no answers; I couldn't help it if my frustration came through in my voice.

Spindlebrock took no apparent notice of my intonation. My eyes followed his as he looked up and down the street. There was not a single soul in sight.

"And now," he said eagerly, removing his wand from his jacket pocket, "we can move on to more pressing matters."

He cast a complicated charm on our luggage, which immediately transformed into small, gravelly pebbles. Astonished and enthralled by the novel spectacle, I stooped down to pick up one of the little rocks, only to find that it would not budge.

"Better put your back into it!" Spindlebrock said with a laugh. "They may look like pebbles, but they still weigh the same as they did when they were luggage."

I poked at the luggage-rocks again, trying to push them along the sidewalk. His patience with with my fascination waning, Spindlebrock continued.

"Don't play with them; no one will bother with them, we'll come back for them later. I know you have more important things on your mind, come with me to a place where we can talk, and I'll answer all your questions to the best of my ability. You've got a lot to say to me, I expect."

This unexpected and overdue recognition of my feelings snapped me out of my reverie. Motioning for me to follow, Spindlebrock started down the road. His pace was brisk and purposeful—the pace of one who knows exactly where he is going. For a few blocks we turned in a new direction at every street corner. Occasionally we took shortcuts through alleyways, or climbed through narrow, litter-strewn passages that ran between houses. Our course seemed so entirely random that it felt as if we were wandering aimlessly. Just as I was about to protest, we climbed through an opening in an old wall and stopped before an ancient looking city block that was crumbling into ruins.

"Adana is full of interesting things, Thomas. Behold, one of the oldest buildings in the country."

I appraised what was left of a deteriorating, age-old building that stood like a monolith in the center of the block. The roof and upper floors were gone, obliterated by time, and the remaining walls of the first floor had not fared much better. Layers of different colored plaster peeled away in large chunks to reveal a patchwork of rebuilt block, brick, and stone. Gaping holes gave the impression that this skeleton of a structure could offer no protection from even the slightest elements.

"There's not much left of it," I observed.

Spindlebrock nodded his agreement.

"There's not much, I grant you, but it's still an important landmark."

We started to walk toward the jumbled mass of stone and mortar; The closer we got, the less it looked like a building. Creeping vines and young trees were pushing up through the earth round about as if to say, "This land is no longer claimed by man."

"I don't think we can go in there," I protested, stopping in my tracks.

"It's perfectly safe," Spindlebrock replied with an almost questioning upturn of his voice. He motioned for me to follow as he went on ahead.

We scrambled through what appeared to have been a wide doorway, and entered a large room. You could push the walls over with one hand, I imagined, they were so decrepit. Old passages leading out of the room had become cavernous holes, revealing the remains of halls and chambers, all in a similar state of ruin. Debris covered the floor, but apart from rubble the room was empty, with the exception of an old wrought iron café table and two chairs, situated in a far corner. A thick layer of dust covered everything.

Spindlebrock picked his way carefully to the old table, and I followed. Coughing, he brushed the dust from one of the chairs, and sat down. I remained standing, puzzled.

"Have a seat, and we'll chat," he requested.

"Here?" I implored.

In reply he only motioned more insistently for me to take a seat across from him at the old table. Hesitantly, I cleared as much of the dust as I could from the rusty iron chair, tested to verify that it could indeed hold my weight, and sat down.

Spindlebrock watched me blankly for a few moments, then scanned the room and sighed.

"This was once the lobby of a grand hotel. It has been many things since that time, but none so luxurious."

He paused, then pointed to the center of the room.

"Over there was laid out the most exquisite Persian rug, with a table in the center that always had an enormous fresh bouquet of flowers. People would stand around it and talk, while others sat here, or spoke with the proprietor."

His gaze moved to the doorway.

"The doors were splendid; Boxwood inlaid with Juniper, with ornate carvings and brass handles. The tone when someone knocked on them was specifically different from that of many other woods."

I looked around the dilapidated room and then back at Spindlebrock. He was often inclined toward elaborate speech, but he was not generally fanciful. His wistfulness intrigued me.

"I can imagine that, yes. Did you read about this place somewhere?"

"No, you won't read about this place in any history book. It was a hotel for magicians, similar in purpose to Bardo's, though quite different in many other meaningful ways."

With piqued interest, I looked around the room again. The possibilities of its prior beauty glimmered in my mind more readily in the light of this new information. For a moment I was almost dazzled at the thought, but my ruminations came back to the forefront of my mind.

"So, this is a safe place for us to talk, then?" I asked.

"It is. I suppose you have some questions?"

Emotion overwhelmed me, thoughts and questions flooded my mind. I blurted out the first few in an unceremonious stream, peppered with harsher language than I will record here.

"What were you thinking leaving me alone in Turkey? Didn't you realize the danger I would be in? What made you think I could handle all of that by myself, without more than a few words of explanation or help from you, or anyone? Why bring me all this way just to abandon me to risk of peril?"

Spindlebrock leaned forward on the table and took his chin in hand thoughtfully for a few moments.

"Those are fair questions. I think, however, they begin with an incorrect assumption."

"And what would that be?" I asked impatiently.

"You assume that I left you here alone in Turk—"

Believing that I comprehended the technicality on which he was leaning, and having no appetite for debate, I cut him off before he could finish.

"OK, fine, you didn't leave me entirely alone. I grant that you left me with Bardo and the protection of the hotel; but that's not what I mean, and you know it."

Spindlebrock leaned back in his chair again. He was calm.

"Let me try again. You assume that I left you at all."

I was incredulous. In my defense, I will note here that the stress of the events was still poignantly fresh, and that I had put off feeling and experiencing that stress for Spindlebrock's benefit, up to this point. I'm not proud of my outburst, but my feelings were now boiling over. I continued my mostly unwarranted onslaught, yelling.

"I assumed?! You told me you were going, you called from Belarus—texted from France!"

"Yes, I did all those things—"

"You wouldn't let me explain anything on the phone, wouldn't tell me what kind of trouble I was in or how I could best avoid it until after I had gotten myself into it! You left me alone, to fend for myself!"

"Granted—"

"You brought me to Turkey, presumably because you had some grand errand for me to do with this letter."

Reflexively, I pulled Crane's letter from my jacket pocket and slammed it down on the dusty table.

"Then it turned out that we didn't even need the letter! I was attacked, kidnapped—do you have any idea? Do you? I fell off a building! These people were trying to take me who-knows-where, and do who-knows-what to me, and you counted on luck—luck! You counted on luck when it came to saving my skin!"

With this last phrase I threw my hands out in disgust. I smacked the envelope on the table one more time, then folded my arms in front of me. Spindlebrock had listened patiently, showing no emotion, only nodding his head.

"I am sorry, truly."

It was a heartfelt and soft-spoken apology, disarming. Spindlebrock waited a few moments, to allow me to speak if I had more to say, before continuing.

"Any assumptions that you may have made were a manipulation, carefully planned on my part. I led everyone to believe I would be in Belarus, and then France, and unavailable to help out here in Turkey. I wanted Crane to think that you were on your own, so we could test the theory of his interest in Conexus, and learn his mind. But, I was there to help you, Thomas, when you needed it most."

"How do you mean?"

"When you left the hotel the first time, and chased that bit of paper into that alley, I was there. I saw the magicians who were charming the paper, and I followed at a distance. When you made your move to disarm the two men on the rooftop, I augmented your charm—I'm pleased that you took the time to learn that little charm from my book, by the way—and I helped you escape without pursuit."

"How? How could you have been there," I fumed, "you were in Belarus."

"No, at that moment I was in Turkey. I went back to Belarus afterward."

"You mean to say you flew back and forth just to help me out? How could you have known?"

"Not at all—and, I did not know. I guessed."

The whole story wasn't adding up. Spindlebrock rushed his explanation in an effort to curtail my rising emotions.

"When that red-headed woman came to speak with you, I watched through the restaurant window intently, and would have intervened if necessary. When you fell from the hotel roof, I was hiding in the bushes near the driveway. I augmented the charm that brute used slow your descent, so that it would actually work—and, I was ready to manage the entire charm myself if he didn't get to it in time. I also created an illusion that Bardo's men were almost on top of you both, when he held you near the tree, so that he would move into a place where Patel could get to him."

I was not grasping what he was saying. The impossibility of it was making my head swirl, but Spindlebrock persisted.

"I already knew where the boat was bound. I knew what story I would give Bardo, and I had a plan for heading you off before any real danger was possible. Thomas, I spent as much time as I could possibly spare watching over you here in Turkey, I assure you."

"But how? How could you get to Turkey and Belarus and France and back so quickly?"

Spindlebrock's face, which had been serious, lit up with excitement.

"Let me show you."

He stood up and walked around the room. He peered carefully through each of the cracked walls, and out through the hole where we had entered. Finally, he returned to the old table and his dusty seat.

"You must promise me, Thomas, to never share the words you are about to hear."

I shrugged and offered my assurances freely. It was a singular charm, especially linked to the dusty ruin we sat in that day. When he spoke it, I instantly had the sensation of being enveloped in a rushing wind that seemed to come from every direction at once. My stomach lurched the way it does when you crest the top of an ascent on a roller-coaster, and I watched as the room seemed to stretch out before me. My vision blurred, the colors around me change kaleidoscopically. All at once my vision snapped back into focus, and I felt as if the entire world came to an abrupt halt, so much so that I started in my chair.

Spindlebrock pushed the letter on the table toward me.

"Put that back in your pocket for now—and absolutely do not get up from that chair for any reason on this good earth."

I nodded absentmindedly, then picked up and pocketed the letter. My attention was fixed entirely on the room around me, which had transformed before my eyes from the broken ruins of a once great hotel, to the luxuriously adorned lobby that Spindlebrock had described, right down to the fresh flowers on the table in the center of the room. People were chatting all around us, lingering casually near the table and in every corner of the room. Large, ornate wooden doors, beautifully carved, opened to admit a traveler from a dark and rainy street.

"What is this magic?"

It seemed to me that since Spindlebrock's charm had caused us to instantly appear in this place, our presence would be as sudden and unexpected to those in the room as theirs was to me; yet, no one paid us any mind at all. For a few moments Spindlebrock and I simply stared at the splendor. Finally, I broke the silence.

"The room, this lobby, it's just as you described. But how?"

Spindlebrock, who had been admiring the Persian rug at our feet, turned to me.

"You asked me how I traveled so quickly. This," he said with a sweeping gesture, "is how it is done."

I looked around, but found no explanation. Spindlebrock continued.

"It's called a confluence, and it's not as much magic as it is a natural feature of the Universe. Like so many things undiscovered, unstudied, or unaccepted by the scientific community at large, it appears more magical than it really is.

"There are points in space that are connected to other points. They join together and move as one—hence their name. If you know how to use them, or have access to a charm to take advantage of them, these confluences can help you move about instantly over long distances.

"For better or for worse, there are very few known confluences to work with. Knowledge of and information about confluences has always been limited; so much so that today most magicians consider them folklore. Similar to Conexus, in point of fact."

"So, you use this confluence, um, phenomenon, to travel to Turkey and other places?"

"I do."

"Where are we now? Is this Belarus?"

"No, but we could use this confluence to get to Belarus if we needed to, it can take us to a variety of places—"

Suddenly remembering that I had heard of the term confluence in a magical context previously, I interjected.

"Wait, the guy with the rainbow hair—Scott—he said they were taking me to a confluence, just before you rescued me."

"He should not have revealed that. Always the careless one, Scott," Spindlebrock said, shaking his head.

"He never bothered to truly understand magical principles. If he knew or cared about—if he respected the thing he was revealing, he would have kept quiet. Yes, they were taking you to this same confluence, though not to this same entry point. Consequently, did Scott reveal anything else?"

"He did let on that W.C. Crane was a man, a fact which I was unsure of."

"Yes, I was unsure as well. Was that all?"

"I think so. It was all that stood out to me at least."

Spindlebrock sat pondering. Eager to know more, I probed.

"You said something about an entry point? What does that mean?"

"Oh, yes. A confluence has three known parts. They are called entry points by those who really know anything about them—which in today's world is only myself, if I'm being honest with you. The few people left that believe in confluences at all, understand them to be focused in only one point—the most obvious point.

"You see, there are always three points. This reality is, again, plainly manifest in the name of the thing. Most people think of rivers and streams when they hear the word confluence. In the case of a confluence of two rivers, you have two flowing bodies of water joining to make one; that is, if my math isn't incorrect, three points. The first two points are the rivers coming in, and the last point is the combined river going out.

"The case of a confluence of space is quite similar. The two points coming into the confluence are not as obvious, however, as the one point coming out, where a much greater energy is produced. Are you following me?"

"Yes, I believe so. Scott was probably taking me to the third entry point, the more evident point, which is apparently known by some. You've taken me here to this point, one of the inlets I suppose you could call it?"

"Precisely."

"And only you know about this particular entry point?"

"I have very strong reasons to believe so. You see, with confluences being esoteric to the point of being mystical even within the magical commonality, the few that do know about them are quite protective of their secrets. The entry point which Scott was leading you to is controlled and protected by a sort of underground clique or union. They believe that they have the market cornered on that sort of travel in and out of Turkey."

I looked around thoughtfully.

"So, you used this entry point to travel such long distances instantly, and kept up the air travel ruse so as not to give away your secret?"

"That is correct."

"So you could watch over me, while handling the situations in France and Belarus."

I began to regret my impatience. For all his faults, Spindlebrock was incredibly mindful in his own way. He was, and ever has been a faithful and constant friend.

"Thank you, I didn't realize all that you were doing," I trailed off, swallowing hard from the emotions that were finally catching up with me. Spindlebrock reached across the table and patted my shoulder amicably.

"Not at all, Thomas. No harm done for my part. It is you that had to endure the affair without knowledge of the unseen aid that surrounded you. You did very, very well in everything."

I cleared my throat and looked around the room again with wonder. Somehow, it seemed to me, we had traveled a great distance in no time at all.

"So, where are we now? You said it's not Belarus; is it France?"

I attempted to catch a bit of the conversation around us, but there were too many voices.

"I can't make out what anyone is saying—and, why does it seem like they don't know we're here? Are they used to people popping up at this table?"

Seeing that I was getting more excited, Spindlebrock placed his hand firmly on mine.

"Stay seated, Thomas," he reminded me. With the index finger of his free hand, Spindlebrock wiped some of the rusty grime from the table.

"Notice this table. It is the same table and chairs we sat down at, right down to the dust. The entire room has changed, as you can see, but you and I and this table have not. If we were to leave this table and these chairs, we would complete the travel, and the people in this room would see us. Until then, we're sort of between the two places."

"So, as long as we sit here, we haven't really gone anywhere?"

Spindlebrock paused for a few moments, looking thoughtful.

"That is partially correct, yes. For the time being, we'll leave it at that. What's important is, we would not want to travel to this place right now, not with this charm."

Taking a deep breath, he continued.

"We should go back."

With that he spoke the words of a charm different from the first, and we traveled back to the dusty ruins in Turkey in much the same manner that we left them.

"That was amazing," I said after we settled. To this day I can see in my mind's eye the last rays of the setting sun as they filtered into the room, wide beams of gold solidified in the dusty air, like fingers reaching out and gently gilding the experience.

Spindlebrock rose from his chair.

"And now you know a few more things than you knew before; and, a few more things than most magicians can claim to know. But, let's talk about some facts that are still unclear."

He paced around the room, kicking up a small cloud while he commenced his monologue.

"You already know, I believe, that all three of the abductions are over and done with; we covered that in the restaurant the evening after your rescue. You know that we took a few young folks into custody, and I believe you realize that we'll deal with them when we get back to Toronto."

Spindlebrock checked off an invisible list in the air as he spoke.

278

"These are thing that anyone involved with the affair would know, of course. Being my companion in these travels, you also know about our deeper hopes: that we would be able to somehow trap this W.C. Crane, or make him reveal himself at least; and, that we would be able, in the end, to undo the damage that he and his cohorts had done to the abducted. That's everything we're working toward, am I correct?"

Spindlebrock had stopped pacing, and stood facing me imploringly.

"Yes, I believe so. You mentioned before you left for Belarus that you thought you had found the answer, with Lilianne?"

"Yes, exactly."

He began pacing again.

"As you recall, one of the missing pieces was a verification of my findings with the study of Lilianne. With your gift, we were supposed to locate Olivia—the one that wrote the letter in your pocket—to have our final test, to see if my findings were worth the trouble. I don't think I mentioned it outright, but my hope was that Crane would be with her, that we would find them both together."

Making his way back to the table, the professor sat down once again.

"If you're ready, we can move on to these important remaining tasks."

He sat on the edge of his chair, eyes fixed on me intently. I had more questions, but the thrill of what still lied ahead was more overpowering than my need for information.

"I'm ready," I responded confidently.

Chapter 21

Olivia and the Aperture Room

To say that I am surprised by something that Spindlebrock does is to embark on a most tediously repetitive task. Guess, therefore, what I felt when upon leaving the ruined building we walked directly across the street, through a single alley, and right back onto the corner where we had abandoned our luggage-rocks earlier. I expressed my dismay at having previously taken such a tiresome route to arrive at ruins that were just around the block. Spindlebrock addressed my concern cryptically, but with patience.

"It is easy enough to walk away from a place that is hidden from the world, but to approach it is often another thing entirely."

After restoring our disguised luggage to its original form, Spindlebrock used his phone to call for a cab. While we stood around waiting, he inquired abruptly if there was anything that I would miss terribly if our luggage was somehow lost or stolen. It was a mildly curious question, but I gave it some thought and responded that I'd be disappointed to lose the souvenirs I had just purchased, and devastated to be parted from my copy of his book.

"You flatter me," he quipped. "Just in case, I want you to keep your Little Book of Traveling Spells and your souvenirs with you. You can carry them in the paper bag you got from the market. Our luggage we'll leave waiting in the taxi when we get to our next stop."

Without argument or question I removed the bag of souvenirs from my luggage and slipped the book in with them.

"Now, I want you to remove the letter from your pocket —don't open it yet."

I removed the envelope from my pocket, and offered it to Spindlebrock.

"No, you keep it. When we get in the taxi, I want you to open the letter and hold it. I think I know where we need to go, so you probably won't need to direct us—but if you think we're off course, give me a signal. Don't say anything about how you're feeling, we don't want to alarm the driver."

The taxi arrived, and the driver received his instructions. As we drove away, I opened and held the letter —I also held my breath. The last time this letter was in my hands I had broken through the author's concealment spell, but had not been detected, nor had I searched any further. This time could not be the same.

The connection was instantaneous and powerful; the horror of discovery, fear, and panic permeated our bond. I clenched the letter hard as we rambled across the city, rejecting the desire to throw it down and escape. Oblivious to all around me, I couldn't tell you a single thing about the route that we took; my mind was shrouded in the thick and painful fog of another person's emotions. Olivia knew that we were getting closer, she knew that I was using the letter, and she was frantically searching for help. She got help, of a kind, but it brought her no relief; the fear never left her, it only increased. As much as she did not want to be found, she wanted even less to seek the only help available to her. She counted the seconds in her mind, filled with agonizing anticipation. I unconsciously joined her, counting in a whisper.

The feelings grew in intensity as we drove, and I instinctively knew we were heading in the right direction. I was dead to the world in the most unpleasant way until we crossed a certain bridge that I had seen previously—the scene of my rescue, passing over the canal—which brought me back to myself. I turned to say something to Spindlebrock, but found his expression too foreboding to risk words. He motioned for me to put away the letter. I did so eagerly, a wave of relief and warmth rushing over me. We pulled up to the entrance of a rather luxurious looking building, with two large men standing near the front entrance; to be clear, they stood such that they were barring the way rather than inviting anyone to use it.

The driver announced our fare. Spindlebrock paid it in full, plus extra so that the driver would wait for us around the corner. One of the men left their post to approach our cab and open the door.

"Gentlemen, allow me."

We stepped out. On seeing the professor, the stern and commanding look on the man's face melted away.

"Mr. Spindlebrock—" he exclaimed. He looked to his companion, who looked all around as if hoping there might be yet someone else they could both appeal to.

"We—we didn't know you were coming," the first man said hesitantly.

Spindlebrock looked them both over, then examined the building and entrance with interest.

"I see not much has changed—no, I didn't know I was coming myself, but a need has arisen."

Without further explanation, Spindlebrock started for the entrance. I followed. The two guards tripped over each other to throw open the doors, visibly relieved that more was not being required of them. The second guard took his turn speaking, his voice cracking a bit as he started.

"Of course, sir, absolutely. I'm sure they can help you at the desk."

We entered the lobby. Though small, it was well-appointed and extremely opulent. No guests lingered, and no one was currently behind the front desk. Spindlebrock tapped lightly on a small bell, then turned and whispered in my direction.

"Do you ever pray, Thomas?"

My thoughts, which were already as creeping and dark as this place felt, snapped back to the pain and fear I had experienced moments earlier in the car, while holding Olivia's letter.

"What? No. No, I don't."

"Why not?"

I was annoyed. Here we stood on the precipice, struggling against a terrible and unknown evil, and this man was wasting precious moments babbling about Sunday school superstition—or so I felt at that point in my life.

"Because, I don't see how a few desperate words spoken to thin air are going to accomplish anything."

"That's an interesting way to put it, all things considered. Most people at least turn to God in their exigencies, even Magicians."

He picked up the bell and rang it more loudly.

Eager for an opportunity to change the subject away from religion, I ventured a question.

"What is this place?"

"It's currently known as The Mazi, though it has had many other names. Pray that you'll never have occasion to find yourself here after today; you'll only witness business of the darkest kind within these walls."

"The guards seemed to know you."

"Indeed. Among other fouler things, this place deals in information and secrets; those are the real currency of magicians both good and evil. Still, I would rather do anything than provide these people with either information or secrets. Generally, if I have any business in a place like this, I trade in potions, which also carry a great deal of value if they are exotic and powerful enough."

He glanced around and tapped the bell again a little harder before continuing.

"Now, I won't have time to explain things as we go, so you'll have to follow my lead."

"Is it safe here?"

"Not especially, but it's at least neutral ground. The proprietors have no interest in getting caught up in the quarrels of the patrons. Wouldn't be good for business. Profit is their game, and they don't care much where it comes from."

An older gentleman came around a corner with his head down, situated himself at the front desk, organized a few

286

papers, and let out a long sigh before looking up at his guests. His eyes widened slightly.

"Mr. Spindlebrock! This is a surprise."

He flipped through the last few pages of a large guest book that was sitting on the desk in front of him.

"I wasn't told you were coming—no, I don't see your name here."

"It's good to see you, Whitmer—you are correct, I am not expected. I was in town when I heard a friend was visiting here at the Mazi. We have some business to finish."

"And this friend, he is expecting you?"

"It's a woman; and yes, we are expected."

The man behind the desk looked doubly surprised. He looked down at the book and back at Spindlebrock.

"I really haven't been told to look for you, by anyone here, and our policies are quite clear on disrupting our clients—"

"I understand. We'll wait here in the lobby until we're called for, but would you do something for me?"

"I will try to oblige."

Whitmer's voice was drawn out and lethargic, with tired manners that were clearly only for show.

"Our host is in the Aperture Room, unless I am mistaken. Her name is Olivia; would you at least peek in there and let her know that we are waiting for her."

"Well, it is most irregular—"

Spindlebrock removed a small vial from his coat and set it on the counter. Whitmer's eyes darted quickly around the room. Understanding the gesture, he quickly pocketed the potion then smiled broadly before continuing.

"I'm sure I can at least check in with Ms. Olivia."

"Thank you. As I said, she will be expecting us."

Whitmer left by the same passage he entered, and Spindlebrock led us to a comfortable set of chairs situated for privacy in the far corner of the lobby. He spoke again in a whisper.

"This is the location of the central portion of the confluence. They call it the Aperture Room. I have my suspicions about how Crane will work things. I must insist that you do nothing, say nothing, and touch nothing."

I nodded. All my questions threatened to burst forth of their own accord; anticipating my pattern, Spindlebrock touched his finger to his lips, then leaned back and crossed his arms over his chest.

By and by, Whitmer appeared once more, entering fully into the lounge and standing before us.

"Olivia has instructed me to welcome you, and to inform you that she will be available shortly. She will send for you when she is ready."

As we waited in the lobby, my mind dashed chaotically through the possibilities of what we might encounter, and how we might be forced to react. A strong sense of dread—the kind that only the ill-prepared are acquainted with—set into my heart. Spindlebrock seemed to be at peace, but I was in torment. Several times I got up and paced around the room, wanting but not daring to vocalize my nightmarish imaginations.

My agony finally ended when Whitmer returned once more and bid us follow him down the wide hallway, the lobby's only apparent connection to the main portion of the building. The carpet was deep red in the wide center walkway, with gold trim near the walls, and very plush, so that our footfalls could barely be heard even by ourselves. Doorways at equal intervals were flanked by large, lush plants, which almost seemed intended to obscure the mysterious entrances from view. I noticed that each set of doors was embellished in a radically different style, one as if it belonged in the Taj Mahal, another seemingly taken directly from the Borgund Stave Church; each was guarded by two men, who were as stationary as the large plants they paired with.

The hallway terminated in a cavernous room whose ceiling seemed higher than was reasonable, and which was the end point for two other hallways coming in from our left and right. Two tall doors made of rough hewn oak with wrought iron trim filled the remaining wall. Spindlebrock stopped several meters before reaching them, and I followed suit. Whitmer, ignoring us both, continued to walk up to the doorway, and, removing a large set of old keys from his coat, proceeded to work the locks until he could open one of the doors wide enough to permit entry. Standing aside, he motioned for us to enter. As soon as we did, the doors closed and bolted loudly behind us.

The Aperture Room was spacious, but uncomfortably cold and poorly lit. It appeared to be arranged as if to seat people for a ball, with tables and chairs dispersed all around the room, leaving a clear space in the center. A chandelier shone down on this ostensible dance floor, making a ring of light that touched only the tables nearest to it, leaving the rest to fade into pitch black shadow. Scarcely had I scanned the scene before me when I noticed a woman standing near an empty table at the edge of the light.

"Please, join me."

Her firm voice echoed in the hall.

Spindlebrock approached and I followed, steeling myself against an unknown and ominous task. Whatever happened, I did not want to reveal my inward hesitancy, which would surely manifest in a stark and embarrassing contrast to Spindlebrock's obvious self-possession. Most importantly, I did not want to jeopardize our purposes, even if I didn't fully understand them.

"I see you finally found me. I was expecting you sooner."

Spindlebrock scanned the room casually as he responded. Outwardly, his guard didn't appear to be up. I knew better.

"It appears we are alone, Olivia?"

She nodded silently.

"Well then, come, let us have a seat at one of these fine tables."

Olivia seemed taken aback.

Spindlebrock made a careless sweeping motion toward the tables.

"Your choice. We'll follow."

As my eyes adjusted to pierce deeper into the shadow, I noted with great curiosity that each of the tables was as different as each of the doors in the hallway we had just left; some appeared destined for a casual French café, while others recalled a more palatial pomp. No two, as far as I could tell, were alike.

The young woman looked around, hesitating. She appeared to be straining, her head tilted as if she were listening intently, muttering to herself all the while. After a few moments, she chose a small, neglected picnic table. It was wood, with three seats which were attached to the table at the base; it appeared excessively weather beaten. We all took our seats.

"A shame, no backs to the chairs. You don't want to chat for very long, it would seem," Spindlebrock remarked dryly while he made a show of arranging himself as comfortably as possible.

"Only as long as we must."

"That's fine, of course. Things to do, all of us. So, let's get down to business then."

Spindlebrock sat upright and crossed his hands on the table.

"First, let's dispense with the pretenses: you know that we would not have dared seek you out sooner, for fear of reprisals aimed at the young people Crane had kidnapped."

"I suppose, if that was your main concern."

"Nonsense," Spindlebrock snorted, "of course it was. Also, I'm curious as to why you were so sure that we would look for you at all. We already captured most of Crane's hooligans, what makes you think you are you so important?"

"That's evident," Olivia's eyes flitted momentarily in my direction, "you're here, aren't' you?"

"What's evident is that you still have terrible penmanship, and that you're enough of a fool to hang out much longer than is advisable in the very same rendezvous that your cohorts divulged in front of my friend here."

Spindlebrock patted me on the shoulder and continued.

"Thomas, my intern, was assured that his stay in Turkey would be a pleasant one, and that he would only be involved in administrative affairs."

"Certainly," Olivia scoffed, "the same way he was involved in administrative affairs in Phoenix."

Spindlebrock leaned forward and rested his chin on one fist.

"Well now, there you make my point for me. In Phoenix, I hardly told him what was going on at all, but thanks to Crane's clumsy, mediocre, and murderous goons, Thomas got dragged in much deeper than was necessary. He was already involved in all of this, as a result, so it made sense to bring him along. I figured if we stayed out of your way in Turkey, he could be here to help mop up after your nonsense."

"And that's really all you needed him for? You couldn't find help from your Turkish friends?"

"I choose my help very carefully, unlike your employer. And now you'll answer a question for me: what, pray tell, is your obsession with Thomas, that you would go to so much trouble to try to kidnap him? Did you intend to poison him as you have the others?"

Forgetting that there was no back to his seat, Spindlebrock started to lean back, caught himself, and sat bolt upright again.

"My employer chooses his help more carefully than you might realize, and he informs them of their duties with precision. I do not need to know what he wants with Thomas Martin, I only need to know that he wishes to see him."

With this statement, Olivia looked down and reached into a small handbag. A moment later, she produced three vials, which she lined up in the middle of the table.

"These three vials contain an antidote, one vial for each of the three young people that were kidnapped most recently, and whom you presume to have rescued. Presently, a potion runs through their veins that even the great professor Spindlebrock could not possibly counteract in short enough a time. Without these vials, they will all three die. Administer these antidotes, and they'll be spared."

Spindlebrock's eyes narrowed, but he did not falter.

"You honestly believe that I couldn't make my own antidote?"

"I'm sure that I don't know anything about it. I only know that Crane believes you cannot, and that I was instructed to offer these to you."

"Well, his potions have been rather more advanced than usual."

He tapped his fingers as he thought out loud.

"And the price, I suppose, is my intern—for reasons that no one at this table knows."

Spindlebrock kept up the facade that he and I knew of nothing that might draw Crane's attention to me. I didn't know exactly what he was about, but I sat as stone-faced as possible.

"I can guarantee he will return unharmed."

"Like Lilianne was returned unharmed? And the others?"

Spindlebrock's voice smacked of disgust.

"Look at you, Olivia. You used to be a bright, vibrant student, with a promising future in the sciences. Now, you're a lackey. You call that unharmed?"

Olivia was unaffected.

"My employer is here, as you have probably guessed. At any moment he will make himself known. You will then have to face him, and it is probable that you will walk away with neither the vials nor your friend. Take the vials and you will be allowed to leave, and you'll see Thomas again. He only wants to talk with him. Now, our conversation is over. What is your choice?"

Spindlebrock glanced around at the empty tables, at the vials, and at me.

"Well, then" he said, reaching for the vials, " I think I'll—absquatulate!"

Immediately following this strange outburst, Spindlebrock quickly rattled off a charm that was reminiscent of the one he had used at the wrought-iron table, in the ruins earlier that afternoon. With a familiar rush, we were all three transported instantly, the picnic table unchanged, to a grassy field. Instead of the early evening that we had just left in Turkey, it appeared to be morning.

As what had just happened dawned on me, I instinctively produced my wand from concealment and leveled it at Olivia. Spindlebrock stood up and pocketed the vials.

"That won't be necessary, Thomas. Both of you stand up quickly, so we can complete the trip."

Both Olivia and I stood up. The sensation was odd, like walking through a short burst of air.

"Now, move away from the table and join me on this side."

Once again, Olivia and I obeyed promptly; I wondered why she was so entirely compliant. Spindlebrock had produced his wand and was pointing it in the direction of the table as we backed away.

"We have to get out of here, it's not safe."

Looking around, I realized that we were in the middle of a field of uncut grass, with the picnic table sitting under the thin cover of the only sparse tree for miles. There was a deserted and crumbling old farm house nearby, a dirt road lined by a bit of drooping barbed wire, and nothing else. The landscape was flat for endless miles, reminding me of the mid-western United States.

"Follow me."

We trailed behind as Spindlebrock headed for the old farm house, his gaze reverting repeatedly back to the picnic table we seemed to be fleeing from. My wand was still drawn, and I oscillated between pointing it at the picnic table and at Olivia.

Spindlebrock climbed in the splintered front door first, avoiding several old and rotted-out steps. After glancing around inside, he motioned for us to follow.

"In here. Mind your step."

The farm house was a wreck, though not quite so far gone as to be unsafe. Through an old, broken-out window I could still see the table sitting in the field. I looked around anxiously.

"We'll be fine in here for a few minutes, Thomas, you can put your wand away."

I looked at Olivia and kept my wand out. Spindlebrock, who was digging around in the drawers of a dusty old buffet hutch, paused and looked at me.

"Thomas, really, it's fine, she'll do exactly as I say."

"I don't understand."

He moved on to the kitchen and began rifling through the cupboards as he spoke.

"Of course. I'll explain everything, but first we need to get as far away from this place as possible and we don't have a moment to spare."

Spindlebrock let out an exclamation as he pulled a set of rusty keys from a drawer. He again beckoned us to follow him out the back door and toward a battered barn, which we all three entered. In the center of the dirt floor, streams of light broke through the failed roof to shine upon a vehicle that looked to be at least seventy years old, with about that many years of accumulated grime. Spindlebrock approached and wiped a thick layer of dust, straw, and cobwebs away from the hood ornament, a winged lady holding a wheel out in front of her.

"It looks like a gangster car," I offered.

Spindlebrock took no notice. Instead, he asked us both to stand back, then proceeded to clean and repair the beastly looking machine with a series of charms. He blew the dust and dirt off the car and right out of the barn, through a wall that was more holes than boards. With another charm he repaired and strengthened the old tires, simultaneously inflating them. He opened one of the doors and cleaned the interior, popped the hood and use a few charms that I am unfamiliar with to work some magic on the mechanics. After just a minute or two and a whirlwind, he pronounced that the car was ready to drive.

At this point I was ready to believe anything, and I followed his command to, "Get in!" as blindly as the mesmerized Olivia. He inserted the key and turned it, and the old car roared to life with surprising fierceness.

"Hold on tight."

Without ceremony, Spindlebrock backed straight through the barn door, flipped the car around, and peeled out of the old gravel driveway and onto the dirt road. In minutes the old homestead was a speck in the astoundingly clean rear-view mirror. We drove to the nearest airstrip, near a town called Tribune, Kansas, where Spindlebrock made a few phone calls to summon the familiar Gulfstream to our aid.

Chapter 22

The Plane Ride Home

When I sat down safely on that jet, I believed that we had gained the ultimate victory over W.C. Crane. There were questions in my mind about a few particulars, but the notion that we had been entirely successful—that we had won—was starting to solidify. I felt exuberant. The flight from Tribune, Kansas to Toronto is short in a Gulfstream, and with our security assured, Spindlebrock was now in a gregarious mood. I'll share some of the specifics of our conversation, which I can still recall in detail.

After obtaining refreshment for all three of us from the plane's small refrigerator, and telling us to drink, Spindlebrock started talking.

"Now, Thomas, that was an adventure."

"Indeed it was!"

"Before you ask your usual string of questions, let me try to cover some ground that might fill things in more coherently."

I consented heartily.

"You've traveled through a confluence—wait; Olivia, you will please take a nap now."

Olivia put down her empty soda can, leaned her chair back and closed her eyes. Her surreal unquestioning obedience was troubling, but I held myself back, hoping that Spindlebrock would provide answers of his own accord.

"Good—now, where was I? Yes, confluence. You've seen two of the entry points of the confluence in Turkey, and used them both in slightly different ways. What did you think of it?"

"It was nothing short of amazing! To think that you can bend the laws of time and space; it shatters physics!"

"I'm glad you are excited. You're right to be awestruck; as I told you before, the phenomenon is not well known, nor often used even by those that know of it. It's like stepping through one of the wonders of the universe.

"You noticed, no doubt, that the Aperture Room at the Mazi had quite a few tables, all different from one another. May I assume that you surmised what that meant?"

"I was thinking that they were tables that went to different places," I ventured.

"Well, to be exact, they were tables that existed at different points. But yes, in their use, they would take you to different places.

"I had assumed, and I believe I am correct—I don't want to wake Olivia, or I'd ask her—that Crane would be using one of those tables in almost the same way that we used the one in the ruined building. He could be present without being visible, hear and see without being discovered. If things went wrong, he could escape without incident, and if things went right he could enter the scene as needed."

"That makes sense. It was a good plan."

"Indeed. You probably also noted that Olivia had some difficulty selecting a table for us to sit at?"

I admitted that at the time I had not really noticed.

"Cast your mind back, and you'll recall that she was mumbling and furtively searching for just the right table. I believe she was in some sort of communication with Crane, though I don't know how, and that he was helping her select a table. Can you guess why it would have mattered which table we sat at?"

"Not at all, unless they wanted to control where we went?"

"Or, if they wanted to attempt to prevent us from going anywhere at all. You see, of all the tables in that room, charms are known for only seven; at least, if you wanted to pay to use those tables, no amount of money could get you more than seven of the charms from the people who own or use that room."

"You're saying that most people only know how to use seven of those tables?"

"I'm saying that apart from myself and maybe one or two other people that have lived over the past century, no one—not one other person—has charms for more than seven of those tables."

"How many do you know?"

"I'll tell you someday. For now, suffice it to say that Crane most likely thought he was guiding Olivia to sit at a table that was not usable. Of course, he was mistaken, but we'll get to that. First, did you notice anything odd about our conversation with Olivia?"

"Well, not really."

"I was, I'll admit, a little taken aback by the directness of it. She seemed to want to take it for granted—and Crane must have also taken it for granted—that you were unquestionably a valuable target in everyone's eyes."

I shifted in my seat uncomfortably.

"Don't get me wrong, Thomas. You're a good friend, but that is not something that anyone would know or assume of someone traveling with me. I have, you see, a reputation in the magical commonality. People don't generally assume that I am capable of making or maintaining friendships."

"I guess I've seen that," I jabbed.

"That's fair, and it's not something that I hide. Rather, I like to encourage the notion. But that's not really what they thought made you a target, as I'm sure you're aware."

"You're talking about Conexus, right? That's what made me a target."

"Absolutely. That would make you a target, but they had no way of knowing for sure that you had such an ability. They could not have known with certainty, yet they acted that way, I felt."

"She never said as much, but I got that impression as well."

"In any case, I'm operating under that assumption. I believe that Crane suspected it from our time in Phoenix, and that it has haunted his mind ever since."

Spindlebrock sat in silence for a few moments before continuing.

"Thomas, you should know and understand the extent of the danger that you would be in if your gift was generally known. The reason I was determined to act as if we had found Olivia solely by using Scott's hint about the confluence, was to put doubt into Crane's mind. We need at least a seed of doubt in there, to counteract the verification that Crane had with Olivia."

"What do you mean?"

"Well, When we were driving in the last taxi, toward the Mazi, what did you feel?"

A recollection of the painfully unpleasant experience came back to my mind.

"Well, I felt fear—and I could tell that she suspected that we were coming, that we had discovered her."

"Which means that Olivia knew, at least in part, that she had been discovered. I suspected that this would be the case, but I'm unfortunately not familiar with the method that was used to conceal her—darkness has so many forms of concealment—and so I don't know what she felt exactly. I think we can assume that she was waiting for a change, and that she was told to contact Crane in the case that it occurred."

"Then why use the letter at all, if you thought it would be a risk? You pretty much knew they would be at the Mazi, why not just show up?"

Spindlebrock looked at me and pondered for a few moments.

"I'm going to answer carefully, Thomas, because I don't want you to take this the wrong way. I understood that having you use the letter meant putting you at risk; I had you use it anyway for two reasons. First, having her concealment charm broken doesn't directly correlate to you having Conexus. There are certainly other methods for

305

breaking such a charm, and hunting people down. Plausible deniability was still a very real option.

"Second, it became increasingly clear that Crane supposed his theories to be fact, and that he was willing to invest himself fully in them. He was throwing every resource at capturing you. I had no reason to suspect that he would stop trying.

Seeing that I didn't quite grasp his meaning, he continued.

"Think it through—he has Olivia, we have the letter. He believes, with an unaccountable level of certainty, that you have Conexus. If we walked away from Adana with the letter, what would he do?"

"He'd find some other way to draw us out."

"Exactly."

"What if we had burned the letter? Gotten rid of it in some public way, so he knew it was gone?"

"Again, think it through. Why would we do such a ridiculous thing? Making a spectacle out of it would have just solidified his theories even more. There was no way to deter him. The only way to ensure that the letter never led to more pain was to rescue Olivia. And besides, she deserved rescuing as much as anyone else, in spite of her handwriting."

With everything said and done, and us safe, I couldn't bring myself to be truly angry. Still, the thought that I had been put at risk on purpose did sting a little.

"You could have consulted with me, before throwing me under the bus, Spindlebrock."

He chuckled, obviously relieved by my levity.

"I think you would have done it anyway. In any case, you learned some things. You're becoming more skilled in your ability, even though you've only used it a few times."

"Do you think they know now, then?"

"Well, my attempts to deny their suppositions about your gift may seem feeble in retrospect, but I still feel it was important to attempt to mask the truth as much as possible. If you consider how we acted and spoke today as the sum of a whole, including all of our actions since we got the letter in Phoenix, I am hopeful that there is still quite a bit of room for doubt in Crane's mind, and that is all I was attempting to reinforce. It's really all we can hope for. Now, as for Olivia, you're probably curious as to what turned her to our side?"

"It was just before we used the table I think, a word you —"

"Don't say it now, she's right next to you. That word—which is an interesting choice on the part of Crane, I think—is a trigger word. It was the same word that we extracted from Lilianne."

"You mean, that's the word, the single word, that you couldn't tell me about before, when you were doing all that research?"

"Precisely so. Combined with the potions that have been administered to these youth, the word becomes a mental control called a trigger, used to initiate a mindless sort of obedience."

"You mean, like hypnosis?"

"Well, I wouldn't use the comparison. The subject is quite conscious of their actions, even though their free will is interrupted. No, it's a complex combination of potions, charms, and mental programming. It's not a mind trick or a brainwashing, per se, it's a practical application of simple concepts combined together for a powerful effect."

"You mean, they'll do what you say, but they still know that they're doing it? They have no choice?"

"Yes, they have no choice, but they realize that they have no choice. In the case of Olivia here, she has been minimally communicative yet exactly obedient. The obedience is not her choice, but she doesn't have to give us anything more than what we demand. With Crane, she was clearly more invested. I suspect that he was a lot more cunning in his approach."

"What do you mean?"

"You see, the trigger word is outside of the conscious inspection of the subject; they don't realize when it's been spoken, they don't recall hearing it. The precise moment when they lose the full control of their self-will is invisible to them. In my case, the word was followed by direct commands, which Olivia could not control, and she knew it. She likely thought that I had charmed her in some way.

"Consider, Thomas, how Crane might have proceeded. After abducting these subjects and administering his little regiment of potions and whatever else, they would return home with no memory of his ploy. At some later date he would arrange an interview wherein he would use the trigger word discreetly, followed by subtle suggestions and steering. He could get them on his side with full cooperation, using veiled force, so that he had their complete buy-in. Do you see the potential in that sort of method?"

"Yes, it's quite brilliant. And you discovered all of this just through your examination of Lilianne's case?"

"No. But, everything I found while helping Lilianne led me to suspect what was going on, and when we extracted the extremely outmoded word—trigger words must not be in common use—I was convinced enough to act."

"It really is quite brilliant," I repeated. "To think, Crane did all of this to amass a legion of lackeys who actually thought they were following him by choice!"

Spindlebrock leaned back in his chair and fell into silent contemplation. After a minute or two of waiting, I spoke.

"Do you mind if I ask a few questions now?"

Spindlebrock looked a bit surprised, but consented readily.

"At that farm back there, where we traveled on the picnic table—"

Spindlebrock laughed.

"You make it sound like a flying table! The table didn't travel, but I see your meaning. I'm sorry, please go on."

"At the farm, you kept a close watch—with your wand at the ready—on the table. If you were worried about being followed why didn't you just destroy it?"

"The table? Destroying one of those tables would be no easy task. I doubt if anyone alive would know how to begin. Even more importantly, I doubt anyone that understood what they were would want to, no matter what the danger was."

I nodded.

"What about the car? How did you know it would be there and that you could get it working? And how did you know where to find the keys?"

"Simple. It's my house, and my car. Everything was right where I left it."

I attempted without success to extract more information about Spindlebrock's old house, his research with Lilianne, and the events in France and Belarus, but Spindlebrock had become distracted, it seemed to me, after mention of Crane's legion of lackeys. Further questions being either ignored, dismissed, or circumvented, our conversation trailed off, and the short flight was finished in silence. Upon landing we turned Olivia and the three vials of antidote over to a magical tribunal that was waiting for us at the airport, then gladly accepted the transportation that had been arranged to take us home.

Chapter 23

A Game of Chess

Our return to Spindlebrock's home was filled with the sweet joy of highly anticipated reunions. Lewis had come directly from Belarus a few days earlier, immediately following the rescue of Paavo Mand. Delphine was comforted by his assurances that all was well, but disquieted by Spindlebrock's continued delay. When we arrived, Lewis had prepared a small feast to welcome us, at the bidding of Delphine, who was too agitated to do anything but direct.

Lilianne was among the welcoming party, and I thought I noticed a cloud of worry over her and her mother that was not dispelled by our return alone. As we ate and talked, their burden seemed to lighten. They seemed particularly encouraged by the confidence that Spindlebrock exuded concerning the resolution of the abductions, the capture of so many involved, and the certainty that all of the effects of their abuses could be reversed.

Over the next month, Spindlebrock included me in every aspect of the final portion of the investigation. The extraction process that he had discovered while working with Lilianne was repeated on the prisoners from the motorboat, all but one: Evalyn had managed to escape somewhere in transit between Turkey and Canada. From the rest of the youth, the trigger word, "absquatulate," was extracted, but their memories were otherwise barren of additional clues relating to Crane or any of the abductions. With no memory of any wrongdoing, they were at first confused and frustrated at their detention; in his wisdom, Spindlebrock held nothing back in his description of what they had gone through and what they had been a part of, which softened their anger into concern and contrition. They were all eventually cleared by the tribunal, released, and provided with counseling and other assistance as needed.

Olivia's case was handled somewhat differently. Not having consumed a Mundus potion, her memory was intact. Still under the mind manipulations that Crane had put in place, and at the command of Spindlebrock's trigger word, she was questioned thoroughly. We learned through her that Crane's full name was William Cartwright Crane—though it is most certainly an alias, as no such person is known in the magical commonality. Her description of his features was below average in detail, she having interacted with him in person only once on their first meeting.

Of Crane's plots, we learned little beyond what we already knew: that he was attempting to gain adherents to his worthy cause. Olivia was visibly frustrated that she could not expound on what Crane's cause actually was, beyond the surface goal of gaining followers. The methods and practices that Crane used were obvious to the point of being stereotypical, and could not have worked without the magical sciences. Spindlebrock's questioning led me to believe that he had surmised correctly on each particular before Olivia answered. He was not pleased at the pittance that we gleaned.

In the end, Olivia begrudgingly underwent the same treatments that the others had gone through, to rid her of the controls and influences that had been placed in her mind. The tribunal was understandably more harsh in her case; her memory was intact, but she wasn't sufficiently remorseful, nor did she seem to grasp the full gravity of her crimes. Since she had no family, she was turned over to the care and protection of Dr. Patel, who was to oversee a lengthy prescribed counseling and observation period, during which time Olivia would live at and attend the University of Magic, Toronto.

With great effort, Spindlebrock located and helped all of the young people from his notebook, who he had previously investigated, starting with Tera Bedisa. Once his quest to restore all these was completed, he immediately published his findings with the University, so that his process could be repeated as needed by skilled magicians the world over.

Word spread quickly of his triumphs, and the magical commonality breathed a collective sigh of relief, knowing that if Crane were to attempt any further abductions, his depraved exploitation could be fully undone thanks to Spindlebrock's ingenuity. Against his own will and to his dismay, professor Spindlebrock met with a hero's reception nearly everywhere he went, but his cantankerous disposition soon established a more usual distance between him and his admirers. Life tends toward normalcy, and after the entire ordeal was through, Spindlebrock went back to his teaching and research, and I returned to my studies.

In my mind we had vanquished entirely. I wish that I could say that my elation was warranted, but time and circumstance revealed to me that not all was well. Spindlebrock, who was not one to pass up the opportunity to enjoy a success, betrayed an ongoing frustration in quiet moments and in small ways. At first I thought that the excessive public buzz was to blame, but Spindlebrock's frustration continued to build. Soon, it was apparent that something else was weighing heavily on his mind.

One Saturday afternoon as we were sitting reading in his lounge, I broached the subject.

"You seem off."

"Huh?"

Spindlebrock looked up from his newspaper.

"Off. You've been this way ever since we got back from Turkey."

"Which way have I been?"

"Off."

"What does that even mean? You do know that the word 'off' has upwards of fifty definitions in a reasonable, unabridged dictionary, do you not? So, what do you mean by it?"

"Just that you're not yourself."

Spindlebrock examined me for a few moments, then lifted his paper again, continuing to speak to me from behind it.

"Nonsense. I'm exactly myself."

"You've been short-tempered, and something is eating at you."

"My temperament has always been abbreviated."

I could not argue the point.

"True enough, but something is definitely eating at you."

"At the moment, you are the only thing gnawing at me, Thomas."

He turned the pages roughly.

"That's because you don't want to talk about it. I, on the other hand, don't want to let it go. Why are you in such a bad mood now that everything has gone back to normal? We won, doesn't that give you some kind of satisfaction?"

Spindlebrock sighed, folding his paper and putting it down next to the lamp.

"You think we won?"

His statement took me aback, and a tremor of unexpected terror briefly chilled my heart.

"Well, isn't it apparent?" I petitioned.

"For a brief moment, I wished that it was."

Spindlebrock drifted off. I waited breathlessly for him to continue. Finally, he came back to himself.

"But then, something you said on the plane made me realize that we had not won at all."

"Something I said?"

"Yes. You said that Crane had done everything only to amass a legion of lackeys."

I recalled the conversation on the jet from Kansas to Toronto.

"Yes, I do remember saying something like that."

"It makes no sense, and yet from our perspective, it is all that Crane actually did. Every effort, every abduction, every ruse, was designed simply to ensnare and program more followers."

"Sure," I replied, dumbly. Spindlebrock turned his full attention to me, his angry gaze penetrating deeply into my eyes.

"Sure? We're sure that this master of potions, this advanced magician with obscure and arcane knowledge of long forgotten portals, this clever and cunning and shrewd diabolist just wanted to amass dumb and mundane followers?"

His voice had risen almost to a shout. I was in a logical corner, but hadn't quite realized it.

"Well, he probably had other plans that he was going to use them for."

"Other plans you say, and yet he made absolutely no effort to prevent them from all falling into our hands to be irretrievably lost."

"Maybe he didn't know that you could cure them?"

Spindlebrock softened, leaning back in his chair, his voice returning to normal.

"And yet he knew that you and I hadn't rushed back to Canada with our prizes, after capturing his lackeys on the bridge and restoring the abductees. We lingered. We sought him out. At that point in the Aperture Room, surely he would have known that we were a threat to any further plans he may have had?"

"Perhaps."

"Surely he would have at least considered the fact that he might never again have influence over these minions he had spent so much time and expended so much energy to gain, and that he might never find a way to gain new ones?"

"Well," I stammered.

"We have to assume that he knew what the risks were, the preponderance of information points to that. When you so naturally and effortlessly surmised that Crane's only reason for all of this was to amass a legion of lackeys, I knew instantly that you were wrong, and that I had been duped. It was in that moment that I realized exactly what Crane's goal was, and that it was he that had won."

My heart sank. Spindlebrock took a long, slow breath before continuing.

"In a game of chess, only the entirety of the game matters. You may win pieces, you may lose pieces, but only the King is of any importance. If you can protect your King, and destroy your opponent's, then you've won. You might sacrifice every piece you have but one; it doesn't matter, because protecting those pieces isn't the goal.

"Crane began by abducting young people. Among all the people in the magical commonality, he chose people in a particular age range. At first I thought it was because they were more susceptible to his methods, or that they might have a particular use, given their positions, their families, et cetera.

"As far as we can tell—and remember, we have had the clear and direct witness of Olivia—these youth never engaged in anything beyond helping Crane to abduct other youths. No nefarious plots to subvert the governments of the world, no schemes to burgle Fort Knox. They only planned and carried out further abductions.

"Then there was the great 'mistake' of capturing Lilianne. Crane, by his own admission in his letter from the funeral, had a deep interest in me as a magician. I was not unknown to him, and I must absolutely infer that my relationship with Delphine was not unknown to him. When he kidnapped Lilianne, he knew that an irrepressible firestorm would descend upon him. He left more traces and made more apparent mistakes, intentionally, so that I would find out his methods.

"And, as if it weren't enough to kidnap the daughter of my closest friend, he attacked and murdered the son of another friend—again, intentionally—when he abducted Talbot. Regardless of his laying blame at our feet in his letter, Crane had this plan in his mind from the start. He realized that it was the only way to galvanize us into an extreme and committed course. It was a sick manipulation.

"After giving me sufficient time to make my discoveries with Lilianne, Crane staged the abduction in Turkey. The Mazi and the Aperture Room are one of only three confluences that are controlled by what I call dark magicians; the rest are either unknown to nearly everyone, or are controlled by more reasonable and less sinister forces. I suspected he would use the confluence, and that suspicion was carefully and deliberately roused when Crane staged additional abductions in France and Belarus, two common end points related to the Aperture Room.

"I should have seen it when Olivia led us to the picnic table. I reasoned, erroneously, that Crane was attempting to sit us at a table that he thought we could not use—you recall, Olivia was somehow receiving instructions from him about which table to choose. In reality, Crane was gleefully selecting a table whose charm was hitherto unknown to him, and which he had reason to believe was known to me. I don't know how he would have known that, I only have troubling theories on the subject.

"I've told you that information and secrets are the currency of magicians. I believe that I also mentioned that in the Aperture, only seven tables were actively used. Now, at least for William Cartwright Crane, there are eight."

Spindlebrock rose from his chair, walked over to one of the windows in the room and started closing the blinds.

"These traveling charms, the ones that activate the tables, are invaluable and dangerous. I believe I alluded to that when we spoke about them before. No amount of money would induce me to divulge their secrets to the wrong magician, and almost no other secrets would be worth enough in trade to tempt me."

He continued to fiddle with one of the blinds, which had a cracked tilt rod and wouldn't shut all the way.

"Crane played out an enormous, years-long chess game to get us into that room and onto that table. He was willing to sacrifice as many of his pieces, and our pieces, as necessary in order to purchase the charm that he got when I activated that picnic table. He knew his opponent well, and he was the better player."

Once all of the windows were shuttered, Spindlebrock turned on the lamp and sat down in his chair.

"But now I am starting to know my opponent, who was heretofore in the shadows. He has—in his ambition—tipped his hand, so to speak. This entire affair was one of gaining a traveling spell—and not the kind that you have in your little blue book."

Spindlebrock leaned forward in his chair and motioned for me to do the same. Speaking in a lower voice, he continued.

"You've been a faithful and honest friend to me from the moment you laid hands on my book. The copy you found was given as a gift to a special friend of mine, who has since passed away. I'm glad that you have it now.

"Our terms were a little one-sided when we first met, Thomas, but I want you to know that your gift is not the reason for our friendship. From here out I will be more than happy to help you in any way I can, as you delve even deeper into the magical sciences, with no strings attached."

Spindlebrock reached out his hand, which I grasped in a firm handshake.

"You are welcome to stay here with me as long as you like. For my part, this business with W.C. Crane is just beginning. If you're interested in helping in our next round of chess, I am certain that I could use your heart, your courage, and your skills."

I was moved by Spindlebrock's display. With great joy, and a touch of hope and levity, I looked behind Spindlebrock at the damaged shutter, snapped my wrist with a flourish, and spoke the repairing charm from his Little Blue Book of Traveling Spells.

The crack in the tilt rod mended itself and the blinds snapped shut as I replied.

"I look forward to it more than anything."

Chapter 24

Epilogue

At the beginning of this book I informed you, reader, that my life had taken a turn. In reality, my life has since wound chaotically around countless metaphorical turns, traveled up and down difficult mountains, through dark tunnels, and over brilliantly lit hillsides, all as a result of the worlds that Spindlebrock has opened to my vision. Thankfully, there is no end in sight—the professor and I are, to this day, fast and true friends.

The personal changes I allude to are not entirely wrapped up in the magical sciences, even if that is where they found their genesis. Spindlebrock, in his innocent cunning, took to reforming every part of my understanding that he could lay hold of. The, "magic that is God," as he likes to put it, is one area where I've experienced radical new thought. Time and space are another. If I were to write a book for every concept he has weaved and twisted into my being, I'd have to abandon every other study and interest in favor of the author's life.

Still, I am keenly aware—having been told as much by my editor—that readers will no doubt be interested to hear what eventually became of our larger dealings with W.C.

Crane. His story is a curious one, with a fascinating and not-unpleasant ending, which I can presently connect with at least two other significant mysteries. You've now read some inside details of the abductions that rocked the magical commonality; you should be allowed to read the rest of the story.

And so, I am determined and committed to finishing what I've started. We can't, after all, get through life with only a portion of the truth of things, any more than a magician can get by with only a small book of traveling spells.

Joseph D. Lyman

Eager to get things going, Joseph was born in a speeding ambulance, on a desert highway outside of Cave Creek, Arizona. His family owned a publishing company, and his Grandfather wrote books, so young Joey decided that he wanted to be an entrepreneur and author.

His early childhood attempts at writing had something to do with ninjas; a degree in business and years of running his own company taught him that writing about ninjas was like drawing boa constrictors eating elephants. Today, Joseph writes about more sensible things. When he's not writing, he's usually playing with his kids, exploring public access Unix systems, tinkering on his guitar, or juggling.

Made in the USA
Monee, IL
18 January 2021